DARK SIDE
OF LOVE

DARK SIDE OF LOVE

Peggy Bechko

Five Star
Unity, Maine

F
BEC

Five Star Romance.
Published in conjunction with Peggy Bechko

Cover photograph by Alan J. La Vallee.

April 1998
Standard Print Hardcover Edition.

Five Star Standard Print Romance Series.

The text of this edition is unabridged.

Set in 11 pt. Plantin by Juanita Macdonald.

Printed in the United States on permanent paper.

Library of Congress Cataloging in Publication Data

Bechko, P. A.
    Dark side of love / Peggy Bechko.
        p.   cm.
    ISBN 0-7862-1314-0 (hc : alk. paper)
    1. Large type books.   I. Title.
PS3552.E24D3   1998
7813´.54—dc21   97-49960

DARK SIDE
OF LOVE

CHAPTER ONE

What was she doing here? Sirena Clark pulled her purse into her lap from beneath the seat in front of her. Reaching into its neat, almost filled recesses, she fished out her small silver compact and gazed into its mirror as if she could find an answer in the brilliant blue eyes gazing steadily back at her. No answers there, she decided, snapping the compact shut with a deep sigh.

"More coffee?" asked a low well-modulated voice somewhere near her ear. A glass coffeepot balanced at the corner of her vision.

Sirena nodded vaguely and held out her coffee cup to the little tray the flight attendant balanced before himself.

"Cream? Sugar?" he queried as he slipped the small tray back within her grasp. He was bestowing on her a dazzling smile that displayed perfectly aligned, brilliantly white teeth.

"Both, thank you," Sirena replied automatically. But her smile for the attentive steward didn't quite reach the depths of her lovely blue eyes as she returned to contemplation of the adventure she'd embarked upon.

Gripping her coffee cup with both hands, Sirena eased her position in her seat and sat back. She had never liked flying in the first place: sitting nearly immobile for hours on end was not her cup of tea; her body ached from the prolonged confinement. But taking the flight from New York in the wee hours of the morning to arrive in Tucson, Arizona as early as possible had been her choice. The plane would be landing soon, nearly on schedule — the end of the first leg of an already exhausting trip. Tackle it all in one big chunk — that was Sirena's idea. Don't stop moving until you get where you're going.

That and the fact that she had traveled this route once before had combined to lend a bit of security to the trip. Someone would be meeting her at the Tucson airport to escort her down into Mexico: not the Mexico tourists delighted in, but a Mexico casual visitors rarely saw — a magnificent sprawling wilderness.

Sirena shuddered with both fatigue and apprehension. Draining the last of her slightly sweet coffee, she let her eyes wander to the window at her left and gazed out over the rolling expanse of desert far below, now bathed in the glow of morning. Her original question repeated itself in her mind, and she almost laughed at her own cold feet. She felt her ears pop softly as the plane banked slightly to the left and began its long descent, the sun's golden rays dancing along its silver wings.

Sirena's previous visit to this remote part of the country — a three-week vacation that had turned into a stay of nearly five months — was at the root of her return. Two years and five months had passed since that trip — an aeon since she'd spent such happy unfettered days — and now the balm of that golden time seemed to be returning to her as she drew nearer her destination.

There was no doubt now that Sirena was a fine painter with a promising future, but there had been a time when she'd felt stifled and uninspired. She had been twenty-four then, and her work had suffered. Her painting had seemed as flat and one-dimensional as she had felt. It was then that the letter had arrived — nearly the same letter as the one that had come to her mother the previous year and every year before that as long as Sirena could remember.

Her mother's second cousin, an old man, lived and worked happily on a ranch of enormous proportions in a wild segment of old Mexico. He had been particularly fond of Sirena's mother when she was young, but Sirena knew little more than that of the background. Her mother never had been one to tell long rambling tales of her childhood. Sirena did know, however, that for a time her mother's family had lived in Arizona, and it was then that Austin Reese had been very much a part of their lives. From what Sirena had managed to learn through the years, gathering what bits and pieces of information she could with the arrival of each annual letter, her mother and Austin Reese had much in common and had shared many experiences. Also, her mother had more than once visited Austin at his ranch, traveling the same perilous route that awaited Sirena. It was hard now for Sirena to envision her mother "roughing it" at any age, but at that time she had enjoyed Austin Reese's company immensely, and each passing year he had urged his cousin and her daughter to visit him.

That time, more than two years ago, Sirena's mother had coaxed her to take advantage of the invitation to get away from the city for a few weeks and find some new inspiration. Never having met her mother's cousin, Sirena had been reluctant. But she had also been desperate. With paints and canvases in tow she had gone for a three-week holiday, financed in part by her mother and the sale of several paintings through a small gallery in the city.

Three weeks had turned into nearly five months, and Sirena's work had blossomed, taking on new power, dimension and life. Austin Reese turned out to be completely different from what Sirena had expected. She had envisioned an old man sitting in a rocker issuing orders to a strapping foreman with dark hairy arms and chest, but the picture painted by her imagination had been far from the reality. Austin, eighty at the time of her visit, had been hitting the leather with the best of them, riding every day with Sirena in addition to managing ranch affairs. He galloped over desert and hills as if he were a cowboy in a western.

It had seemed to Sirena then as if she'd found home. When the day came that she had to leave, she'd sworn to return as soon as she could. But time had passed swiftly, and the paintings she'd brought back from the Sierra Madre had sold quickly at that same gallery in New York, snatching away her visible proof of what she'd accomplished in Mexico. She was left with only fading shreds of happy memories, and each day carried her, like a time traveler, farther from that special period in her life.

Now she was returning — but to what? Austin Reese had died a little more than a month ago, leaving all his vast holdings to her. Sirena had felt the shock waves of that revelation from the roots of her hair all the way to the soles of her feet after the telegram had come. She didn't know the exact size of the ranch Austin Reese had carved out of the desert and mountain wil-

9

derness, but it had to encompass thousands of acres. And there were stipulations to the will — stipulations Sirena was not yet sure she could live with. Because that was precisely what was meant: she would have to live on the ranch to inherit.

The plane gave a sickening lurch; a result, Sirena knew, of updrafts from the broiling desert floor far below, a common occurrence in spring and early summer. The seat-belt sign came on, and her knuckles turned white as she handed the coffee cup back to the steward hurrying past. A tall attractive man making his way toward the rear of the plane flashed a friendly smile at her, his probing dark eyes focusing on the empty seat beside her. Despite the roller-coaster feel to their ride, he didn't seem to be having any trouble keeping his feet beneath him.

Sirena met his gaze unflinchingly and gave him her most aloof smile in reply. It was difficult for her to give way when someone met and held her eyes. Few men seemed to understand that, and many times her directness had been misinterpreted as a come-on, when in reality it was nothing more than an unwillingness to show weakness, to shy coyly away from a man's appraising gaze.

It was amazing, Sirena reflected, the independence that seemed to have been bred into her. She remembered vividly her father's death when she was only six. The tragedy of his passing, preceded by a short illness, had caused her to jump from childhood into maturity with amazing speed. Her own naturally independent nature had propelled her into being more self-reliant.

Though Sirena's mother appeared self-sufficient on the surface, the simple fact was that she never recovered from her husband's death, for their marriage had been a true love match. Because of her mother's inability to cope, Sirena had quickly begun to take over more responsibilities as each year passed. Insurance and investments had left Sirena and her mother quite comfortable financially. Even so, Sirena had realized while still a child that all her mother's dating, all her seemingly frivolous travel and apparently unconnected wanderings, were geared to one impossible end: finding her beloved husband all over again.

The timbre of the engines changed subtly, and Sirena could

feel the plane slowing as it dipped and rode the air currents, the flaps outside the window lowering and vibrating with the strain. Her usual apprehensions clogging her throat, Sirena struggled to calm herself, listening vaguely to the announcement of impending landing that came over the speakers in a tinny, almost singsong voice.

In a few minutes the plane would be on the ground, and Sirena breathed a sigh of relief, but her comfort was short-lived as her active mind took the matter from there.

Once they were on the ground, then what? According to the telegram, she was to be met at the airport — but by whom? The last time Austin Reese had greeted her in person; this time there was no Austin. Her journey, in fact, had barely begun. The drive down into Mexico to the Reese ranch took a good ten to twelve hours, providing the truck didn't break down and the arroyos weren't flooded by recent rain, rare though that was. Thinking ahead, Sirena had brought enough clothes for several months, as well as a full set of paints, fresh and new, plus rolled canvases. She intended to give ranch life a fair trial before deciding.

There was no doubt in Sirena's mind about her own managerial skills; she would get the hang of things soon enough. What tugged at the back of her mind, filling it with indecision, was the ranch's location. She would be hundreds of miles from a large city and more than twenty from the nearest village. Most of her life Sirena had been a city girl, surrounded by people and things. The fact that she had always been wild about horses, nearly bullying her mother into providing riding lessons in Central Park, had done nothing to prepare her for the reality of country life. She was not too sure she could handle this total change in her life.

Sirena's mother had laughed at her apprehensions, insisting she had been born to it and urging her not to pass up such an unexpected opportunity. As far as her mother had been concerned, it was all cut-and-dried. Sirena would live her life down in Mexico on the huge ranch Austin had left her. She would paint all year and spend a month or two out of each back in New York for a gallery showing and sale of her accumulated

11

work. Of course, during the year she could ship selected paintings back to New York for sale; while that might not be as easy as shipping from New York, it was certainly not impossible. Those had been the words of wisdom Sirena's mother had imparted to her just before boarding the jet to Europe with her latest companion, a Manhattan lawyer.

It was the way her mother had always been: caring, concerned about Sirena's future, but brusque and often following the simplest or most auspicious course of the moment. Much of that same personality that brightly told Sirena to take a blind plunge into a new life was reflected in her own flighty behavior. Maybe, Sirena considered, she was her mother's daughter more than she cared to admit.

The soft bump of the plane touching down on the runway jarred Sirena from her musings, and she was thrust lightly against the restraint of her seat belt before the plane slowed to a lumbering taxi that would take it to the gate for disembarking. Up ahead Sirena could see the low-slung profile of the Tucson airport crouched beside the network of runways that radiated out from it. Already the ground crew was scattering, running around like so many busy ants, rolling out the stairs and guiding the big jet in.

Sirena's mind, though, was far from the busy scene, rushing on ahead to the ranch that awaited her. A jumble of thoughts assailed her: thoughts of her mother and her own past years. By now her mother would be somewhere in London, even as she herself was preparing to penetrate the interior of Mexico, half a world away. How could she ever have guessed that her jogs along the bridle paths in Central Park would someday bring her here?

Over the loudspeaker the pilot was rattling off the airline's thanks, the local temperature, the present time and instructions for those continuing the flight, but Sirena paid little attention. Collecting her purse from beneath the seat in front of her — the only thing she hadn't checked as baggage — she automatically rose with the others and made her way toward the door, jostled gently from the rear. She felt an odd apprehension growing within her, and her mind raced as she slowly followed

12

the bobbling line of people to the door that led to fresh air and sunshine beyond. It was not too late to turn back. She could take the next flight back to New York, sign the papers relinquishing any claim to the ranch in Mexico and forget the whole thing had ever happened.

Sirena knew she could do that, but in the same instant she knew also she could not. This was a challenge, and she had never been one to run from a challenge. One way or another she would see it through to its conclusion. She set her softly squared chin and turned her blue eyes to the future.

Her thoughts marshaled about her, Sirena decided the best approach was to head immediately for the lower level and baggage claim; whoever was meeting her would undoubtedly be there. He or she would not be in the crowd of people hovering just inside the glass doors, eagerly straining for a first glimpse of a friend or relative arriving on the plane. Eyes set forward, spine erect, Sirena marched across the concourse with the other passengers, caressed by the warmly wafting breeze and brilliant early-morning sunshine. The group burst through the double doors to the cooler interior in a flood.

The meeting of the two crowds of people, those waiting and those arriving, was like the clash of an incoming and an outgoing wave. Sirena bobbed and weaved her way through the press of people, eyes never moving from the point she had set for herself somewhere up ahead. Her mind already focused on the long trip ahead, she never saw the hand that reached out to grasp her arm gently but firmly.

"Sirena Clark?" asked a low mellow voice, questioning and yet already sure of her response.

"Yes," Sirena admitted, lightly pulling away from the man who'd accosted her, testing his grip. But the stranger seemed unprepared for the moment to turn her loose.

She shifted her gaze from the deeply sunbrowned strong hand that grasped her arm and met a pair of compelling gray green eyes flecked with a brooding black. As their eyes met and held, a jolt — actually a shock — ran up the length of Sirena's spine, and she wondered at her dramatic reaction to a total stranger. It was as though her skin had turned super sensitive where his rough fingers brushed lightly against her flesh. Her mouth, she realized, had gone suddenly dry.

A smile curved the thin lips set in a face that to Sirena seemed far from handsome. His eyes as they regarded her appeared to change color, flecks of gold leaping into their depths to do battle with the black that lurked at the bottom of the twin gray green pools. It was as if he could read every thought that went through her mind.

Ridiculous! Sirena knew her mouth was dry from the flight. As to the rest, flying did funny things to her nerves. This was merely a delayed reaction; she just knew it was so. This tall arrogant stranger had made no move to remove his hand, and yet the tumultuous feelings were already receding. The flutterings of her heart began to quiet, and Sirena decided she wasn't too pleased with the proprietary air he had so instantly assumed with her.

"I didn't catch your name," she said coolly, drawing away enough to make it quite clear she was going to have her arm back. She waited expectantly for his explanation and apology.

Aristocratic head thrown back, the stranger gave a low rumbling laugh from somewhere deep in his chest. His reaction caught Sirena completely by surprise.

"That's because I haven't told you yet." His features were dark, matching his thick raven hair and suggesting at least some Mexican ancestry, yet he spoke with only the faintest accent. "I'm Ramón Savedel," he explained with a solemn little bow that would have been courtly had it not been for the sarcastic edge to his words. "I've been sent, as promised," he went on smoothly, "to pick you up here and deliver you to the Reese ranch. If you want to go elsewhere," he added dryly, "you'll have to make other arrangements. I don't have the time to oblige."

The compelling gray green eyes appeared almost to glow as he swept her with an insolently appraising look from head to toe, and Sirena got the distinct impression he did not have much use for her. But he didn't even know her; how could he dislike her? She shrugged mentally. It *was* possible. She herself was already feeling a considerable dislike for Ramón Savedel and the accompanying fact that she was going to be spending the next ten or more hours with him.

"Mr. Savedel —" Sirena put ice into her words "— I would hardly expect you to do more than agreed. I wish only to reach my destination as soon as possible, with as little annoyance as possible."

Sirena felt the color mounting in her cheeks along with her temper, but there was nothing she could do about it. Ramón Savedel was deliberately baiting her; she was naive in many ways, but she was not blind to something as blatant as that. Why he was baiting her she didn't know, but she was determined not to rise any further to it. She was going to have to spend many long hours in the close confines of a vehicle with this man, and already she knew the experience was bound to be an unpleasant one.

"Ramón — please call me Ramón. And I'll call you Sirena." The stark angularity of his chin and deeply chiseled features was somehow softened by the grin that quirked the corners of his lips. Sirena had the distinct feeling he was mocking her.

"Ramón, then." Sirena gritted her teeth and managed a smile that was not quite sincere. She would have preferred to snap back in reply and inform him that he could call her Miss Clark, but the journey had already taken on a promise of difficulty and it did not seem prudent to make matters worse. With a little luck, after he delivered her to the Reese ranch she would never have to see him again.

The crowd around them had mostly dispersed, leaving only Ramón Savedel and Sirena Clark standing in the broad corridor of the airport. Sirena, usually supremely self-confident, felt suddenly awkward and out of control of the situation. The fact that there was no situation to be in control of did nothing to ease her tension.

"I think we'd better go get my luggage," Sirena said at last, her voice sounding strangely hollow to her ears. "If you have so little time to spare —" she threw his own remark back at him "— we'd better get moving."

"Whatever you say." Ramón's voice was as smooth as silk and just as caressing. His eyes were shuttered now, revealing

15

nothing to Sirena's questioning gaze. "Right this way," he added, gesturing to the small sign that depicted a cartoon cowboy making a mad dash in the direction of the baggage claim.

Much to Sirena's relief he didn't try to touch her again. She didn't care to know if his simply touching her now would have the same results as only a short time earlier; she was perfectly content to attribute her original feelings to flight nerves. Sirena was not one to tamper with a matter laid to rest.

No words passed between them as they made their way down the long corridor, winding around and through pockets of weary travelers draped with cameras, heavy burdens of luggage clutched in their hands. Sirena never in her life had been one for small talk. Still, the silence weighed heavy, and she was relieved to reach the stairway that led to the lower level, where her baggage would undoubtedly be awaiting her arrival by now.

"May I have your claim tickets?" Ramón was perfectly polite, but something about his tone didn't encourage conversation. There was a manner of stiff formality about him, yet at the same time he seemed to be actively courting a dislike for Sirena, a total stranger to him. There was a puzzle here to be solved. Of course, Sirena reasoned, it could be merely an instant personality clash. But if there was not something more than met the eye, she would be vastly surprised.

Sirena handed over her claim tickets as requested, though she could see there was no need. There was no one posted to check the baggage claim tickets against those attached to the bags. In fact, hers were the only ones left in sight, slowly turning on the heavy black belt that carried them along.

Ramón frowned. "All yours?" he asked over his shoulder as he stooped to pick up the first one and latched onto a second following only a short distance behind.

"Yes," Sirena replied. Why did that admission make her feel somehow guilty and awkward?

Muttering complaints to himself, Ramón collected her assortment of bags, the cases containing her art supplies and her portfolio. "I like a woman who travels light," he remarked

16

sarcastically, tucking a couple of bags under his arms, slinging one over his shoulder and picking up a couple more with his hands. That left only the portfolio and Sirena's lightweight disassembled easel for her to manage.

"If I stay at Rancho Reese," Sirena said tightly in icy tones, using Austin Reese's name for the ranch, "I'll be needing all of that and more."

"For what?" Ramón asked quietly, turning with his burden toward the door and swearing mildly upon discovering the automatic mechanism wasn't working that day. "There aren't any discos down there, or museums, or libraries, or even galleries," he went on in spite of the predicament he found himself in: a door to open and no free hand to manage it.

With her lighter burden, despite her growing dislike for Ramón Savedel, Sirena attempted to dart ahead and open the door for him. But he was too quick for her. Even overloaded, he forcefully pressed his lean athletic body against the door to push it open, bracing himself to hold it for her at the same time.

Forced to pass within precious inches of his slender aristocratic frame, Sirena noticed for the first time the thoroughbred build of him, his height as he towered above her. Once again she felt the strange, almost animal magnetism she'd experienced earlier at his touch.

"Excuse me," she murmured as she passed him with lowered eyes. She was amazed by her own uncharacteristic behavior — by the unconsciously demure attitude she adopted before this overbearing man.

Outside the door she straightened and faced him squarely as he struggled through the door on his own. If he wanted to be a martyr, she resolved, let him. She would no longer attempt to dent his masculine pride by offering her help.

Ramón didn't bother to get the car and bring it around. Instead he continued out into the parking lot, leaving Sirena to follow or stay as she chose. Even loaded down with luggage, Ramón Savedel strode across the pavement like an Olympic runner. His long legs carried him easily across concrete dividers and miniature cactus gardens that separated one drive from another, as well as the long-term parkers from the short termers.

Toting her light burden, Sirena hurried along behind, swearing at the dressy high-heeled shoes she'd chosen to wear on the plane. They slowed her stride now and made her appear a stumbling idiot unable even to stay on her own feet. She glared at Ramón's broad back moving across the parking lot ahead of her and wondered if he was at all aware of her as he swept along to their destination.

Then Sirena saw the vehicle he was heading for and almost groaned aloud. It was a Jeep, a small one with only minimal luggage space at the back, and that, she noted as she stumbled up, was already half filled with a huge jug of water and a bulky canvas sack.

"Lucky I brought some rope," Ramón said evenly, already fishing in the depths of the Jeep's open trunk. "We'll have to tie on some of these bags." He paused and gave her that same sweeping appraisal she had suffered earlier inside the airport. "Sirena, did you bring any other shoes with you?" he finally asked, his voice infused with the patience of a saint.

The tone rankled, but Sirena nodded. "Yes, shoes as well as boots. I *have* been to Rancho Reese before," she reminded him tartly.

"I know." Ramón's eyes sparkled, and Sirena tried to remember having seen him previously when she had been there with Austin. "That's all the more reason you should have had the good sense to wear them," he went on, his accent a bit more noticeable now. "Do you know which bag you packed them in, or would we risk scattering women's dainties all over the surrounding cacti if you dared open it? Because if there's any chance of your reaching them, I suggest you do so. The next time we step out of this Jeep the country will be far from suited to your present footwear."

Sirena flushed. She was more than half tempted to send this pompous Ramón Savedel on his way without her and find some other manner of reaching Rancho Reese on her own. The man was insufferably rude. She hesitated, cheeks flaming.

No, Sirena decided, this was no man to back down or run from. He sorely needed a lesson, and turning her back on him would not bring it to him. "Just what the hell is your problem?"

she demanded scathingly, hands braced on her hips, her entire being rebelling at his tone and obviously negative opinion of her. It was impossible for her to accept his blatantly disparaging attitude in silence.

The gold in the depths of Ramón's eyes seemed to flare for an instant. "I have no problem, as you put it," he replied silkily, "that your taking yourself back to the city where you belong wouldn't cure." Then an expression akin to pity shone in his eyes. "You're a city woman, and yet you want to play at running a grand *rancho*. You will never stay long enough to learn what it truly means to be *patrona* of Rancho Reese, but as long as you do stay, we'll be seeing a lot of each other."

The thought flashed through Sirena's mind that she would most certainly do her best to make sure they did not spend time together after this trip, but she kept it to herself.

"My shoes are in that bag." Sirena stiffly indicated the one he had slung over his shoulder, changing the direction of their discussion. The garment carrier was equipped with an attached zippered pouch inside for extra shoes. "If you'll just give it to me, you can pack the rest in the back while I get them out and change." Sirena's voice was frigid as she experimented with giving orders. Then, lifting the bag wordlessly from Ramón's shoulder, she moved to the passenger's seat to sit down. At least now she knew where she stood with this grim stranger. He obviously, for reasons of his own, did not think she should inherit Rancho Reese or even be here at all. And he was making it quite clear he didn't care if she was aware of his feelings.

Ramón quirked an eyebrow in her direction and tossed the heaviest of the bags into the back of the Jeep.

Defiantly Sirena lifted her chin, a challenge in the depths of her blue eyes. It didn't matter to her what Ramón Savedel thought of her. She was here — and she didn't intend to let him interfere with her plans. With an air of being in control once again she efficiently unzipped the garment bag, reached in and withdrew the thick-soled walking shoes she had packed. Rezipping the garment bag with a flourish, she left it within Ramón's reach to load with the rest of her things. Then Sirena removed her flimsy open-toed high-heeled sandals and tossed them nonchalantly into the open space directly behind her seat. Without another thought to them, she snuggled her small feet into the more comfortable and supportive leather walking shoes, and as her toes basked in the newfound comfort, she wondered why women, just for appearances' sake, wore the shoes they did.

The answer she knew as well as the question; it was as old as the ages. Vanity. Through the centuries women had pulled, pushed, laced and locked themselves into almost anything they believed appealing to the male eye. Well, Sirena decided with a wry glance over her slim shoulder in Ramón's direction, *she* did not have a male eye she wished to please. High-heeled shoes were ridiculous, and she intended to avail herself of all the comforts so well remembered at Rancho Reese. Where footwear was concerned, that meant lovely flat open sandals. Huaraches.

Sirena sighed as Ramón finished tying the last knot, giving everything an extra good tug to make sure it was secure. She did up the laces on her shoes, unaware of the view of shapely leg she displayed for his probing gaze.

Swinging her legs into the Jeep, Sirena glanced down at her feet. The shoes were not exactly flattering to the dress. She sighed again. It was all too likely that once back in New York she would change her mind about uncomfortable shoes; that simply was the way things were. Of course, she could wear a dress more suited to the shoes, or slacks. The light clingy dress she had on now befitted comfortable plane travel, but its designer had had nothing like what lay ahead in mind. Sirena didn't know where her brains could have been when she'd dressed for the trip late the previous night.

Down to minute details Sirena remembered the route they would be taking from the Tucson airport to their final destination in Mexico. Undoubtedly they would go east from the airport, then turn off on the Sonora highway south to Nogales, which was about seventy miles south of Tucson.

At Nogales they would cross the border into Sonora and drive south on highway 15. It would be more than one hundred and fifty miles on that leg of the journey to Hermosillo. All that would be an easy drive. It was when they took the dirt-road cutoff near Hermosillo and began threading their way southeast with nearly another two hundred miles to travel that the going would get rough. Rancho Reese lay below Madera in Chihuahua, cradled in the bosom of the Sierra Madre Occidental. Vast expanses of the ranch bordered the Rio Sirupa. It was desert, mountain and valley set in a crazy-quilt pattern that brought change with each passing mile. The journey by Jeep yet ahead was going to take longer than the trip by plane she had already endured.

"Ready?" Ramón dropped into the driver's seat, the light Jeep swaying with the sudden added weight, and turned over the ignition before Sirena had an opportunity to reply.

The Jeep started with a solid roar, and Ramón nonchalantly jammed it into gear, pulling out into traffic. Sirena grabbed for the handhold set in the dash and braced herself in her seat as he whipped the small vehicle around a tight corner and accelerated. There was a definite desert morning chill in the air, giving Sirena another reason to curse her choice of dress for this trip. She hadn't expected a limousine to greet her at the airport, but neither had she expected to be met by an open Jeep. Grimly she set her teeth against their chattering. The June sun would soon be climbing, and its burning warmth would bring on a new problem.

"There's an old jacket behind your seat." Ramón spoke loudly to be heard over the roar of the wind created by the Jeep's passing. "You look as if you could use it."

"Thanks," Sirena murmured, though some strange unpredictable part of her rebelled at thanking this man for anything.

Marveling at her own peculiar feelings where this stranger was concerned, she quashed an inner urge to say something biting. For some reason, Ramón Savedel swept away her normal rational approach to everything and left Sirena feeling off stride and unreasonably angry about it.

The whole thing was absurd, she decided as Ramón whipped the Jeep off a local road onto the nearly deserted interstate, where at the early-morning hour few were stirring. The light hem of her dress fluttered in the breeze, caressing her legs with feathery strokes that seemed rather distracting under the circumstances. Twisting around in the seat, Sirena felt for and grabbed the offered jacket. She knew what Ramón thought of her, of her urban upbringing, but she was going to make a determined effort to be friendly. She was not just another city girl looking for adventure in the wild mountains. And — she formulated the thought without realizing it — he would know that soon enough.

"Do you live down near Rancho Reese? Are you a neighbor?" Sirena asked as she shrugged into the heavy jacket and wrapped its generous width about her slender form. She wished it was long enough to tuck down around her legs, for the wind was whipping at her skirt hem in a dangerously revealing game of peekaboo. "Or are you making the trip from Tucson to take me down?"

"That's one helluva long trip for a Sunday-afternoon drive," Ramón said with a laugh. He glanced at Sirena with a mocking smile, his eyes flashing.

"Well, then," Sirena persisted, "why are you doing it?"

"I owed Austin Reese a favor," he replied, "that's all." His words were blunt, but his tone hinted at some further reason.

"Is it really?" Sirena retorted.

Though she had no idea what she was fishing for, she enjoyed the clouded disturbed look that passed across Ramón's arrogant features. It was as if he suspected her of knowing something he thought she shouldn't. Keeping her eyes focused straight ahead, her long graceful fingers fighting to hold back the silken mass of her auburn hair swirled about by the wind, Sirena let a knowing smile curl the corners of her lips.

"Austin is dead," she said quietly. "He wouldn't know one way or another if you paid him your debt of honor."

"No, he wouldn't," Ramón admitted, guiding the Jeep into its turnoff to the south onto the Sonora highway. "But I would."

Sirena laughed softly at his reply. "That's true." While not having any great liking for Ramón Savedel, she had to at least admire the character of a man who would pay his debts, no matter what. "Still —" Sirena wouldn't let the matter rest "— it couldn't have been a very large debt for you to be able to repay it with one trip up to Tucson and back."

"This trip doesn't make up to Austin Reese by a long shot," Ramón returned. "Not that it's any of your business," he added dryly. Half turning to her as the Jeep raced along at a breath-taking speed Sirena found more than slightly uncomfortable, Ramón quirked a black eyebrow and twisted his lips sardonically. She had slipped, revealing — to his obvious pleasure — her decided lack of knowledge where his relationship to Austin was concerned.

"And don't think the debt passes on from cousin to cousin." Ramón's words had a bite, and his eyes the pierce of a lance. "In this arrangement I do what Austin asked of me, not you. Given half a chance, a woman like you might get the wrong idea."

"A woman like me!" Sirena almost stood up in her seat, her voice going hoarse with the anger that rushed through her like a runaway freight train, her throat threatening to close on the words she spoke. "Tell me, just what kind of a woman am I, Mr. Savedel?" Sirena's lips felt stiff, and her eloquent eyes glittered with an anger that went much deeper than anything she'd known in recent years.

How could this man do this to her with a simple off-the-cuff remark? How could he categorize her without even knowing her? Sirena fumed as she waited, blue eyes boring into the side of his head for his answer.

"You know what kind of a woman you are," Ramón said icily. "Do you want it spelled out for you? All right, you're a fortune hunter. Rancho Reese, despite its rather unique location, is no small plum. You know you could have signed off. You could have stayed in that nice comfortable apartment in New York City. The inheritance would have fallen to others — others who are considerably more deserving. But now here you are to claim what you see as rightfully yours. After playing fairy princess for a few months in Austin's hacienda, you think you can come back here and run things."

He glanced sharply to where Sirena sat as still as a statue, staring straight ahead into the glow of the morning, her creamy skin bathed in a gold-and-rose light that caught in her auburn hair. She looked like a beautiful witch, her skin kissed by the early-morning sun. Her chin was cocked at a defiant angle, her hair streaming out behind in a glowing curtain of silken flame-licked bronze.

"You *are* planning on taking over the reins and running things, aren't you?" Ramón pressed. "A ranch doesn't run itself; it takes a lot of hard work. You can't daintily paint with one hand, keeping it clean and lily white up at the hacienda, and at the same time wrestle in the dirt with the rest of us to keep a working ranch going. You'll have to excuse me for being blunt, *Miss* Clark, but I just don't think you're suited to it." His eyes moved over her in silent swift disapproval. "Even if you are deserving of it — which is something else I don't believe."

Ramón shook his head and gave the road another glance as they continued on their twisting roller-coaster ride. "Poor Austin must have been getting senile just before he died to leave that place to you," he finished flatly.

A sign with the name of a town whipped suddenly into view from behind a small hill and disappeared just as quickly. The town itself was lost in the blink of an eye, since Ramón made no move to slow the pace of the Jeep speeding south. They were only a few minutes from the border.

Sirena could feel explosive anger boiling inside of her. What had been active dislike for Ramón Savedel could easily turn into a well-trenched hatred. They had not known each other much more than an hour, and already she felt she could cheerfully throw him from the speeding Jeep. He had no right to pass judgment on her — and no right to so insult the man to whom he claimed he owed so much. Sirena wanted to scream at him, to tell him in strident tones just what she thought of him, but that wasn't her style. Besides, that sort of behavior was no doubt exactly what he expected of her.

"How dare you speak like that about Austin Reese!" Sirena ground the words out at a volume that barely topped the whine of the Jeep's engine. "You claim to be his friend, then you insult him like that?" In silence Ramón guided the Jeep into a tight right turn that seemed almost to double back on itself as he headed into the Nogales on the American side of the border.

"Basically," Sirena went on, no stopping her now, "it's none of your business why Austin Reese left his ranch to me and none of your business whether I come here to live and accept the terms of the will." Sirena put ice in her voice and, she hoped, doubt in his mind. Her words showered on Ramón like splintering glass. "Furthermore, I don't give a damn what you think about me or anything I may do. You're an insufferably rude man, and I doubt we have anything further to say to each other!"

There was no time for a telling silence to settle in the wake of Sirena's sharp words as the huge gates at the border loomed up ahead. It did not appear to be too crowded: the cars were moving along at a steady pace, passing through the gates with little delay.

Ramón made no reply to Sirena's stinging verbal attack but merely curled his lips in a mocking smile that grated on her nerves and spoke volumes. His opinion of her was set; it would not change easily. He eased the Jeep to a halt before the border entry station and leaned a bit to one side to exchange a few words with the uniformed guard. The guard obviously knew him, for he greeted him with a broad grin and threw a casual glance in Sirena's direction. As they conversed in Spanish, she had the uneasy feeling the conversation was mainly about her. Of course, that was an absurd assumption, and Sirena kept her eyes straight ahead, only nodding politely in the direction of the guard when it appeared the conversation was at a close.

Sirena made her decision almost instantly after Ramón's accusation. She definitely would not suffer this man's presence beyond the border crossing. At the earliest opportunity she would leave him to make her way to Rancho Reese. Surely she could hire some form of transportation in Nogales.

Slipping the Jeep into gear, Ramón let out the clutch and jumped the vehicle ahead into the heavy traffic of the Mexican section of Nogales.

"We're across the border," Sirena pointed out succinctly. "Now if you'd just let me out and unload my baggage, I'll make my own way from here to the Reese ranch. I won't be needing your services any longer, so you can count your debt to Austin paid."

Ramón responded with silence, adeptly dodging a car as it

25

pulled out of a steep side street. His foot slammed the gas pedal to the floor, and he changed gears like a racing driver, goosing out of the Jeep's engine every last ounce of pickup it had. The area near the border was crowded with tourists, and as Sirena kept her eye open for a likely hotel, she noted the hilly alleys that fed into the main artery. Having made her decision to separate from Ramón, Sirena realized it was going to take longer to get to the ranch than she'd originally planned — an annoyance, but better than the situation she was now forced to endure.

"Whenever you get the opportunity, please pull over." Sirena's voice was brittle, and she tried to put a vibrant tone of command into her words. After all, she reasoned, for him to keep her against her will could be construed as kidnapping.

Ramón most certainly had heard her words, but he showed no intention of pulling the Jeep over to the curb. Colorful Nogales was slipping quickly away on either side of them, and before long they would be outside the city, threading their way south along temporarily good highways that would soon dissolve into dirt tracks. Then would definitely not be the time to abandon her driver, and Sirena was determined to carry through on what she had decided so abruptly only minutes earlier, despite having only a vague notion of how she would proceed from here on her own.

Sirena glared at Ramón. She was not going to repeat herself, and if he was trying to bait her again, she was determined not to go for it. Before they'd left Nogales altogether, he would pull over, maybe even double back, once he saw she was not going to be harassed and bullied by him.

Lips grimly compressed in anger, Sirena sat silently beside Ramón Savedel as he drove like a madman through the narrow streets. He dodged cars and pedestrians with the same adroit skill, one muscular brown hand locked on the steering wheel, the other on the knob of the stick shift.

"Sure do like a quiet woman," Ramón observed as they left the outer limits of Nogales behind for the rolling desert beyond.

Sirena jerked her gaze around to his face and in that instant knew he had no intention of turning back. For a frozen moment the realization sent a chill up her spine, and a feeling of help-lessness washed over her. She did not know this man. The farther they got from Nogales, the less likelihood there would be of her finding any help. With the exception of an odd village or two, from here on the country turned wild, and Sirena dreaded the thought of being alone out there with Ramón.

"Stop this Jeep right now and let me out," Sirena ordered determinedly. "I told you in Nogales that I'm not going with you. I want to go back — immediately!"

"Too much trouble to turn around," Ramón said with a grin as the Jeep continued to career down the road at breathtaking speed under his steady hand.

Sirena glowered at him, but it was painfully evident that neither sharp words nor a devastating look was going to have any effect at all on this man. Action was the only answer.

"Why are you so determined to get away from me, anyway?" Ramón questioned her in a velvet tone. "Did I hit a little too close to the truth for you to take?" He glanced her way, then returned his gaze to the long stretch of road that unraveled before them. "Just sit back and relax. I'll get you to *your* ranch soon enough."

"I don't take orders!" Sirena snapped. "Especially not from you!" And with one deft movement she reached over, flicked the key to the left and jerked it from the ignition.

Instantly the Jeep engine died, and Sirena jumped nimbly from her seat, carrying the keys along with her. She headed back the way they had come before the Jeep had had a chance to roll to a complete halt. Bleakly she reflected on her momen-tary gratitude to Ramón for his sarcastic comments on her footwear back in Tucson. Feet safely cradled in the soft leather of her sturdy walking shoes, Sirena stepped out with a long swinging stride along the edge of the road.

She intended to toss the keys to the side after a few steps, but then she became increasingly aware of the sound of heavy footsteps coming resolutely after her. Anger renewed itself as a burning knot within the pit of her stomach, and right alongside it, piercing her with its icy point, was a barb of fear.

Impulsively she considered flinging the keys in Ramón's face and suggesting he safely escort her luggage to the ranch to the south, while she herself would go back to Nogales and handle things on her own from there. But the impulse never manifested itself in action. In fact, it was all Sirena could do to quell the urge to run as those footsteps bore down on her. The same hand that had gripped her back at the airport, gently restraining, now wrapped itself around her arm in a band of steel, pulling her up short with a wrench.

"The least you could do if you're going to walk out on a man is return his jacket." Ramón's words were harsh and cutting. "It gets cold out in the desert at night."

In her agitation Sirena had completely forgotten the jacket she'd donned back in Tucson for the open Jeep ride.

"Take it, then!" she snapped, attempting to shrug out of the garment as his fingers curled tightly around her arm.

"Oh, no." Ramón's voice had turned silken. "I like it just fine where it is . . . for the moment." His eyes glittered with a smoldering fire, and his steady gaze told Sirena much more than words as he used his greater strength to draw her steadily closer to him.

CHAPTER TWO

Where men were concerned Sirena was far from broadly experienced, but the look in Ramón Savedel's eye was one she had seen more than once in her life. There was no mistaking it. A small shiver of fear rippled along the surface of her skin, raising goose bumps in its wake, as she stared up into the fathomless depths of his eyes.

"Let me go!" she demanded as he drew her inexorably nearer. Some inner reservoir of strength gave force to her voice and determination to her exhortation.

With disturbing ease Ramón plucked the Jeep's keys from Sirena's unresisting fingers as she continued to stare at his chiseled features, sun-browned and harsh in the glare of the full-morning light. Even though nervous and unspeakably angry, she still managed to feel ridiculous clad in her fancy afternoon dress, a heavy fur-lined denim jacket that fell way below her hips with sleeves far too long and her solid but unflattering walking shoes. Her silken hair was caught childishly beneath the collar of the jacket, and Sirena seethed as she strained against the man's hold.

Still gripping her, Ramón easily encircled Sirena's waist with his free arm. She was grateful for the thickness of the heavy jacket that separated their bodies as he drew her up tightly against him to overcome her resistance.

There was no escape from his grasp save his releasing her of his own volition, and though the urge was strong within her to strike out at him in anger and frustration, Sirena stilled her struggles. Her heart was beating wildly, fluttering within her breast like a captured bird. She was sure Ramón could feel it even through the thickness of the jacket that separated them.

Gasping for breath, Sirena felt the quivering of her knees and knew real fear when she stared into Ramón's cold unwavering gaze. The arrogance of his features, the stubborn tilt of his chin branded him as a man who would dare almost anything, and she was here with him alone.

"That's better." Ramón's voice mellowed as his initial anger seemed to soften, and his grip on her transformed itself almost into an embrace.

All Sirena's senses were tautly alive and tingling. She nearly choked on her efforts to breathe, though her very recent physical exertion had been light. A liquid warmth seemed to be spreading throughout her body, filling her mind with a light airy bubble that threatened to snatch her senses away. She felt as though she were shrinking from him within the oversized confines of the jacket that had suddenly become much too warm to bear as his face, starkly angular and darkly handsome, filled her vision.

"That was a damn fool stupid stunt you pulled back there," Ramón said sternly, gray green eyes glowing with the flecks of gold igniting and flaring within their depths. Anger was there, but also something else. An almost pantherish sensuality lurked behind the flaring of the gold.

Sirena's limbs felt weak and languid, but from somewhere she found the strength to repeat her demand. "Release me immediately." She made her voice as low and rude as possible. "I told you, I'm going back to Nogales. I'll handle things my own way from there."

Ramón's face loomed close above hers as she stood enveloped in the intoxicating indefinable male scent of him. She could feel a strange new emotion growing inside her with a throbbing power that seemed almost to rob her of her strength, raising from the primitive depths of her an urge to melt within the strong circle of his arms.

With a cynical smile Ramón quirked an eyebrow but did nothing to loosen his hold on her.

"I'm not going to release you . . . yet." Ramón breathed the words like a flutter of butterfly wings into her ear. "Not until we have an understanding between us." His tone sharpened and his grip tightened as Sirena, almost as a reflex at his remark, began to push against him to force her freedom.

"You're an overbearing tyrant of a man!" she accused, thrashing wildly in her imagination for the insults that best suited his outrageous behavior. "A despicable dictatorial barbarian! Does it fuel that male ego of yours to prove your strength is superior to mine?" She spat the words angrily.

"You're forgetting who I'm doing this for," Ramón returned evenly. "It's not for you — it's for Austin Reese. I promised him I would collect you from the airport and bring you safely to the ranch. I have collected you, and now I'm taking you there. From that point on you may do whatever you wish, my little termagant, but for now I'll give you a choice." The cruel curve of his lips returned; Ramón was clearly enjoying his physical superiority over her.

Sirena blanched, but with one arm locked firmly in his grip and the other hand braced against his broad chest, there was very little she could do save await his dictum.

"You can get back in that Jeep with me and ride upright, or you can try something like what you just pulled again and find yourself tied up along with the rest of the baggage," he finished mildly, but his words were like a slap.

Never in her life had Sirena been treated in such a way, and never again would she permit it, she resolved as she stood immobile in his cruel embrace. If she ever got the chance to make him pay for this indignity, he would indeed pay dearly. White-hot anger was already breeding the seeds for revenge.

Trying to read in his eyes whether he would in fact carry through on his threat, Sirena stared up into Ramón's face. He would, she decided, and would also enjoy doing it. Once she reached the ranch, she would be in the driver's seat — an opportunity she would relish when it came. She didn't know what kind of trouble she could stir up for Mr. Ramón Savedel, but she would do her best to check every angle once she was safely at her destination.

"You've made your point," Sirena conceded. "Now let me go."

"I would," Ramón chided softly, "but if I do, you'll fall flat on the ground."

The bitter humor of his words chilled Sirena. She suddenly

realized she'd been leaning her full weight against his encircling arm, that she'd practically fallen against him. Her back stiffened and a high flush colored her cheeks. It was left to Sirena's imagination to figure out what was going through Ramón's mind at her reaction.

What was worse, her own behavior gave her cause to doubt herself. The man was infuriating, a bully — in every way the kind of man she'd avoided like the plague since high school. Arrogant and superior, he was full of his own ego. His very attractiveness seemed somehow to make that all the worse. And the awareness that she had, without realizing it, begun to respond to him, made her cringe with self-disgust.

"I'm perfectly able to stand on my own," Sirena told him defiantly. "You're —"

"Very well." Ramón released his hold on her so abruptly Sirena hardly had time to collect herself, stumbling back a step or two before she could regain her balance. The suddenness of the act forced the uncompleted thought from her mind.

"Shall we, then?" Ramón questioned, gesturing broadly in the direction of the Jeep. He gave a small mocking bow.

Glowering, Sirena walked briskly in the direction of the vehicle, feeling somehow like a prisoner. That was not so, she reasoned; she was on the way to claim her inheritance. Nothing Ramón Savedel could do or say would change that, and it didn't matter to her *what* he thought of her or her motives.

Brilliant blue eyes glittering with suppressed anger flicked in Ramón's direction as he swung into his side of the Jeep, hardly casting a glance at Sirena to see if she was indeed following his instruction. Evidently he entertained no doubts whatsoever that she would do as she'd been told. That fact sent the blood coursing through Sirena's veins with renewed anger. He was so *sure* of himself, so sure of her. It was too much. She would live for the hour when she'd be free of him for good.

In stony silence Sirena took her seat, waiting tensely as Ramón turned the key and the Jeep surged once again to life. With less than his usual smooth acceleration, Ramón guided the Jeep back onto the pavement, speed gathering as his foot rested heavily on the gas pedal.

Her hair whipping in the wind, Sirena shrugged out of the heavy jacket, leaving it draped around her shoulders, for a touch of nighttime chill still punctuated the rising warmth of the air around them. By the time the sun traced its path overhead the heat would become quite intense, and Sirena reveled in the first kiss of the sun upon her undeniably pale skin. If she were careful, she would soon have that delicious golden tan she'd acquired on her last visit.

It didn't matter that none of her friends and acquaintances would be around to admire it. Just the lift she got when she looked in the mirror and discovered her new self would be enough. And there would be plenty of opportunity for her to ride horses — a pastime she loved. Sirena was an excellent rider, a fact Austin Reese had been astounded to learn. Peace and beauty abounded everywhere, on the ranch proper and in the wild countryside that surrounded it. Maybe this was a good idea; maybe this really was where she belonged. She just had to get there first.

The only thing that would be missing was Austin himself, and to Sirena that was a pretty big something. Austin Reese had been the ranch. It could feel unbelievably hollow without him, a shell of what it once was. Sirena could vividly remember the bustle of work going on around the ranch, the yells of the men as they worked outside and the quick movements of the housekeeper, Anita, as she puttered about within the walls of the sprawling hacienda, cooking and cleaning.

All except Austin would be there when she arrived; of that much Sirena had been apprised. A sum of money was also part of the estate, to be used to keep the ranch running and the employees paid for a period of time while the details of who was going to take over were worked out. Just how much money there was had not been revealed to her. That information, the will stipulated, was to be withheld until Sirena reached the ranch itself and chose whether to accept her inheritance with its terms. The amount didn't matter, since Sirena would have control over it only if she stayed on and used it for the running of the ranch. Sirena just hoped it would be enough to keep things going until she could learn the business side of the ranch's operation. She hated even the possibility of putting the proud ranch into debt.

Sirena knew from the will's contents that Austin had appointed someone he was very fond of to guide her and familiarize her with the ranch's operation. She supposed he would be there waiting for her, to help her avoid any economic pitfalls that might confront her. While reading through the sheaf of papers explaining the arrangements in detail, she had skimmed over the name of the person who would be helping her, but for the moment she couldn't call it to mind.

Austin Reese had wanted to make as sure as any man could that his legacy would be nurtured and treasured. He had been a strange and complex man. But at least, Sirena reassured herself, she would not be faced with immediate money problems on her arrival, and she would still have those friends she had made during her previous visit: Miguel Vargo, or Mike, the ranch foreman; and Anita Lopez. There were a few others she remembered, as well, distant neighbors she would enjoy meeting again. What did Ramón Savedel have to do with it all, she wondered again.

Sirena settled back into her daydream with a deep sigh, closing her eyes against the sight of Ramón so close beside her. The steady drone of the Jeep as it hummed along the road was almost hypnotic, and she gratefully fell into the half trance the cocoon of sound offered.

When they stopped for a quick lunch, Sirena finally found out what Ramón had in the canvas sack that had filled half the back of the Jeep when he'd arrived at the airport to pick her up. There was bread and cheese, carefully wrapped to keep them from drying out, hot peppers, which Ramón obviously relished, and whole tomatoes, which they liberally salted and ate out of hand. There were also apples and nuts, as well as plenty of surprisingly cool water. Far more food was in the bag than what the two of them could consume in one meal, and Sirena wondered a bit about the tremendous quantity, though she said nothing about it.

In fact, neither one had much to say about anything over the meal they shared in the glare of the noonday sun. Ramón had about him the look of a man who was waiting, and Sirena made it her business not to address him in other than the most formal terms when it was absolutely necessary.

The desert winds were blowing softly, and the temperature was soaring. There was no thermometer, but Sirena judged from past experience that it had to be in the nineties. Ramón's jacket lay tossed casually aside as they finished their meal, the bread drying out in their hands even as they ate. Climbing back into the Jeep, they hit the road again, and suddenly it seemed as if Ramón were as eager to reach the ranch south of them and be free of her as she was eager to be free of him.

The tightening of Sirena's skin reminded her of the extreme dryness of this country, and she cursed herself for not having tucked her bottle of moisturizer into her purse instead of packing it in one of the suitcases. Between the wind of the Jeep's passing and the intensity of the sun, Sirena knew her skin was going to burn. There was nothing she would be able to do about it, and reflecting on her escort, she didn't care to ask any favor of him.

Settling into her earlier posture, slumped low enough into the seat to give her head and neck support from the back, Sirena closed her eyes and blocked out the world as the miles rolled beneath their wheels. Ramón stopped again, this time for gas, but during the entire transaction Sirena didn't bother to stir.

Within a few minutes they were on their way again. Sirena was completely unaware of Ramón's flickering gaze directed at her with growing frequency as the open road presented him with unending opportunities. She could almost feel the faintly rosy sheen settling across the surface of her soft creamy skin, but she had no desire either to meet Ramón's gaze or converse with him, so except for the sway of the Jeep she remained as she was, unmoving and enduring.

Eyes closed against the brilliant sun overhead as well as Ramón, Sirena could not see his continuing appraisal of her. Even with eyes wide open she would never have been able to read his thoughts.

"Heads up — this is where we turn," Ramón warned above the whir of the Jeep engine, the thrum of the heavy overland tires on the asphalt and the grinding of the gears.

Sirena barely had time to jerk herself upright in response before the front wheels of the Jeep dropped off into what felt like nothingness, a sensation followed by a bone-jarring jolt that snapped her jaws together. Jounced and jostled out of her reverie, she pressed her suddenly aching back up against the seat to give it some support. And this, she remembered only too well, was one of the better dirt roads they would be driving down. From here on things only got worse. Ramón downshifted and accelerated without further comment on their state of affairs.

A large dust plume rose up behind the Jeep, and Sirena was just grateful they weren't in the center of it when she saw, coming from the opposite direction, a massive and lumbering old truck headed straight for them. She sighed in resignation. If the dust wasn't going to get her one way, it would get her another.

"You could have given me a little more warning," Sirena said irritably as the truck engine suddenly surged to fill the void of silence that had separated her and Ramón, the metallic roar of it competing with her for attention.

Ramón nodded curtly and smiled, guiding the Jeep dangerously close to the edge of the road at breakneck speed. He passed the truck with a hairbreadth of space between them.

"You're crazy!" Sirena snapped when she could stop choking and gagging. Dust seemed to have filled every free breathing cell of her being and sucked the moisture from her lungs and nostrils.

The ruts deepened, and Ramón slowed the pace of the vehicle. "Were you born in New York?" He asked the question as if he hadn't heard Sirena's last outburst. "Are you used to moving around?"

Sirena had no idea of what he was getting at, but she decided to ignore the remark and concentrate on the erratic course the Jeep was following beneath Ramón's guiding hands. "I've lived in New York ever since I can remember," she finally responded, answering only the first, more innocuous question.

There was no avoiding him now by retreating into her

dreamworld of darkness and rhythmically soothing sounds. At least not the darkness behind her eyelids. The darkness of evening was another matter; that was not too far distant. Sirena was sure they would not reach the ranch until well after sunset, and the last few miles would drag by at a turtle's pace as they picked their way through the wilderness and into the ocean of mountains that made up the Sierra Madre Occidental. Before too much longer there would be no roads at all, and they'd be forced to thread their way along on a well-worn trail known only to those who lived in the area.

Sirena shrugged back into the jacket she'd worn earlier as the sun disappeared behind a mountain peak that rolled off to their right. The chill that inevitably accompanied the desert night began to make itself felt in the rushing of wind that encompassed the Jeep. Ruts and bumps were beginning to feel a natural part of the ride, and Sirena attempted to focus on the more positive aspects of her situation. The most positive was the fact that the journey had to end eventually!

The road narrowed to a one-lane trail, and Ramón did very little to slow his pace. The sun set in a glorious spectacle of purples, pinks and azure blues, lighting up the sky with an iridescent glow that washed down over the mountains in a river of light.

"Then why did you come here?" Ramón asked suddenly, as if they'd been conversing all along. He flicked the Jeep's lights on, guiding the vehicle over the ruts with only one hand — a feat that made Sirena nervous and put her on the edge of her seat. "You know the terms of the will," he went on. "This is one hell of a long way from New York."

"Painting is my life, Mr. Savedel," Sirena said by way of explanation, more for her own frame of mind than for Ramón. "New York is not. And I've done some of the best painting in my life here. Does that answer your question?"

"It's a romantic answer, a damn good one, too, but there's another," Ramón probed, not able to leave the matter alone. He downshifted abruptly, fighting the sudden lurch of the Jeep as one wheel dropped into a pothole and the other banged up against an impossibly large rock. The vehicle felt as if it were twisting itself in half beneath them, and Sirena reflexively clutched her seat.

Warily she eyed Ramón's dark countenance, the hard planes and angles of his face as he ground his teeth along with the Jeep's gears. He jerked the wheel to the left and gave the valiant little engine another surge of power. The vehicle leaped forward, headlights stabbing a shaft of light along the narrow path before them.

Despite the lurching unevenness of the ride, Sirena was coming to realize there was not a time when Ramón was not in complete control; when those hands, large and powerful as well as long, slender and aristocratic, were not completely responsive to the rough road beneath their wheels. Body locked upright, feet playing the pedals like a fine-tuned instrument, Ramón let the cynical smile that Sirena hated curl the corners of his lips.

"Could be, too," he said tightly, again as if there'd been no interruption, "that you thought once you got down here and laid claim to what was yours, you might be able to find a way around the terms of the will . . . suck the place dry and go back to your city."

Sirena gasped — but not from the shock of Ramón's words; she would have expected as much from him. It was the Jeep. The headlights picked out the rock dead ahead an instant before they hit it. The momentum made it too late for Ramón to stop, and the Jeep bucked like a maddened bull, sending the world into a crazy spin for a suspended moment. Ramón fought the wheel like a madman, jerking it first one way, then another in a battle to keep the vehicle upright. With a resounding crash the Jeep came back to earth on all four wheels again, and almost instantly it felt as if one of the tires had sunk into a sandy hole.

For a split second Sirena was too rattled to contemplate the implications of the subtle lurch of the Jeep to the right. She wondered why Ramón, in his apparent insanity, wasn't immediately shooting along their way once again.

Ramón began to swear softly under his breath, cutting himself short before he could take it too far for feminine ears. Their predicament hadn't yet sunk into Sirena's consciousness, and it amused her that Ramón hesitated to swear heartily in her presence after all the other things he'd been more than willing to say to her, especially considering what he thought of her in general. Her bright blue eyes twinkled in the darkness where their humor couldn't draw Ramón's attention.

"We've got a flat." Ramón made the announcement as though a flat tire were a terminal condition, while his eyes sparkled with his own peculiar brand of humor.

"Will it take long to fix?" Sirena asked innocently. Her tone was studied, masking the urge she had to giggle at the extra work suddenly facing Ramón.

If Ramón had read her mind, he couldn't have come up with a more disturbing answer. "All night," he said flatly.

"What?" Sirena demanded. "What do you mean, all night? It's only a flat tire; you just told me so yourself. How could it possibly take all night to fix?"

Ramón switched off the ignition and sat indolently back in his seat as the silence of the surrounding mountains and desert descended upon them.

"It'll take all night," Ramón informed her, "because I can't fix the tire until I have some light, and it won't be light until morning." He threw the words at her as if lecturing a slightly backward child.

"Don't be ridiculous!" Sirena flared. "You must have a flashlight in this Jeep somewhere. I'll hold it for you," she offered stiffly, leaning forward to check the glove compartment.

"There is no flashlight," Ramón informed her as Sirena pawed through the contents of the overloaded glove compartment. "I forgot to put one in this trip."

"Forgot?" Sirena brought herself up short in her search, a fleeting vision of his having planned this from the beginning filtering into her mind through a descending veil of paranoia. She could feel anger welling up within her, tying itself into a firm knot in the middle of her chest. Taking a long deep breath, though, she felt some of the building tension ebb.

"We can't just sit here all night," Sirena protested. "They're expecting us tonight, aren't they?" she asked, referring pointedly to the handful of workers at the ranch aware of her impending arrival. "They'll be worried."

Ramón chuckled as if savoring a private joke. "They won't worry about it tonight, probably not tomorrow, either. Now tomorrow night . . . they might begin to wonder. This is wild country, Sirena. Any number of things could delay us along the way, and it's not a snap to pick up a telephone to let them know we're going to be late. You don't happen to see a telephone booth anywhere around here, do you?"

"No, I don't," Sirena said cuttingly. "But I do see a strong capable man who could certainly change a tire if he put his weak mind to it. Why, you could build a fire and fix the flat by the firelight!" she finished smartly.

"My, my, you certainly do have a sharp tongue. Not the most appealing of traits in a woman as lovely on the surface as you," Ramón returned easily. "But that doesn't change a thing. A romantic notion you have there, changing a tire by firelight, but not very practical. In case you haven't noticed, there are no city lights here to help brighten things up. A fire would cast only a flickering glow from the distance I'd be forced to build it at. I'm not going to risk life and limb just to please you, trying to change that tire on a rough surface by a flickering light. All that just so you can get where you're going a little sooner." He grinned at her and shrugged. "Besides, I could use some rest."

He was laughing at her. Though Ramón was not an easy man to read, Sirena could tell that much easily. She stepped out of her side of the Jeep, her skirt slipping momentarily up above her knees, then dropping back as she straightened. Around them the blackness was complete, pierced only up ahead by the headlights of the Jeep.

The tire, as far as she could make out, was about as flat as any she'd ever seen; the rock they'd hit had apparently forced a blowout. She bent over to touch the disabled tire and could feel the rough edges of a gaping hole in the rubber. In that much Sirena had to admit Ramón was right: the darkness would make changing the tire a dangerous affair. And perhaps her firelight idea might not work as well as she had thought.

Ramón flicked off the headlights and Sirena nearly had to

reach out and touch the Jeep to be sure it was still there. There was no moon this night, and the stars seemed farther away than Sirena could remember viewing them, even through the dim dirty conditions of New York, where their distant sparkle had competed with the lights of landing jets and towering buildings.

It was evident to Sirena that she couldn't change the tire on her own. That left the only alternative Ramón had already pointed out: she would have to resign herself to waiting until morning.

A chill breeze blew from out of the surrounding mountains, sending a shiver down the length of Sirena's spine. Hugging her arms tightly about herself, she locked her jaws against her chattering teeth. She was exhausted from traveling most of the previous night and then all of this day by Jeep into rough forbidding country; her energy was at a low ebb. And now this! She was hungry and she was tired, and there was little prospect of either need being satisfied. The all-consuming darkness that had fallen in a curtain about them in the wake of Ramón's turning off the headlights had been far from a comfort.

"We'd better get the Jeep off the road," Ramón broke the silence, hopping out of the driver's seat, "and make ourselves comfortable. It'll be a while until morning. If someone should happen along during the night — unlikely though that is — we wouldn't want them to run into the Jeep in the dark."

Ramón hadn't even finished what he was saying when he positioned himself behind the disabled vehicle and began to push. He had no doubt left the Jeep in neutral, because it started to roll immediately in spite of the flat tire. Sirena jumped quickly to one side.

"Do you have any warmer clothes in your luggage? I'll probably be needing that jacket you're wearing before too much longer," Ramón reminded her.

How chivalrous, Sirena thought to herself, but made no comment, deciding the less said between them this night the better. "It's going to be cold," she commented instead, "no matter what we do."

Ramón chuckled. "I've spent many nights out in the open. Believe me when I tell you we won't freeze. I'll turn on the headlights for a few minutes so you can find a place in the shadows to change," he volunteered. "But don't take too long; we don't want to add a worn-out battery to our problems. It's a long drive to the ranch from here, but an even longer walk."

Sirena selected one of her bags from the back of the Jeep after Ramón had loosened the ropes that bound them. She knew she'd packed some jeans, heavy cotton slacks, long-sleeved shirts and woolen pullovers in that bag. It was beginning to feel as if she would need every layer she could find. The icy nip of the air did not bespeak a June night.

"Keep an eye out for snakes and spiders," Ramón called after her. "And don't worry — I'm not going to look," he added as Sirena lugged her heavy bag into the shadows that bordered the shafts of brilliant yellow light from the Jeep's headlights.

When Sirena felt she was far enough away from the Jeep, she put the heavy suitcase on the ground and opened it. It was hard to see anything and impossible to keep a wary eye out for either spiders or snakes or anything else that might happen to creep or crawl. Sirena cringed, but it was evident that for this short period of time she was going to have to trust her fate to whatever good fairy watched over babes in the wilderness.

Hurriedly Sirena rummaged through her neatly packed bag, pulling out jeans, a long-sleeved shirt, a heavy pullover and a pair of cotton long underwear she'd packed for the trip after remembering her last time in the chilly mountains. She slid hastily out of Ramón's jacket and stripped to her flimsy underthings, feeling the goose bumps rising along her flesh in a rolling wave. Teeth chattering, Sirena drew on the garments one at a time in rapid succession, feeling the warmth building between layers. She tossed the flimsy traveling dress she'd worn into the open case; then, closing the suitcase, she used it to sit on while she took off her shoes to pull on the warm woolen socks.

Lack of sleep made Sirena feel almost bubbleheaded as she walked back toward the beckoning lights of the Jeep and the small sense of security they offered. She loathed giving up the heavy jacket that she'd draped about her shoulders after she'd changed. This was the warmest she'd felt since being met at the airport at dawn that morning — save, that was, for the few hours of intense sun that had managed to give her a pinkish burn.

It occurred to Sirena that she must certainly be crazy to have got herself into a position like this. She was the one who had always unabashedly admitted to her penchant for creature comforts and had protested even the setting of the thermostat to a lower temperature to conserve energy. She chilled easily, feeling the cold knife all the way to the bone when it came. This was a country of extremes. The desert; the lush, almost tropical forests on the mountains; the heat of the desert day; the cold of the desert night. How had she talked herself into this? And why was she stuck out here with this insufferable man?

Ramón was nowhere in evidence as Sirena dropped the heavy suitcase at the back of the Jeep. No doubt he had his own preparations to attend to; and in spite of her nervousness at being alone in the desert darkness, Sirena found her companion's brief absence a decided relief.

"I'm over here," Ramón called to her before Sirena had a chance to pursue her line of thought any further. Glancing around in the direction of the voice, she spotted a faint flickering of light.

"Turn off the Jeep's lights and come on down," he instructed her, and his voice seemed to hold a friendly note lacking earlier.

Reaching inside the Jeep, Sirena did as he asked and started to walk slowly in his direction, made wary by the sudden change in his manner. Her ears were not deceiving her; she was not one to be easily caught off guard. Since Ramón had picked her up in Tucson, her nerves had been alternately drawn taut as a bowstring, then eased by the beauty of the wild country that surrounded them on all sides. She had decided he was doing his level best to make this journey as hard on her as possible, and she was not going to put up with any more of it. She was going to Rancho Reese and that was that. What she did once she arrived there was none of Ramón Savedel's business, and she would make sure he was aware of that fact as soon as he had completed his mission and delivered her at the doorstep of the hacienda as he'd promised Austin Reese.

Sirena cocked her head, elevated her chin and started to pick her way slowly over the rough ground to where Ramón had built a small fire. He was waiting for her to join him, but the expression in his eyes was impossible to distinguish.

In the past Sirena had certainly done her share of hiking, riding horseback and winding up an energetic day's activities around a campfire. She remembered vividly a trip she and a group of friends had taken just after high-school graduation. They'd ventured into the Adirondacks and spent a marvelous time exploring, both on horseback and on well-marked hiking trails. That special trip, and frequent walks down Mianus Gorge in New York's lovely Westchester county, made up some of Sirena's fondest memories. The gorge was a startling pristine wilderness nestled in the valley of the Mianus River. Beautifully abounding in wild flowers, ferns, moss, towering trees and small waterfalls, it was about two and a half miles long, which made for an enchanting leisurely excursion. Sirena had always taken along a picnic and found many reasons to linger there, basking in the natural beauty of the area. So although she had never considered herself an overall outdoor girl, she had enough experience to recognize a well-built fire when she saw one.

The flickering reddish orange flame was a beckoning finger of warmth in the chill of the night, drawing Sirena on. She wondered how Ramón had been able to build it in those few minutes she'd spent off in the shadows. The fire was surrounded by a narrow mound of dirt evidently scooped out of the hole it had been built in and a circle of large rocks. A stack of short branches was heaped nearby and a handful of kindling left beside the friendly flames. Apparently it had not taken much to get the flame to catch.

"I'm afraid this isn't going to throw much warmth, but it should brighten things up a bit," Ramón said encouragingly. His dark head was bent over the results of his efforts as he fed the hungry flames from the stack of wood he'd collected.

Long athletic limbs outstretched alongside the fire, Ramón gestured to the spot opposite him. "Make yourself comfortable," he offered easily. "We might as well have something to eat. There's plenty of food remaining in the bag and water

44

enough for tonight. There'll be some left over for breakfast if neither of us gets too greedy."

A new flash of her earlier paranoia shot through Sirena. The food — she'd forgotten all about it. *If* Ramón had in fact planned this little camp-out, he would have thought of extra food and water. But, she reasoned, there was no way to plan a blowout such as they'd had; and despite what he thought of her, that would not be a reason to get himself stranded out here with the object of his anger and disgust.

"I had Anita pack plenty — always do when I go out of the area. Breakdowns happen more often than any of us care to admit." Ramón's tone was almost benign in light of their past exchanges.

The ease of his manner now that he was out from behind the wheel of the Jeep left Sirena feeling a bit unbalanced. Warily she lowered herself to the ground to sit cross-legged before the fire, jacket draped about her slim shoulders, and as she did so, Ramón observed casually, "You look a lot more comfortable in those. Here —" he held up the food bag, offering her the pick of its contents "— help yourself." Then he reached for the jug and poured the water.

"Thank you." Sirena felt stiff and somewhat awkward. She had been prepared to sit down, spend an irritating evening with a man she disliked, grab a few hours of restless sleep and be on the way again with the dawn. But now something else was happening, something she wasn't yet prepared to understand. Ramón Savedel was being *nice* to her for the first time since they'd met. Oh, he had always been polite, to a point, but he hadn't yet deigned to be *nice*. The change made Sirena decidedly uneasy. She reached into the bag for her share of the cheese and bread — a pretty unexciting repeat of lunch, but welcome nonetheless — and managed to accept the brimming cup of water with a steady hand. Then she doffed the jacket she'd been wearing, attempting to hand it around the small fire to Ramón.

"Brrr, you're right." Sirena rubbed her arms briskly against the sudden chill that assailed her even through her heavier clothes. "The fire doesn't do much to warm things up," she

45

continued with a weak smile. "Or even brighten things up," she admitted ruefully, referring tentatively to her earlier suggestion of fixing the tire by firelight.

"We could try body heat," Ramón offered wryly, one dark eyebrow cocked. "No?" He answered his own suggestion before Sirena could make an attempt to conceal the half-amused half-appalled look that crossed her face. "I didn't think so really." With a strange expression lighting his eyes he stared at Sirena as though it were the first time he was really seeing her.

He shifted his gaze to catch hers square, and Sirena felt the shock of their meeting tingling all the way throughout her body. A small smile quirked the corners of his lips, and she once again had the odd feeling that somehow he had climbed inside her head and knew now what was going on there. Of course, since she herself didn't know for sure what was going on in there, save for the sudden onrush of confusion, that thought was particularly silly.

A warm blush was spreading its way up her throat and into her face, staining her cheeks a bright crimson. Sirena could only hope the rosy glow of the flames would camouflage her sudden surge of emotions.

"You're a puzzle, Sirena," Ramón said. "And I must admit, ever since childhood, to a flair for puzzle solving." His words echoed Sirena's thoughts on her own abilities.

Chewing her simple fare thoughtfully, Sirena managed to return his regard with a level stare. Why, she wondered, did she care what this stranger thought of her? Why did she find herself interested in the complexities of his personality? And why did part of her actually want to like him, despicable though he'd been in his high-handed treatment of her? It didn't make any sense; but then, attraction between two people rarely did.

Attraction? Sirena had been prepared to let a growing dislike mature into something more extreme, and yet somehow Ramón Savedel, without doing anything or even seeming to alter his attitude toward her, was drawing a feeling from her that she wasn't yet prepared to recognize. The churning inside her head and heart was an unfamiliar experience — and a shocking one.

When she'd heard her girl friends describe such feelings in the past, she'd considered them positively juvenile.

Sirena was twenty-six and had never known a man intimately. She had remained elusive, independent, reasoning with herself that she had neither the time nor the inclination to get wrapped up in that flood of adolescent emotions so many seemed to pursue throughout life. A wry little demon inside Sirena pricked her, saying it was all a fairy tale anyway; love didn't really happen like that. What then, the demon pricked her again, was she saving herself for if she didn't believe it? Why had she not plunged into affairs as so many of her friends had, flitting from one partner to another as if love were a form of recreation? Sirena didn't grope for the answers. She knew only that Ramón unexpectedly stirred within her emotions new and never before experienced . . . emotions she didn't want to acknowledge — not now, not with *him*.

Her long legs folded comfortably beneath her, Sirena regarded Ramón uncertainly from beneath lowered lashes. She had to admit that in his own way he was a handsome man. His eyes were piercingly alight and yet at the same time brooding. Thick brows of bluish black gave character to his face, and long curved lashes of the same color partially shuttered his enigmatic eyes. The stark angularity of his finely chiseled features was softened by the firelight, and the tousled hair that curled over his collar added to his dangerous pantherish good looks. His physique was rugged, long athletic limbs supporting a well-muscled frame that seemed well used to outdoor activity. In the wild nighttime setting he appeared relaxed and comfortable, and his sensuously full lips and slow smile gave him an aura of animal magnetism that was hypnotic in its intensity.

Whether Sirena wanted it or not, Ramón stirred sensations inside her, and she moved to quash them.

"I am what I am, Ramón," Sirena told him, using his first name in spite of their recent verbal fencing matches. "And I won't make any apologies or excuses for it. If you're looking for some secret hidden away deep inside, you aren't going to find it." Sirena put more bite in her words than the retort to his earlier comment warranted. "Furthermore, just to set things straight, I don't give a royal damn what you think of me or my motives."

Ramón raised an eyebrow at her outburst, disbelief clearly mirrored in his eyes. That simple reaction from him rankled, but Sirena was determined to stick to what she'd said. She wasn't going to allow him to affect her in any way. Whatever this feeling was that he stirred within her, it had nothing to do with the reason for her coming here and would have even less to do with any future action she chose to take. If Ramón Savedel had the idea he could read her like a book after only a few hours' acquaintance, he was going to find he was very much mistaken.

Not once during their exchange had Ramón reached for the jacket, which now lay by Sirena's feet, away from the fire. "You'd better keep that," he said silkily, gesturing toward it. "You look as if you really need sleep, and without that jacket you aren't going to get much of it. Shivering will keep you awake."

"I don't sleep well on planes," Sirena admitted, "but I'm not taking your jacket. I'll catch up on my sleep when we reach the ranch."

"I haven't withdrawn my earlier offer," Ramón told her with an impish grin that left no doubt in Sirena as to what he had in mind. He leaned forward a bit, as if anticipating quick capitulation.

Sirena bestowed a frigid gaze upon him that was much colder than the air surrounding them, and yet the memory of that single contact back at the airport when he'd met her was a strong one. If she let her mind dwell on it, she could still feel that peculiar tingling his touch had ignited. But she was determined not to let her mind dwell on it. For whatever his reasons, Ramón had apparently declared a truce for now. Of course there was always later to think about. . . .

"Seems a shame to waste a night like this," Ramón went on. "I wonder what you'd do if I came across that fire and joined you?"

"A question like that doesn't deserve an answer," Sirena snapped, "especially since you're not going to do it." She wasn't really sure of what she was saying. After all, she knew Ramón Savedel no better than he knew her.

All that talk earlier of a debt to Austin Reese could be so much soft soap he was selling her. Sirena couldn't be one hundred percent sure he wouldn't unfold that tall frame of his and cross the fire in one stride to her side. She shuddered to think what would happen then, but somehow managed to cover the twinge of fear and confusion that filled her. After all, she was sitting in the darkness on a cold moonless night, in the middle of a desert, in a foreign country, with a strange man.

Sirena was beginning to wonder again why she'd been so naive as to accept a ride with a perfect stranger, believing in her assured little world that it could be none other than the ride promised by telegram. She had naturally assumed Ramón had been sent by whatever authorities handled Austin Reese's will and had forwarded her the documents in New York. Though even now there was no reason to think Ramón wasn't assigned to escort her to the ranch, Sirena realized she could have gone by intuition and refused his offer. She had no obligation to accept the transportation provided; she could have worked out her own arrangements to reach the ranch, though it would have been considerably more complicated from her end and her funds had as always been severely limited. Everything so far had been provided by Austin's estate, and though her mother was fairly well-off, it was a matter of pride with Sirena not to accept money from her.

Pulling herself up short, Sirena stopped her useless speculation and backtracking. What was done was done, and she was here now. True, Ramón Savedel was an enigma: a threat one minute, a friend the next, and an inquisitor nearly always. But just as long as he wasn't a sex maniac, Sirena reflected, all would work out in the end. They would reach the ranch tomorrow, and she would be free of him.

"Don't worry, Sirena," Ramón said with a deep-throated chuckle, "I'm not going to attack you beneath the starlit sky, although any man in his right mind would be sorely tempted."

Regarding him dubiously, Sirena managed a weak smile in response to his backhanded compliment. With a devilish grin

Ramón climbed to his feet, sending renewed shivers of apprehension up her spine, creating a chill within her that had nothing to do with the cold.

Chin elevated, Sirena strove to keep an unruffled exterior as Ramón moved closer to her. His words told her one thing, his actions another, but she was not going to go screaming off into the surrounding darkness with her fear driving her like a whip.

Ramón dropped to his knees in the dust beside Sirena, searched for a soft spot, then started scooping out the sand with his cupped hands until he'd created a shallow trench more or less the length of her body. Sirena felt her heart move into her throat. The absurd thought came to her that if he was planning on assaulting her, then murdering her and leaving her body here, he wasn't going to do a very good job of burying her from the looks of things!

Her rational side at war with her irrational fears, Sirena sat back in fascinated silence as Ramón completed the work he had started. To distract herself, she watched the play of heavy muscles beneath the fabric of his shirt and the strength in his hands, so obviously accustomed to hard work. This man had been a friend of Austin Reese, the same Austin Sirena had come to care for deeply. If Austin had seen something in this man that made him worth calling a friend, then he couldn't be capable of the wild acts her vivid imaginings were conjuring up. If nothing else, Austin Reese had been a good judge of character.

Still, an apprehensive skeptical voice whispered at the back of Sirena's mind, *everybody makes a mistake sometime.* . . .

Climbing to his feet once again, Ramón towered above Sirena where she sat motionless by the flickering fire. Her eyes, the pupils large, reflected the glow of the firelight. Ramón bent and picked up his jacket from where she had placed it, then invited casually, "Roll in." He gestured to the shallow indentation in the earth.

"What?" Sirena gasped, still in the dark as to his intentions.

"There's your bed." Ramón lowered himself to his heels, bringing himself once again to eye level with Sirena. "It'll keep

50

any wind that might come up during the night off you and retain some of your body heat. Should keep you warm with this." He held up the jacket.

"I told you . . ." Sirena began, some of her courage returning in a sudden flush as he pressed the bulky garment into her hands.

Ramón raised a hand to still her protests. "I have an old blanket I dug out of the back of the Jeep before you got back. The jacket isn't quite as smelly. Now you'd better get some sleep; morning comes early in this country."

Once again, as Ramón's hands brushed against hers, Sirena felt shock waves coursing through her entire body. A sort of primitive magnetism about him, an overwhelming virility that struck an answering chord with her, set her teeth on edge and made her feel like a snarling cat poised and ready to fight off a marauding tom. Except she was not sure how much of a defense she was prepared to put up. Sirena felt her cheeks flame once again and hoped the undulating glow of the fading fire would be enough to conceal from Ramón her unsettling feelings. But as she sat struggling to compose herself, he was up and moving to the opposite side of the fire, leaving her to do as she saw fit.

"What about snakes and creepy things?" Sirena ventured, her voice unsteady with the power of the strange emotions that surged through her.

"I wouldn't worry too much about them," Ramón reassured her with a chuckle as he scooped out his own trench close to the fire. "They're probably asleep by now."

The humor of his remark eluded Sirena, and she shot him a look that would have been deadly had he been glancing her way to receive it. Anger quickly flushed away the last of the peculiar sensations that had tingled through her.

Sleeping on the ground had never appealed to Sirena, not even when she'd been young and all the other kids thought sleeping outside in a homemade tent of sorts was a real treat. Sirena had always preferred the warmth of her own bed; and the New York environment with a tiny square of yard behind her childhood home certainly had not harbored the same kind of wildlife as the Sierra Madre. Her eyes apprehensively probed the ground around them, faintly lighted by the small fire that flickered between them.

Finished with his undertaking, Ramón stoked the fire, rolled into the blanket he had brought from the Jeep and stretched out in his earthen bed, closing his eyes instantly.

Shivering convulsively, Sirena realized she was very cold. Since Ramón had the blanket, there was no reason for her to allow her pride to make her suffer. She wrapped the extra-size jacket about her slender form, hugging it to her as she leaned into the rising warmth of the campfire. In a few moments the chill passed and she followed Ramón's example, retiring to the bed he had fashioned for her.

Wrapped tightly inside the jacket, Sirena pillowed her head on her arm and closed her eyes. Warm visions of the hacienda that would soon greet her passed through her mind like a reel of movie film. Luxuriating in the strange warmth that her earthen bed seemed to provide, she dropped off quickly into a deep dreamless sleep.

CHAPTER THREE

Ramón was right: morning did come early to this country. When a firm hand gripped her shoulder and gently shook her back to the land of the living, Sirena felt as if she were being forced to abandon something incomplete. She wanted to mutter in protest, turn over and go back to sleep, as she did sometimes at home, but here there was no alarm clock to shut off, only that persistent shaking that filled her subconscious with the sensations of an earthquake.

"When you finally sleep, you really get down to it, don't you?" Ramón's voice was chiding and vibrantly awake. "Come on," he coaxed, "wake up! Tire's changed. We'll be leaving in a few minutes."

Sirena sat up and blinked. "Changed? Already?" She knew she was not making much sense, but then the fuzzy jumble of images that filled her mind didn't make much sense, either.

"I already had my breakfast — yours is waiting in the Jeep for you. You can eat while we drive. If you want to get there for lunch, we'll have to make some time."

Climbing to her feet, Sirena brushed the night's dust from her clothes. The day snapped into clear focus at last. There was a bite to the air that brought back reminders of the night past — she glanced in the direction of the fire and saw that nothing remained but charred bits of wood at the center of the circle of raised earth.

Within a few minutes they were back in the Jeep, Ramón turning over the engine and easing it into gear. The past night seemed no more than a dream to Sirena as she sat quietly in her seat, the bag of remaining bread, cheese and fruit in her lap, munching a cold breakfast that was quickly filling her empty stomach. To wash the food down, she sipped some of the remaining water from a cup.

The black night that had cloaked them yesterday when Ramón had taken the cutoff from the main road had erased from Sirena's sight the magnificence of the wild country around them. Now she saw an unbelievable ocean of mountains rolling off on all sides, low peaks nearby, the higher ones stretching out to infinity. The sun, a dazzling ball of brilliance, hung suspended in a flawless blue sky above the eastern crest of the mountains. Despite the dryness of the country there was a greenish cast to the hills, and the cuts and rises that surrounded them appeared to be so many green folds of darker and lighter shading, reminding Sirena of a crumpled piece of child's construction paper tossed carelessly aside. Far in the distance were peaks still capped with snow, glistening a startling white beneath the climbing sun.

The land had a subtle roll, much like the configurations of drifting sand dunes, and yet the earth was solid. A low carpet of scrub grass made the distance appear as a beckoning green meadow, and the distant jagged peaks, though seeming to threaten to tear giant rips in the sky, appeared somehow peaceful and benignly omnipotent. The odd contrast sent a thrill of adventure rushing through Sirena's veins.

She glanced sideways, careful to avoid Ramón's gaze. His profile was distinctive against the pale blue of the early-morning sky as he adeptly guided the vehicle over the changing terrain. The hands that controlled the steering wheel and grasped the shift knob were hard hands; sinewy, deeply tanned capable hands that bore no rings or even signs of rings worn in the past. With an effort Sirena tore her eyes away, her mind devilishly remembering and replaying the picture stored there of those sun-browned hands moving and commanding, the play of the muscle beneath the skin.

Ahead the land rose forbiddingly, and Sirena's heart caught in her throat as she recognized this breathtaking pass, seemingly impenetrable. But Ramón showed no hesitation. The road disappeared as they pressed on, fading first to a rutted trail, then to a barely visible path that only a trained eye could discern.

This country was not for the weakhearted. Again Sirena was assailed with doubts about herself and her mission here. When visiting the ranch so short a time ago she had felt she belonged — but had she really? Ramón's attitude toward her and her city background angered her. He seemed so unwilling even to give her a chance. And yet small doubts of her own niggled at the edges of her consciousness. Whether she did really belong was a question that only time could answer.

Nosing ahead, the Jeep crunched over the rock-strewed ground, its hood cocked at an upward angle as the climb steepened. Ramón kept both his hands on the steering wheel now, his jaw set, eyes moving ahead, watching the twists and turns of the faint trail he followed. There was no reason to shift gears; it was just a steady slow climb, and the Jeep was performing well.

Sirena clutched her seat. Though the angle of the Jeep kept her pressed back, she still had to guard against the sudden lurches and bounces. Trying to keep an apprehensive look off her face, she forced a half smile to her lips and froze it there. The expression came out as more of a grimace than a smile, but Sirena didn't have a mirror at the moment to observe it, and it was doubtful she'd have been too surprised had she seen it. She could feel the blood leave her cheeks and the fluttering of her heart within her breast as they approached the top of their climb.

Then suddenly the land opened up before them into a grand sweep of grasslands, dotted in wild profusion with the blooms of a golden flower that reminded Sirena of the California poppy. As the ground leveled off into a broad plateau that stretched out into the far distance, its end not within Sirena's view, the green was almost overwhelming. Of course, it wasn't quite as much a shock as the first time she'd seen it. As a city girl the word "desert" had conjured up images of endless stretches of barren blistering sand, only rocks to break up the monotony of the sand dunes and maybe an occasional cactus to call friend.

Much to Sirena's pleasure, Austin Reese had gone out of his way to make sure she learned about the country her first trip out. Never in her life had she experienced such a sense of freedom, such beauty everywhere she looked. That was what had brought her back, Sirena realized. That was the real reason

55

she had come now: to renew the fascination and the love affair that had erupted between her and this wild sprawling wilderness that few had a chance to experience. And in its midst rested an oasis of beauty and grace, of quiet and solitude, of the modern and the traditional, in the form of Austin Reese's ranch. The contrast had been startling and beguiling, and after she'd returned to New York it had never released its hold on her. She'd always known she would come back here, though she would have preferred it to be under happier circumstances.

It seemed to Sirena almost a sacrilege to crush a double trail across the billowing expanse of green. As the Jeep threaded its way through the wild country, she enjoyed the feel of the wind rushing through her hair. She had long since given up trying to keep it in place with her hands, and until this ride was over, combing did no good. This wasn't the time to worry about her appearance, she decided.

Ramón increased the Jeep's speed, and wary thoughts of another blowout crossed Sirena's mind. If it happened again, there would be no spare with which to exchange the damaged tire. The idea put her nerves on edge, but evidently it had no such effect on Ramón, who continued to drive in his nonchalantly manic style.

The hours passed, and Sirena felt as if they were adrift in a gentle sea as the green of the thick grasses swayed and rippled around them. The sun continued its slow and deliberate climb, the warmth of it penetrating until Sirena shed the bulky jacket once again and began rolling up her sleeves.

Bronzed by the sun, skin toughened by the wind, Ramón didn't appear to take much notice of the change in the temperature. In the chill of dawn he had driven the open Jeep without benefit of a jacket or even the blanket he'd used during the night, and now the rising heat that was quickly bringing a light film of perspiration to Sirena's brow didn't seem to faze him at all.

They descended the plateau much as they had ascended, the Jeep at an almost impossible angle, Sirena clinging this time to her seat to keep the bumps and bounces from throwing her out over the windshield and hood. Ramón, surprisingly, had not had much to say since they'd started out that morning, and an uneasy silence had settled between them.

Much to Sirena's amazement, she now recognized a few of the landmarks. They were drawing near to the end of their journey.

"Just over the next rise," Ramón announced suddenly, once again as if he'd read her thoughts. He jockeyed the Jeep around a deep rut and through the swiftly flowing waters of a stream that meandered across their path. Pointing in a southeasterly direction, he explained, "We'll see the hacienda as soon as we come around the base of that hill over there."

The hill, patchy green in spots, blocked their view, and Sirena remembered well how the ranch buildings themselves nestled into the bowl of a small valley, protected from the worst of the elements. She remembered, too, the magnificent trees that lined the banks of the creek that flowed through the hacienda's courtyard and the ones that marked the perimeters of the ranch yard. She had fallen asleep each night with the wind whispering through the leaves of those trees. How lovely it would be to do so again.

As Ramón guided the Jeep forward, the road appeared more clearly in the distance, taking on the appearance of a rutted country lane once again. Jeeps were used frequently for many of the jobs on the ranch these days, and the road leading to the main buildings had naturally worn in a bit more distinctly than some of the others that crisscrossed the ranch and surrounding wild country. Sirena experimented with thinking of it as home. The thought brought a pleasant sense of warmth flooding through her, and for the first time since her plane had landed back in Tucson, she felt herself begin to loosen up and relax.

"Feeling like a land baroness yet?" Ramón asked caustically.

Sirena bit her lower lip as she tried to think of a suitable reply. She wasn't going to allow him to ruin this moment. For a brief instant she thought to ignore him completely, but she knew Ramón would not let her silence pass that easily.

"I told you earlier — I don't care what you think of me," she said sharply. "Why shouldn't I enjoy it, since *I* own it?" In spite of her resolve to do otherwise, she couldn't help adding a half explanation. "I happen to love this place — not that you'd understand anything like that."

The Jeep hit a particularly jarring bump, cutting off any further words Sirena might have had to say and returning Ramón's full attention to the road. Then abruptly the road leveled as they hit the bottom of the dip. Ramón's tension eased visibly, and he turned his head to glance at Sirena.

"Nobody said you shouldn't enjoy it, Sirena," he told her quietly. "Austin Reese had every intention that you should. But do you really know that there's a lot more to it than moving into a grand hacienda and playing the great *patrona?* You have to love more than the place. You have to love the land. You have to love what the years are going to force you to put into it, the pieces of yourself the land is going to claim. Can you do that, Sirena?" There was the ring of warning to his words.

Ramón's ideas were ridiculous! No wonder he believed she could never hope to live up to them! The man seemed to think of Rancho Reese as a shrine to nature herself and the greater powers that be. It was just a ranch. Beautiful and no doubt needing plenty of hard work, but a ranch nonetheless . . . a legal holding of thousands of acres. Sirena loved the wild beauty, but now she realized Ramón was expecting — no, *demanding* — much more of her.

"Well," she managed through stiff lips, barely able to dampen her anger at his condescending attitude, "pretty soon you won't have to worry about any of that. You can wash your hands of me and the ranch completely." She straightened and shifted her stony gaze ahead.

Gradually the ride became a bit more even as the Jeep's wheels found the broader smoother expanse of the ranch road, and Sirena loosened her hold on the seat. The end of their enforced companionship was near. Ramón chuckled softly, the sound of his laugh mellow and somehow nearly caressing.

"My, you are in a hurry to be rid of me," he chided her gently. "Well, I hate to tell you, Sirena, but *I'm* part of the conditions of the will."

"You're what?" Sirena demanded, half turning in her seat

to stare at Ramón. His deeply tanned face was animated with humor, his dark eyes sparkling with the revelation he had saved for so long. Then the name Sirena had skimmed over so lightly when reading the terms of the will flashed through her mind. Ramón Savedel!

"Surely you read all the fine print in those papers you received. Austin Reese named me in the will to be your adviser and assistant until you understand the workings of the ranch. I agreed to it when he made up the document." Ramón glanced Sirena's way, then back to the road in front of him, guiding the Jeep toward the narrow creek crossing that lay ahead.

Just beyond the creek a small knot of people had gathered in front of the glistening white arches of the magnificent hacienda. They must have heard the sound of the Jeep's approach.

"So," Ramón went on with an impish grin, "I'm yours until I decide you can handle things on your own."

Sirena's jaw dropped at Ramón's revelation. She still couldn't believe it was true. She had known about the assistant Austin had arranged for her to have, but Ramón's name when he had introduced himself in Tucson had not struck a familiar chord. Her mind had been in such a blur since leaving New York that it simply hadn't registered.

"No comment?" Ramón prodded as the Jeep dipped toward the water.

Sirena opened her mouth to reply cuttingly, but she never got the chance. All that came out was a startled cry as the Jeep continued its descent, turning into an empty air drop as an entire section of the crossing gave way beneath them in a sudden rush.

The world lurched crazily, then hung as if suspended by a string for an instant before the Jeep plunged headlong into the shallow stream. The drop was only about four feet, but it seemed to Sirena like a multistory fall. It ended in a mechanical grunt and an unimpressive splash. She barely had time to gasp before the bank of the stream collapsed beneath their front wheels and the Jeep came to rest abruptly on the silty creek bottom. With a terrific force her head snapped forward, forehead meeting dashboard with a blinding crack that exploded a million stars behind her eyelids.

Blinking, Sirena was not sure whether she was awake or unconscious. The knot of people from the hacienda appeared in a rush at the far side of the creek. Among them was a tall man with angular features, aristocratic and aloof, his dark eyes seeming to rivet on hers even across the distance that separated them.

Her mind groping for familiar things, Sirena pushed back her surprise as the face snapped into focus. Ramón. It was Ramón. But that couldn't be. It couldn't be Ramón; he was sitting in the seat beside her. In fact, he was softly calling her name, and his voice held an unexpected note of concern.

"Sirena . . . Sirena, are you all right?" The voice tugged at the corners of Sirena's consciousness, demanding her attention.

If Ramón was sitting next to her, speaking to her in such muted tones, how could he be at the far side of the stream, as well, hesitating there, hovering on the opposite bank a moment before striding into the shallow waters of the creek, heading for the mired Jeep? A deep throbbing clammered for attention on the right side of Sirena's forehead, and shock waves were still rippling through her brain, making it impossible for her mind to grapple with the simple problem now confronting her. Ramón couldn't be in two places at once.

And then he was touching her, laying a hand on her shoulder, using the other, large and strong, yet gentle, too, to cup her chin and turn her head toward him. Through the confused muddle of her mind Sirena could see the look on Ramón's face, read the concern there — and something else, as well. What was it? She could almost feel it, yet she couldn't identify it.

"Sirena," Ramón repeated her name, long slender fingers holding her chin firmly, his eyes gazing into the depths of hers.

"I-I'm all right," she stammered at last, raising a hand to touch the rapidly rising bump on her forehead.

Ramón removed his hand from her chin, and Sirena felt a soft wave of regret wash involuntarily over her. Automatically she turned away so that he couldn't read the look in her eyes. Even if it was merely the reaction of a muddled mind, she couldn't risk his seeing it.

"Are you both all right?" Another voice intruded above the quiet flow of the stream's waters around the front wheels of the Jeep. The voice was definitely masculine, impeccably polite, with the most aristocratic of Mexican accents Sirena had ever heard. The tones were similar to Ramón's, but in some way more clipped and quietly commanding of attention because of the inflection given each word.

"We're fine, just fine." Ramón's reply was short and irritable, a trait Sirena had come to identify with him during their short acquaintance.

Sirena's gaze fell squarely on the tall slender man standing patiently in the swirling stream waters, waiting for her response. She gave a start that brought forth a muted chuckle from Ramón despite his apparent bad temper in the wake of the accident. "Sirena, this is my twin brother, Rualto." Ramón introduced him.

It was like looking at the mirror image of the man who sat next to her. Sirena couldn't believe her eyes. Except for one or two tiny lines between the brows and the slightly stronger accent, she would not have been able to tell the two of them apart.

"And you, Sirena." Rualto, his face creased by a pained frown, used her name as if it were a most delicate musical instrument. "Are you all right, as well?"

"I think so," Sirena answered him. "It's just a little bump on the head, nothing broken." She managed a faint smile that she hoped would erase the frown on Rualto's face, the face that looked so much like Ramón's.

"Not a very pleasant way for a beautiful woman to be welcomed to her new home," Rualto said gallantly. "If I may be so bold. . . ." He reached around Sirena and swept her into his arms from the Jeep's seat before she could marshal her thoughts to protest. With a long stride he started for the opposite bank.

"That wasn't necessary," Sirena protested in embarrassment as Rualto deposited her on the ground beyond the water's edge. "I could have walked myself." Ramón meanwhile hopped out of the driver's seat and circled the Jeep, examining the position, the damage and the cause, in no particular hurry to join the others.

Rualto laughed at her muted protests. "One of us was already standing in the water; there was no reason for us both to do so," he assured her.

"It was very kind of you." Sirena had her legs beneath her again, and the pain in her head from the whack had died down to a quiet, if steady, throb.

With a warm chuckle Rualto spread his arms in a welcoming gesture. "Welcome to Rancho Reese — or is it possible it will soon be Rancho Sereno?"

Sirena smiled. She didn't know much Spanish, but she knew that word. It meant serene, and she did not miss Rualto's play on her name.

"*Señorita!* It's so good to see you again." Anita Lopez bustled forward to greet her. Her familiar face was a welcome sight indeed.

During the five months Sirena had spent at Rancho Reese on her last visit, she and Anita, Austin's young cook and housekeeper, had become good friends. She was especially glad of that now.

"Señorita Clark," Miguel Vargo greeted her with a wave as he strode purposefully in their direction from the stable. His once black hair was now nearly white, his face deeply tanned and wrinkled. Miguel hurried forward in a loose-legged manner that defied the years he carried upon his slender yet upright frame.

"We thought you would arrive yesterday," he said when he was close enough to be heard without shouting. "Was there trouble?" The look of concern on his face was genuine.

"Just a flat tire." Now that she was here, Sirena found the whole thing amusing. "Ramón didn't have a flashlight, so he waited until it was light to change the tire."

Miguel cast Ramón a doubtful look, then returned his sunshiny smile to Sirena. "Well, at least you are here, even if your arrival was not too smooth," he commented, eyeing the listing Jeep and Ramón carrying a load of her baggage to the creek bank. "A few days ago there was a bad storm, and the water must have washed out the bank. I'm very sorry, *señorita*."

"You must be hungry!" Anita declared, her small slender frame taut with her eagerness to be helpful. "I have a hot meal for you at the house," she went on before Sirena could do more than smile and wave aside any guilt anyone could try to shoulder concerning the accident. Her soft accent was lilting and friendly, a sound Sirena had longed to hear during her entire trip down. "I've made cheese soup, *burritos* and strudel for dessert!"

Sirena laughed softly at the young woman's choice of menu. Anita had been with Austin for years — since the age of thirteen — and was a complete whiz in the kitchen. She cooked not only Mexico's traditional dishes but almost every other country's, as well. Austin had always treated her as the gem she was, and through the years she had become his good friend and confidante. Anita's bright youthful optimism had always lighted up the hacienda, and being so close in age to Sirena, the two women had had much in common, sharing ideas and confiding in each other on Sirena's previous visit.

"Don't let it go to your head," Ramón said quietly into Sirena's ear. "Anita is probably worried about losing her job here now that Austin is gone. To her, Rancho Reese is home. After all, she was only a girl when she first came here."

"Don't be absurd!" Sirena snapped, careful to keep her voice low so that Anita, who was already leading the group toward the sprawling hacienda, couldn't hear. "Anita and I are friends. We got to know each other quite well when I was here last time. I wouldn't let her go."

"Ah," Ramón went on, "but Anita doesn't know that for sure."

Sirena's eyes flared. "Then I'll make it my business to see that she does."

"Don't allow my brother to annoy you any further." Rualto stepped up close beside Sirena, cupping her elbow in his large capable hand. There was an expression in the depths of his dark glittering eyes, so like his brother's, that was impossible to identify.

Rualto was pleasant and polite. And why shouldn't she enjoy

his company after the many hours of strain spent in Ramón's disapproving presence? Rualto seemed undemanding and far less critical than his brother. So much alike, the two of them, and yet so different.

Rualto was laughing softly at Sirena's side. "We shall have to devise a way for you to tell my brother and me apart — and quickly!" he teased. "I should not like to be blamed for his obnoxious behavior."

Sirena grinned. "There's little likelihood of that," she quipped as they walked, leaving Ramón behind to become unofficial bag boy in charge of the small mountain of luggage he'd criticized upon her arrival. She could feel Ramón's burning eyes fastened upon her back, and she could envision the sardonic quirk of his lips as his snap judgment of her was verified. To him, it must seem that she was playing the part of the grand *patrona* sweeping onto her *rancho*. Well, let him!

The sight of the hacienda close up once again brought a smile to Sirena's lips. Nothing had changed; it was just as she remembered it. The house gleamed whitely beneath the brilliant sun, rising to two stories on each of the wings and lowering just a bit at the front where the reception, living room, kitchen and dining areas lay beneath well-remembered, beautifully vaulted ceilings. The terra-cotta tile of the vast expanses of roof, along with the stately trees that lined the drive, served to soften the stark whiteness of the main house, and the heavy iron gates set in the whitewashed adobe wall that surrounded the place provided an elegant accent. Huge picture windows overlooking the wild country beckoned Sirena closer, drawing her toward the cooler confines of the hacienda's interior.

"The horses are beautiful, as always." Miguel — or Mike, as Austin Reese had always addressed him — came up on Sirena's opposite side as she and Rualto walked briskly along the road that led to the house. "I hope you'll be riding soon — and often, as you did before."

Sirena had no doubt Mike meant what he said, and she felt a warm glow suffuse her. This was the way she had remembered Rancho Reese. Warm and welcoming, magnificent yet comfortable.

"You are a fine rider, *señorita*." Mike offered the compliment in a quiet, almost hesitant way.

"Thank you, Mike. I will be riding soon — and often." Sirena's brilliant blue eyes lighted up with the thought, full lips curving upward in a special smile for the ranch foreman.

Heavy footsteps came up rapidly behind her as she spoke to Mike Vargo. Ramón.

"You bet your life she'll be riding, Mike," Ramón said brightly. "She has a whole ranch to inspect, and I intend to see she inspects every square inch of it, just as Austin would have wanted her to. In fact, *did* want her to, as expressed in his will. Sirena and the horses will be seeing a lot of one another."

Mike seemed a bit startled by Ramón's passing remarks, but he made no comment. Not so Rualto.

"Don't allow my brother to annoy you too much," Rualto said by way of comfort. "There is much more involved here than you know, but in time you will learn. He doesn't feel you are suited to this work. That is *his* opinion."

Grinding her teeth, Sirena stared at Ramón's back as he easily passed them and made his way into the house ahead of them. "And you?" Sirena couldn't resist asking of Rualto. "What do you think?"

"I think this was Austin Reese's ranch, his to do with as he saw fit, and he saw fit to leave it to a very beautiful woman." Rualto was never one to falter with the charm.

As they passed through the huge iron gates, Sirena's gaze fell on a quietly aristocratic woman standing patiently in the outer portico beneath the arch, awaiting their arrival.

"Our mother, Carlotta Savedel." Rualto introduced Sirena with a flourish. "This is Sirena Clark. Our ranch borders yours on the east," he elaborated. "Our mother wished to be on hand to greet her new neighbor."

"That was very kind of you." Sirena stepped away from Rualto, extending her hand warmly to have it clasped in the older woman's cool one. "I'm so pleased to meet you."

Sirena uttered the banal phrase with a sincerity she felt very deeply. This country was not as tame as the urban setting she was used to, and Sirena was acutely aware of the fact that neighbors here could be one of the most important aspects of life. In that sense it hadn't changed much from the days of the old West.

"You are staying for lunch, of course," she went on, extending the invitation she knew Anita would have already prepared for, leaving Carlotta to accept what she had no doubt already expected to receive. In fact, Sirena realized, the aloof middle-aged beauty had to have already spent the night in the guest rooms of the *hacienda*, had she, in fact, come there with her son to welcome her to Rancho Reese. Hospitality went without question when ranches were at the very least a good half-day's drive apart.

"You are most kind." Carlotta spoke the words with a soft silky accent that made it plain to Sirena's trained ear that English had obviously not been her first language.

"I just wish I'd met you when I stayed with Austin those few months a couple of years ago," Sirena went on.

"Ah." Carlotta removed her hand, clasping it with the other before her, dark eyes regarding Sirena in veiled appraisal. "I was not very well then." Her voice was refined, the words delicately spoken, coming from finely chiseled lips set in a flawlessly smooth alabaster face.

For some reason Sirena didn't believe what Carlotta was telling her, but she held her peace in spite of a nearly overwhelming desire to ask, just as sweetly, if Carlotta's two sons had been ill then, as well. It was not as if she had been there on a two-week vacation. Five months was a very long time for good neighbors to stay away.

Austin had mentioned the Savedels in passing, Sirena remembered. He had spoken briefly of the widow and her two sons who owned the ranch bordering his on the east. At the time she had thought she detected a note of affection, or at least liking, when he had mentioned them, but he had seemed to have no inclination to talk about the family in detail. Actually, he'd only spoken of them at all in answer to Sirena's questions regarding friends and neighbors in that wild land.

"Shall we go inside?" Sirena offered graciously, becoming

66

aware of her own disheveled travel-worn attire in contrast to Carlotta Savedel's immaculate appearance.

Self-consciously her hand went to her hair, which had not been thoroughly brushed in more than a day and half. All of her toilet articles were in her bags. Sirena had never dreamed she would be confronted by guests immediately upon her arrival.

Leading the way through the intricately carved doors into the beautifully tiled entry hall of the house's cool interior, Sirena got the distinct uncomfortable impression that Carlotta was accustomed to performing such hostess duties at the Reese ranch. Rualto hung back with a slight smile curving his full lips. Clearly he was trying to be supportive in what he recognized to be a trying situation for Carlotta.

The inside of the stately home took Sirena's breath away just as it had the first time she'd seen it. Not one article of furniture had been moved. Austin had always liked things to be comfortable, and for him to be comfortable he had to know where everything was.

Carlotta headed straight for the formal massive double doors that opened from the entry hall into the living room, rather than taking the shorter route Sirena remembered as being to the left of the entryway through the open front gallery, with its fabulous cresting arches and magnificently lush potted plants. With a brittle smile she tagged along, feeling almost as if she were the guest and Carlotta the hostess. Things would sort themselves out in time; no matter how rude this woman was, Sirena was determined not to make an enemy of her the first day at Rancho Reese.

Beyond the double doors the mammoth living room sprawled in brightly sunlit welcome. The stone fireplace, an old friend, dominated the north wall of the room; large enough for Sirena to stand up in, it could accommodate logs the size of small trees in the winter. On either side of the fireplace stood large sofas, stark in their simplicity, with wood frames hand hewn from the tough mesquite wood Austin had favored. The plump rust cushions provided the perfect background for the brilliantly hued embroidered pillows strewn casually across them. A small square table sat at the far end of each sofa, and at the head, facing the fireplace, was Austin's favorite high-backed wood chair, the fine cordovan leather burnished to a high patina.

Two massive cabinets, glass fronted and softly lighted from behind, displayed the fine collection of ancient Indian pottery and artifacts Austin had collected through the years. They occupied the walls to either side of the fireplace, quietly imposing in their presence. A beautifully carved chair, its arms decorated with arches and scrollwork intertwined with small animals, stood next to the cabinet on the outside patio wall across the massive room.

Closer to Sirena and on her right was a glowingly oiled game table, gleaming in the sunlight that spilled into the room. The stately chairs placed around it were of wood so dark it was almost black, and the seats and backs were of supple leather. Immediately to her left as they entered was yet another pair of sofas, these more the size of love seats, facing each other with a long low table between them. Plants were everywhere, green and lush, and everything about the room spoke of comfort and the symmetry Austin had loved.

How well Sirena remembered, too, the formal dining room, and beyond that the kitchen, large and airy, with its small breakfast table behind a bubble of glass that overlooked the courtyard. She and Austin had breakfasted there every day of her stay, and she would do so again.

But for now Sirena absorbed herself in the beautiful living room, with its magnificent furnishings and massive beams that ran across the length of the room nearly twelve feet above her head. A sense of serene permanence could be felt everywhere she looked.

"You mustn't allow us to keep you from freshening up." Carlotta's voice, benignly commanding, broke into Sirena's reverie as they stood just inside the doorway of the vaulted living room. "We wouldn't expect you to remain so uncomfortable throughout lunch." The sweep of Carlotta's coolly appraising gaze uttered the uncomplimentary volumes her lips did not, and her sympathetic suggestion came across like an iron fist in a velvet glove. "We can entertain ourselves quite well until you return."

There was no gracious way around it. Carlotta Savedel had just politely taken over Sirena's household, and it rankled. Trying hard not to remember some of the backbiters she'd had the misfortune to know back in New York, Sirena reminded herself that Carlotta could merely be trying to help.

"You're most thoughtful, Carlotta. Thank you very much," she said, keeping her cool exterior.

One hurdle to get over, she told herself, one more thing to get through before she would be left alone and at peace with the aristocratic old house and immense ranch Austin had bequeathed to her. Sirena doubted Carlotta would be staying another night. By nightfall she would be gone; and by that same calculation, she reflected, so would Rualto.

"If you'll excuse me —" Sirena hesitated a moment longer "— I'll be back in a short while."

Carlotta Savedel, Sirena had to admit, was an imposing figure. She stood slim and straight, her spine stiffly erect, holding her head at a proud tilt. She seemed to be examining the rest of the world under the microscope of her own standards — and finding it extremely lacking.

The pale alabaster of her skin was starkly emphasized by the blue black of her hair, which cascaded loosely down the middle of her back. Despite its autocratic sternness, her face was somehow ageless. She was dressed simply in the woven leather sandals so common in Mexico, a simple, crisply ironed white shirt and a full black skirt. She had to be in her middle forties, but her hair was the color of that of her sons. She wore no real jewelry, no rings or earrings, only a delicate gold chain at her throat with a tiny cross hanging from it — a symbol of her faith, not an ornamentation. Anita and Mike Vargo surely would know more about Carlotta. When the woman was gone, Sirena was going to have a lot of questions to ask.

Turning on her heel, Sirena moved with a certain amount of grace and pride toward the long hallway that led to the bedrooms and guest wing. Anita intercepted her as she turned a corner.

"Señorita Clark," she called softly as she came up behind her.

"Enough of that 'Señorita Clark,' Anita. Call me Sirena, as you did last time. Now what is it?"

Bright green eyes filled with warmth and humor fastened on Sirena, and a beautiful smile creased Anita's round sunny face.

"I had Ramón put your bags in the guest room you had when you visited," she said a bit hesitantly. "We didn't clear out Señor Austin's room since we didn't know what you'd wish to keep, and I wasn't sure whether you would wish to sleep there before you took care of that. I hope you don't mind."

"Not at all, Anita," Sirena responded gratefully. "I'm glad you thought of it. I wouldn't have been comfortable in Austin's room, not with all his things there as he left them. I'll be most content in the guest room."

Anita beamed, pleased she'd done the right thing. "I'll be getting back to my lunch," she said simply, eyes reflecting her genuine pleasure with the sudden breath of life in a house so recently touched by grief. Her feet whispering along the floor, Anita hurried back to the kitchen. It wouldn't do to have the lunch too crisp or long overdue with Carlotta Savedel in the house. It wouldn't do at all.

Sirena could well imagine what a shock the reading of Austin's will had been to the household. She knew, too, that while Ramón made her angry, he was right to a certain extent. But whether the Savedels agreed with Austin's choice of an heir, the fact remained she was there now, and Rancho Reese had been left to her care. She would do her best to run the ranch with the same love and efficiency Austin had put into it. Anita and the others, Sirena affirmed in her mind, would not have to worry about their place in the scheme of things as long as she was able to keep the ranch running.

Heading down the long hall toward the room Anita had selected for her, Sirena decided it was going to take some getting used to — this business of being head of a household such as Rancho Reese. It irritated her a bit to admit that Ramón had been correct: she did have a lot to learn. Without a doubt she was going to have to buckle down and master a great deal of it in a hurry.

Sirena had the distinct impression Anita hadn't wanted to tell her in front of Carlotta that she'd given her a guest room instead of Austin's suite. Maybe she was wrong, but the feeling was one she was having difficulty shaking: already it seemed as if Carlotta had far too much power in this house. She had an uneasy suspicion that her coming to the ranch and taking over was going to be like wrenching power from the older woman. Sirena had never been good at subterfuge and power plays, so the old faithful direct approach was going to have to do the job.

Though she was not overly fond of the idea of having the wool pulled over her eyes, Sirena intended trying to be fair to everyone. Pride of ownership was welling up from somewhere deep inside, and she was determined to make a go of what Austin Reese had left for her.

Long legs carrying her briskly along the tiled hall, rubber-soled shoes squeaking softly as she walked along, Sirena realized her thoughts were scattered, and she struggled to organize them. She didn't even see Ramón when he stepped into her path.

The collision was abrupt and brief. Sirena jumped back as if she'd been scalded when she realized into whose arms she had inadvertently walked. Startled by the sudden contact, she could feel her flesh jumping as Ramón favored her with a dazzling smile.

"Alone again so soon?" he quipped. "My brother's charm was not enough for you?"

"If you must know, I'm going to my room to get cleaned up for lunch," Sirena snapped. "And it wouldn't hurt you to take advantage of one of the guest rooms to do the same," she ended haughtily, her nose wrinkling in distaste.

"Ah . . . Carlotta," Ramón said quietly, his voice filled with deeper knowledge.

"What?" Sirena was fast losing what little patience she had left after a night in the desert with Ramón and now the unexpected guests who seemed to have more influence in her home than she did.

71

"I simply mean it was Carlotta's idea that you shed your layers of grime after having spent the night with me in the dirt." Ramón described the situation accurately, if tactlessly. "Carlotta is a wizard at giving commands without sounding as if she is."

"Your mother . . ." Sirena began, almost reflexively going to Carlotta's defense.

"My mother," Ramón pointed out with no emotion, "is a tyrant. She firmly believes she should have been *patrona* of Rancho Reese long ago and could at this moment probably cheerfully scratch your eyes out."

Automatically Sirena glanced over her shoulder in the direction from which she had come.

"Oh, she's not there, like a shadow attached to your shoulder," Ramón assured her. "That will be my job and pleasure in the future. We're going to be seeing a lot of each other, Sirena. Take my word for it." He smiled broadly. "Now was that an invitation to lunch I heard a short while back?" He was innocently referring to Sirena's sharp suggestion that he clean himself up.

"Do I have a choice?" Sirena asked coldly, throwing out the rules of hospitality, glad for the moment that they were alone.

"No," Ramón returned with a grin. "I wouldn't want you to be charmed beyond endurance by my silken-tongued brother. So as long as they'll be staying for one of Anita's delightful lunches, then I suppose I'll be forced to join all of you at the table. I can watch you play the role of grand *patrona* there at close hand. Who knows what magnificent plans you might come up with for the *rancho* over lunch? You might decide to change the draperies in the living room or maybe install stereo throughout the hacienda. I wouldn't want to miss it." Ramón spoke the words softly with calculated charm.

"You're insufferable," Sirena protested hotly.

"Oh, am I?" Ramón quirked a questioning brow in doubtful reply to Sirena's outburst. Then he turned on his heel and walked with an easy grace down the long hall in the direction of the living room.

Sirena sighed. What had that delightfully charming, warm and gentle old man got her into?

CHAPTER FOUR

After a good night's sleep Sirena could feel her scattered senses marshaling around, her control of the situation returning. As anticipated, Carlotta and Rualto had departed after lunch the previous day, leaving behind a decided chill in the air, but relief where Sirena was concerned. Finally she was alone. At least nearly so, for Ramón had stayed on as he had promised — or was it threatened?

Sirena was not entirely sure, but she was now certain of one thing as she sat at Austin's massive desk in his handsomely appointed study: that Austin had indeed and in great detail appointed Ramón to guide and counsel her until she had a full understanding of the ranch's complex operation. He had even gone so far as to place Ramón in charge of the ranch funds until he determined Sirena was capable of handling the job. Of course, Sirena had gleaned that information from the papers sent; it was only the identity of her guardian that had at first eluded her.

When Sirena had arisen at almost eight-thirty, the sun had already been shining brilliantly in the clear blue sky, and Ramón had been nowhere in sight. In the dazzlingly bright breakfast room, its windows facing the courtyard replete with towering trees, trickling stream and beautiful birds, Anita had informed Sirena that Ramón had eaten early and gone out somewhere; she hadn't been certain where.

Sirena had eaten breakfast in peace and blissful solitude, and now she let her gaze wander at will around the large, comfortably furnished study. The smells of leather, polished wood and cherry tobacco, Austin's favorite, permeated the room. Papers Sirena had dug out and examined were spread all over the desk top in a sort of jigsaw clutter that made some sense to her, even if it would to no one else. She had done a considerable amount of reading and was already becoming aware that there would be a lot of paperwork clamoring for her attention. The file drawer of the massive desk was crammed with papers, and Sirena hadn't yet even started to peruse the actual file drawers that occupied a back corner of the room.

All in good time, she reasoned; she was going to be here a long while. The unbidden thought surprised her. As yet she hadn't decided if she was definitely going to stay, if she would be able to live with the terms of the inheritance. She smiled to herself. Well, she supposed, to make that decision she was going to have to think of it as home and try it on for feel.

Daydreams, Sirena mused, *nice, safe, happy daydreams.* And why not? There was a safe and happy feel about all of Rancho Reese. She flicked a glance over her shoulder toward the door that led to the bedroom alongside the study. The combination of four rooms — bedroom, sitting room, study and private bath — had been Austin's suite. It was completely furnished with square, starkly carved furniture, highly polished and gleaming beneath the soft light that filtered in through the windows. Nothing about the rooms was unhappy or, strangely, even sad. It was the way Austin would have wanted it. A gentle warmth seemed to fill every corner of the room, and Sirena found very little that she would change in the decor. Perhaps she could add a few pieces of furniture more suited to her own size than Austin's and replace his personal possessions with hers. Within a very few days she would settle in and put her own stamp on her surroundings. There was time, though, time for everything.

Sirena pulled another envelope from the desk's shallow center drawer and recognized Austin's familiar scrawl across its white surface. The envelope was carefully sealed and addressed to her, but there was a stipulation, one boldly written beneath her name. The envelope wasn't to be opened unless she was in crisis or about to be married. The strange combination amused Sirena. Had Austin equated marriage and crisis to be one and the same? And why, she wondered, had he gone to such lengths to try to ensure everything would go exactly the way he wished after he was gone?

Sirena placed the envelope to one side, following Austin's

wishes, aware that he had known full well she would do so. Did Ramón also know the contents of that letter, she wondered wryly. It would appear from Austin's papers that he knew almost everything else about the ranch's inner workings. Attempting to put Ramón from her thoughts for the moment, she reached for the formal will and the sheaf of papers attached to it just as the door swung abruptly open.

"Up so soon after your arduous journey?" Ramón greeted her mockingly as he strode into the room, completely at ease within his surroundings. "And looking for a loophole already, I see." His words carried a sting Sirena would not have believed he could make her feel.

"Don't you believe in knocking?" she snapped in retaliation, brilliant blue eyes flaring with the anger that surfaced whenever Ramón was near.

Angry with herself, as well, for allowing him to stir such a violent reaction within her, Sirena glared at him. How dared he look so composed, so virile, so overwhelmingly at home as he swaggered into her office with a mocking smile on his lips? Yes, Sirena decided, it was *her* office now, no matter what anyone else might think, and she was going to make sure they all knew it.

"No, I don't, as a matter of fact," Ramón returned, his mouth twitching with a half-suppressed smile. "What was I interrupting — a tryst with your lover?"

Sirena glanced away and fought the urge to blush. It was strange, the effect Ramón seemed to have on her, and she didn't like it at all.

"I suggest you knock in the future," she said through stiff lips as she put aside the papers she'd been holding and rose from her chair. Somehow she felt that standing up would help her to be on a more equal footing with this strange overwhelming man, a man who in some way made her feel she was staying at Rancho Reese at his sufferance.

"Certainly, *patrona*." Ramon's voice was silken and caressing, his amused eyes flicking over her in a searching appraisal that spitefully brought the flush she had fought at his entrance high into her cheeks.

"That might be the first truly human thing you've done since I met you," Ramón said, referring to the flush Sirena could not hide. "But believe me, Sirena, I didn't come here to fight with you or embarrass you. I just wanted to tell you I have the horses waiting out front and Anita has packed a lunch. You're so eager to run the ranch, I thought the sooner you got out of your soft castle tower here, the better." There was insolence in his gaze, an inexplicable mocking look in the depths of his eyes as he took in her inappropriate dress for riding.

At the same time Sirena assessed Ramón's appearance. He was wearing a fresh shirt and a clean pair of jeans along with a high-crowned broad-brimmed cowboy hat and well-worn boots, ready for the trail. Attired as she was in flat sandals, a light cotton wraparound skirt and short-sleeved white blouse, Sirena felt at an odd contrast to him.

"You're going to have to adjust better than that," Ramón sighed with mock patience. "You should be dressed and ready for anything at this time of the day."

"You forget," she reminded him tartly, "I've seen almost every square foot of this ranch already with Austin." Sirena was puzzled at her own attitude. Why was she hesitating? A long quiet ride in the countryside would be lovely whatever the excuse. She gazed fixedly at Ramón and knew the answer. She wasn't sure she wanted to be alone with *him* again.

Ramón laughed at her stare. Folding his sunbrowned arms, he waited.

Sirena was mesmerized by his gaze. Her tongue touched her dry lips, nervously moistening them. Peculiar and unexpected sensations arose from deep within, and she was alarmed at her response to Ramón Savedel's undeniable physical magnetism, to the sheer overwhelming maleness of his presence. She had never felt this way previously. Unfamiliar quiverings assaulted her beneath her cool exterior. Sirena was sure the trembling of her lips would give her away and Ramón would recognize the tumult of emotions that assailed her now as she stood rigid before him. She shuddered. If he reached for her now. . . .

"Is my tie crooked, or did I forget to shave this morning?" A boyish grin fretted at the corners of Ramón's mouth as he managed to subdue his deep-chested laughter. He didn't give her a chance to reply but instead turned toward the door. "You haven't seen the ranch from the viewpoint of a *patrona,* only as a guest. Get changed." He threw the command out as casually as if he were addressing one of the workers on the ranch. "I'll meet you down by the corrals in fifteen minutes."

Anger surged forth to fill the peculiar void Ramón's abrupt departure had created within Sirena. She was tempted to stomp down those stairs and tell him politely he could go to hell; she would ride over the ranch when she was ready. But that would be playing into his hands, proving to him what he had said about her being a fortune hunter, wanting only what she could take from the ranch and not the responsibility. And to be truthful, she did want to go riding. The fresh air would be a welcome balm, and the horses were waiting. It was too beautiful a day to let petty anger stand in the way of her enjoying it, and she could use a break from all the papers that covered the desk. Perhaps while riding she would get a glimpse of Ramón's better side — assuming he had one. If they were to carry out Austin's last wishes, they were going to have to spend a lot of time together, and Sirena didn't look forward to being completely miserable.

Sooner or later Ramón would have to see that she was serious. She would make him understand that she was not looking for a convenient loophole to let her out of her obligations where Rancho Reese was concerned. Sirena stepped out from behind the desk and started for her room to change. She couldn't even imagine why she cared what Ramón thought, but she knew she did.

Anita was coming down the hall toward her when Sirena emerged from the study and intercepted her with a smile in greeting.

"I'll be out riding with Ramón, and I don't know when we'll be getting back this afternoon," she said quietly, "so why don't you just take the rest of the day off. I can manage a light dinner for myself."

"Oh! But I couldn't do that," Anita exclaimed. "You arrived only yesterday — I couldn't leave you today."

"Nonsense!" Sirena smiled brightly. "Of course you could. You've been taking care of this house ever since Austin died, without a single day off, and then on top of it you had to manage company before I even arrived. You deserve a day off. Take it, Anita."

"If you're sure. . . ." Anita hesitated, dipping her head.

"Of course I'm sure!" Sirena assured her. "Now scat. I'll see you tomorrow. Go find your young man," she teased, "and have a good time."

Green eyes sparkling in her round face, Anita turned and disappeared in the direction from which she had come. Sirena didn't see the strange look that had first passed behind the excitement in Anita's eyes or the momentary confusion the young girl displayed.

Hurrying now, Sirena returned to her room and shed her skirt and blouse, draping them across the bed as she stepped to the closet. Few of her clothes hung there, since she hadn't had time yet to unpack completely. Her jeans were there, however, as well as the long-sleeved plaid cotton shirt she wanted. Her boots, well worn and gleaming from the new coat of polish she'd applied before leaving New York, stood on the floor beside the one pair of sling-back high heels she had managed to unpack the previous night. She slid the belt of plain brown leather that came quickly to hand through the loops of the jeans and left the buckle undone and dangling while she hurriedly did the shirt buttons up to the highest one below the collar. Then she dropped to the seat of the dressing table, picking up her brush. She would have to tie her hair some way.

With no further thought Sirena brushed her fine auburn hair until it gleamed, then grabbed hold of it and twisted it into a thick braid that hung down the middle of her back. A final glance in the mirror was enough to tell her the results were satisfactory. Snatching up her hat at the last instant, she dashed out the door into the hall, rushing for the side door to head for the corrals, her heart light within her.

Sirena was about to run toward the corrals when she brought herself up short. What was she doing, bending to Ramón's command to be there in fifteen minutes as if she were some young schoolgirl eager to please? Whether Ramón cared to acknowledge it, Rancho Reese was hers. And though she might not know enough yet about its inner workings to be giving the orders herself, she saw no reason to obey Ramón's, to jump every time he opened his aristocratic mouth!

Deliberately Sirena slowed her pace, hesitating inside the door, letting seconds and minutes tick by before opening it. Then she strolled outside, heading in the direction of Mike Vargo's well-kept stable.

The stable was situated several acres from the main house, to keep down both the smell and the flies that stables and corrals tended to attract. Sirena could see figures moving in the distance and make out several horses saddled and waiting. It wasn't easy for her to keep to the slow pace she had set herself, especially not with the habit of walking fast along New York streets. Moseying along at this pace would have got her run over in a crowd back home. Here, if it weren't for the urge to move faster that continually pricked her, it seemed comfortable, almost peaceful.

"Ah," Ramón said as she arrived at the corral, "a most unusual species — a female who arrives on time."

Sirena blinked. She had? How could she have when she'd been stalling all the way from the house? The last thing she'd wanted was for it to appear as if she were making an effort to comply with Ramon's demands.

"It takes a lot less time to dress," Sirena returned sweetly, almost in reflex, "when you're going to be with someone you don't care to impress."

Ramón quirked an eyebrow, his expression one clearly of disbelief. His self-assurance irritated Sirena nearly beyond endurance, but even as she felt her anger begin to rise, she felt, too, the strange thudding of her heart, the warmth of a blush as it spread up into her face. His eyes crinkled a message to hers, and that same boyish smile she'd seen tugging at his lips earlier twitched there now. Once again he seemed to be reading all her thoughts with no trouble at all.

"Shall we go?" he asked her, gesturing toward the horses that stood waiting patiently. He moved with an indolent stride that somehow drew her along with him toward their mounts.

Sirena was acutely aware of Ramón close beside her as she gathered the reins in her hands and placed her left foot in the stirrup to swing aboard. She executed a little skip for momentum and began to straighten her left leg to carry her into the saddle when she felt a hand braced against her hip, propelling her easily onto the horse's back. A sudden spreading tingling sensation of warmth and want surged through her body, and she involuntarily jerked away from the unexpected contact.

Her eyes going round and large with surprise at the stirrings within her, she turned her gaze on Ramón. Her spine stiffened with renewed dignity. "That wasn't necessary," she informed him frostily, her hands signaling her mount to step away as Ramon's long fingers lingered on her thigh. "I'm completely capable of getting up on a horse without any help."

Ramón's lips twitched again, as if he were afraid to reveal any humor to her other than the sarcastic wit he chose to display with nearly every meeting. "You shouldn't rebuff a helping hand when it's offered," he said quietly, turning to his own horse. "It may not be offered again."

The words sounded almost like a thinly veiled threat, and Sirena felt like a chastened child. What was it about this man that set her raw nerve endings to tingling and her heart to fluttering within her breast like a wild bird wanting to be free? How was it he could, with so few words or gestures, send her soaring to wild euphoria and almost in the same instant come crashing into a heated anger she'd never before experienced? She didn't know how, but there had to be a way to quash the feelings that surged to the surface each time she was with him. The two of them seemed to have got off on the wrong foot once again, but the whole day lay before them, and Sirena was determined that the rest of it would go differently. There had to be a way to create a friendly business relationship with this man.

The day was beautiful, the sun shining down from a clear blue sky. A few stray puffs of cloud floated gracefully above the distant mountains whose snow-shrouded peaks glistened whitely. Ramón led off from the corral at an easy trot, and

Sirena immediately recognized the excellent qualities of the horse she rode. As in the past, Mike had chosen well for her.

Sirena leaned forward in the saddle a bit to enable her to stroke the silky chestnut mane of the mare. The horse tossed her head at Sirena's gentle touch, enjoying her rider's hand.

"Your mare's name is Chispa," Ramón informed her as they guided their horses across the creek the Jeep had had such trouble negotiating the previous day upon their arrival. Then, altering direction, he headed for the chain of mountains that loomed east and southeast. The high wall appeared to be impenetrable, but Sirena knew better, and the soft green of the rolling slopes beckoned to her.

"Chispa," Sirena repeated, laying her hand along the mare's neck, feeling the strong arch there, reveling in the play of the muscles that rolled fluidly beneath her. "What does it mean?" she asked a bit timorously, enjoying the sense of companionship springing up between them as their horses carried them along. She was almost afraid an unexpected incident might again turn Ramón antagonistic.

"It can mean several things," Ramón said easily. "But when Mike named her, I believe he was thinking of a small diamond. She is among the best your ranch can produce." Sirena didn't miss the emphasis Ramón put on "your" when he spoke of the ranch, but his words were quiet, not abrasive, and when he half turned in her direction, he displayed for her an expression that passed for a smile, even though the corners of his sensuous lips still insisted on a sardonic twist.

"Care for a short gallop?" Ramón offered when the ranch house was far behind them and the countryside had become a gentle roll that would be easy on the animals.

"Oh, I'd love to!" Sirena's bright eyes glittered with excitement. She leaned forward slightly in the saddle, lightly touched her heels to Chispa's sides and let the mare go before Ramón could say anything more.

Chispa, as if she had been spring-loaded, leaped forward, chestnut mane flying, long legs stretching out for the turf that lay in front of them. Her hooves pounded a rhythmic tattoo that Ramón's horse close behind her echoed. Sirena sat the fluid gait of the horse with ease. The wind tugged at the brim of her hat and tossed the thick braid that hung down the middle of her back. From the rear she thought she heard a deep-throated laugh of exultation, but she ignored it and concentrated on her riding. Rolling gently in the saddle, she could feel the surge of the horse's muscles beneath her own as her legs gripped the little mare's sides. Her left hand held the reins and her right lay alongside the chestnut's neck in encouragement, gently stroking and patting as Chispa's strides continued to lengthen.

Ramón drew up alongside her, directing their course toward an arroyo that dipped between the hills. The tops of the water-loving trees were barely visible above the crest of the hill.

The feeling of complete freedom was heaven to Sirena. The wind whistled past her ears; the sun shone full on her face, and the powerful striding of the animal beneath her created a fantasy world that sent her blood racing through her veins.

For a few seconds Ramón's horse took the lead, directing their strides onto the sandy bottom of the arroyo. Suddenly Chispa's silken strides were transformed into an airborne glide, as if her small hooves were not even making contact with the earth. The soft sand absorbed the shock of each stride and cushioned the ride even further as Chispa tugged eagerly against the reins, begging to go faster, to move out of the rocking gallop into a full run.

Sirena reveled in the mare's obvious enjoyment of the ride. The horse was breathing well, her strides coming easily, effortlessly, as they leaned into a broad turn. Trees and tall grasses sprang up on all sides of them as they moved deeper into the canyon. Sirena knew she would be sore the next day, but in the excitement of the moment that didn't matter. She felt she fit in the saddle as snug as a hand in a glove. With a joyous laugh that came from somewhere deep in her city-girl's liberated soul, Sirena gave Chispa her head and turned the mare loose.

With one bound the small horse was again even with Ramón's striding steed, and the next took her ahead at no urging from Sirena. Chispa jerked against the reins, and then suddenly she was free, running wild as her ancestors had done in these mountains long after the Spaniards' arrival with the first of her kind.

Sirena experienced an incredible primitive thrill as Chispa stretched out on the wild run. Tall trees turned into a green blur on either side of their passing as she flowed easily with the horse's swift stride.

From behind her Sirena could hear Ramón's yelp of concern and the sudden increase of his own mount's pace, but she ignored it. She was enjoying the ride far too much to bow to his domineering commands. She felt exhilarated, alive, as if she had partaken too liberally of an intoxicating drink. She was asking nothing of her mount. The animal was running for the sheer joy of running, and Sirena was not ready to stop her yet; she was not ready to give up this splendid feeling of joyous abandon.

Then suddenly Sirena felt a new emotion gripping her. Like a block of ice freezing, forming in the pit of her stomach, paralyzing fear wrenched her. A shock ripped through her body, bringing sweat to the palms of her hands and a piercing cold to the same soul that had only moments earlier been rejoicing in newfound freedom.

The left rein, the lifeline that connected Sirena to Chispa, telegraphing commands, had snapped at the last toss of the mare's head. Sirena had been too caught up in the wonderment of her flying stride over the land to notice exactly at which instant it had happened, but now she was holding the limp detached piece of leather, dangling it from a sweaty palm that was rapidly losing its grip on the remaining rein. She felt her mouth go dry. Easing back in the saddle, she tried to telegraph her intent to Chispa, tugging gently on the remaining rein, which now slipped continually in her hand.

So that was why Ramón had bellowed at her, Sirena realized. He must have seen the rein separate near the bridle when she had passed. She had to stop Chispa, she knew, but she wasn't doing a very good job of it. The mare was running with the bit in her teeth, and the gentle persistent tugs on the remaining rein were having no effect other than to pull the horse's head and cause her to swerve sharply, not slacken in speed. Sirena could feel panic beginning to rise in her chest, tying itself into a stiff knot that threatened her breathing. She tried talking softly to the fleet-footed horse, shifting her body weight to a rhythm that encouraged a slower gait, but nothing seemed to be having an effect.

Sirena gritted her teeth. She was going to have to let the mare run herself out, and that was certain to be a long harrowing ride.

"Don't fight her!" Ramón's voice cut into the surging of the wind around them as he guided his horse up close beside Sirena's, keeping a firm hand on the reins and leaning over to reach for Chispa's bridle. Sirena blanched at the maneuver. She had seen horses at the track running too close to one another go down in a tangled heap of legs, riders and saddle leather. One small misjudgment and there could easily be a broken leg or even a broken neck. Sirena could feel her heart beating frantically, her face set in a frozen mask of terror.

"I've got her," Ramón called through clenched teeth. "Hold on, Sirena. I'll have her stopped in a minute."

Sirena could see the strength in Ramón's long fingers as he grabbed the broad cheek strap of the bridle in one hand and the reins of his own horse in the other. Taking in the slack, he was slowly, steadily shortening the strides of both horses, though Chispa protested with more than one sharp shake of her fine head. Stride by stride they slowed. Sirena's frantic gaze fixed itself on the play of Ramón's shoulder muscles beneath the taut fabric of his shirt as he continued to exert his strength over the will of the stubborn mare, drawing her to a halt alongside his own horse. Before she could gather her thoughts, Ramón was off his horse, letting the reins drag to keep the animal from wandering, and alongside Sirena, helping her down from the saddle, strong hands easily encircling her waist.

His arm around her, Ramón guided Sirena to the grassy bank of the arroyo. She could feel her own breathing coming very fast and knew that if he removed his arm, her knees would surely buckle.

"Sit down." Ramón's voice was firm, the slight accent Sirena was so often aware of lending authority to his words. "You're all right," he reassured her, the usual mockery gone from his tone, the bottled-up anger he nurtured somehow dissipated. "It's all over," he crooned, sounding like a stranger to Sirena's ears.

"I'm — I'm all right," Sirena responded. But that warm strong arm did not move away from her, and Ramón pulled her down to sit on the soft grassy bank beside him, drawing her close against his side. He held her there, the steady beat of his heart quieting the rapid tattoo of her own as if it had somehow cast an irresistible spell.

A strange enervation was creeping through Sirena's limbs, and she began to tremble in Ramón's embrace. Weakly she tried to push away, then sighed and relaxed against him, her mind crying out in protest to what she was allowing. Her body was responding unashamedly to his. Her mouth went suddenly dry, and she moistened her lips with the tip of her tongue.

Sirena turned her face enough for her blue eyes, which were clouding with an arousal she had never felt before, to meet Ramón's gray green eyes, which had darkened with passion. For once he was looking at her warmly, without anger, without mockery. His smoldering gaze sent a liquid heat coursing through her veins as he groaned from somewhere deep in his chest.

"Oh, God, Sirena!" Ramón murmured huskily. His lips descended to capture hers in a sweet gentle kiss that robbed her of any remaining shreds of will. His hand brushed the hat from her head, and he drew her closer to him. "I've wanted you from the moment I saw you," he breathed into her hair.

"Ramón . . . Ramón, no." Sirena weakly attempted to stop what was happening between them, to deny what had been there almost from the moment they'd laid eyes on each other back in Tucson. She struggled to still the wild race of her pulse that his roaming hands ignited.

"Shhh," Ramón chided her gently, "shhh, *mi amada*." And his lips returned to their delicious torture of hers. His kiss deepened, caressing, demanding, drawing from her uninitiated body a trembling that swept through her with a sweet surprise.

85

"This has nothing to do with the ranch. This is for us alone. . . ."

His meaning was clear. However he felt about her inheriting Rancho Reese, it had nothing to do with this strange, almost electric physical attraction between them. And in her own confused weakness Sirena couldn't fight his logic.

One hand remained wrapped about her slim waist, holding her to him as if she might choose at any instant to flee, while the other moved up to her hair, loosing the tie that held it. It flowed over her shoulders and down her back in a gleaming auburn curtain that picked up the stray beams of sunlight, and he wrapped his hand in its flame-shot silkiness. Gently he used his grip in her hair to pull her head back, laying the smooth white column of her throat open to his kisses as he pushed her back onto the grass.

Sirena felt her entire being tingling and going weak as his mouth crushed hers, his heated hunger prying her lips apart, tongue probing, plundering the sensitive depths. Strange and unexpected sensations raced along her nerve endings. She felt her sensitized flesh jump as his hand brushed the separated halves of her blouse aside. Hard and sensual, his fingers intruded upon the flimsy lace that remained to cover her smooth soft breasts, her last line of defense.

Sirena's head swam with the flood of new sensations. His mouth left a trail of liquid fire wherever it roamed, scorching her to her innermost depths. The firmly muscled length of him held her there, pinned to the sweet-smelling grass that surrounded them as he rolled on top of her. His shirt fell open, and she could feel the prickle of his tightly curled chest hairs against the curve of her breasts. The passion raging through his body startled her, and even more frightening was the answer she felt in her own. It was as if a door tightly closed for years was suddenly opening within her, melting away the resistance that threatened to stiffen her limbs, slyly beckoning him on.

His knees were intruding between her legs, his hand straying to her hip, sending shivering ripples of pleasure throughout her body even as he continued to kiss her. A soft moan Sirena was not even conscious of making escaped her mouth, and Ramón chuckled softly before his lips moved to follow the line of her jaw and his hand moved to the button at the top of her jeans.

Sirena gasped as his knuckles slid across the smooth flesh of her stomach. Her eyes flew wide as the fog of sensation lifted with a shattering abruptness. What was she doing? Sirena had never allowed this to happen before. Never, she had believed, would she experience this wild stirring of the senses. She had always intended to save herself for the day when she truly loved a man, but now. . . . Now suddenly all that was falling apart. What was happening to her?

Then the truth began to seep into her consciousness, sending her reeling, as though from a stinging blow. She was on the verge of falling in love with this man, this mocking stranger, this dark-haired lover who admitted even as he touched and caressed that this was only desire. He made no mention of love.

No, Sirena's mind rebelled. She could not be falling in love with this man, must not be falling in love with him! He didn't love her — would never love her! He thought of her only as a fortune hunter, a grasping woman out for all she could get. She couldn't allow this, knowing what he believed. He would simply use her. It would mean nothing more to him than momentary gratification.

Shock waves thundered through the heated tingling fibers of her flesh as Ramon's hand skirted along the waistband of her jeans. His fingers teased the sensitive flesh of her stomach, caressing her, then found the stout button at the top of the jeans no obstacle at all as it slid out of its fastening. Feebly Sirena began to protest, her mouth freed of his as his lips sought her breasts, mouthing more determined protestations when her hands began to push at his broad sun-bronzed chest.

"No!" Sirena cried out weakly, twisting in his embrace. "No! Stop!" She struggled determinedly against her own desires as well the unrelenting strength of his. She could not let this happen.

Sirena knew her protests had reached Ramon's ears, for his mouth moved again to capture hers, stifling any further words that threatened to form there. As his tongue played with her lips, his hand started to move lower.

Far back in her mind Sirena became aware of distant hoof-beats coming in their direction, moving nearer with each passing second, but all she could focus on was Ramón. She twisted and fought, and for what seemed an eternity he was oblivious to her struggles. His strong virile body molded to hers like the interlocking half of a jigsaw puzzle, pressing her into the soft earth and muffling her struggles there. Sirena felt a sob of frustration rising in her throat. Would he ever stop?

Then abruptly Ramón jerked away, raising his head. The weight of his body continued to hold Sirena pinned helplessly beneath him, and one hand was still wrapped in the bountiful silkiness of her hair.

"Damn! There's someone coming." His hand released its hold in her hair, and he rolled off her. "You'd better make yourself decent fast," he suggested with a wry twist of his lips as he climbed to his feet and turned from her, no doubt to gain control over the rampant arousal of his body.

Shivering, Sirena fumbled the buttons of the blouse into their holes and shakily fastened her jeans. Could she have stopped him? Would he have stopped if he hadn't heard the hoofbeats drawing nearer?

"How could you?" Sirena demanded, the anguish she felt masked in the bite of her words as she worked swiftly to stuff her long shirttail into her jeans. "I asked you to stop. How could you?" Her face was still hot and flushed, but she could feel the ebbing of that liquid fire that had burned through her veins only seconds earlier.

"How could I what?" Ramón asked through tight lips that spoke of passions barely leashed. His breath still came in harsh ragged bursts. "Take what was offered me?"

Sirena gasped, climbing to her feet to face him. "Offered you!" she cried through lips still swollen from his kisses.

"Yes, offered," Ramón cut her off roughly. His eyes glittered, and that old mocking smile twisted the corners of his lips, replacing the softened look Sirena had seen earlier. Now he was all angles and hollows, hard and unyielding.

"I wouldn't have kissed you if you hadn't wanted to be kissed," Ramón said coolly. "You welcomed it. You melted against me and returned that kiss. I am not a recluse, Sirena — I've seen women in such a state before, begging with their eyes to be kissed . . . and much more. You weren't exactly fighting me."

"You took me by surprise," Sirena protested. "It was a shock. It took me a few moments to react. But you certainly knew I was fighting you at the end. Why didn't you stop? *Would* you have stopped?"

Ramón gave a low chuckle, the sound of it rough and somehow cheerless against Sirena's ears. "Were you fighting *me*, Sirena, or were you fighting yourself? Would you have continued to fight if I'd kept on?" he challenged. "Don't deny you've felt what's between us. You wanted this as much as I." Ramón's eyes searched her flushed face with a searing intensity. "You're a beautiful woman, and you're not a child. There must have been other men. And feeling what's between us, why *was* it so wrong that you wanted me to stop?"

"Why must there have been other men?" Sirena hissed, tossing her mane of unbound hair back behind her shoulders. Her eyes were sparkling pools of blue ice, frosted over by the anger that rose within her.

A voice inside Sirena, her woman's soul, screamed her indignation. Ramón had been prepared to take her there, in the soft grass, not because he felt any love for her but because he believed she had been with other men. What difference could it make, he no doubt reasoned, if he had his pleasure with her, as well?

"Oh!" Sirena gasped, but bit her tongue against any further comment, for the rider both of them had heard approaching was now in sight.

Ramón stared at Sirena as he towered above her, his lean athletic body almost radiating animal heat. Expressions of disbelief, then puzzlement and finally conscience-shaking revelation chased one another across the planes and hollows of his darkly handsome face. Tentatively he reached out to her, but she had already turned away, having seen only disbelief stamped across his aristocratic features and mirrored in the depths of his eyes.

Rualto drew his horse up in the arroyo near Ramón's and Sirena's. "Am I interrupting something?" he asked innocently as he sat astride his magnificent black mount. His gaze wandered from Sirena to his brother, and the look in his eyes suggested he knew exactly what he was interrupting.

"I saw there was trouble with the horses," he offered by way of explanation. "I covered the distance between us as quickly as I could," he added with a shrug.

"You're all right, Sirena?" Rualto was solicitous as he drew his spirited black horse closer to the raised embankment so that he was eye to eye with Sirena where she stood on the raised grassy bank. "My brother has not, er, taken advantage of you?" he asked wryly, his gaze sliding over to Ramón.

Sirena laughed a little uncertainly, the sound of it hollow to her own ears. A muscle worked in Ramón's hard jaw, and she marveled again at how much alike the two brothers were in everything but manner. Rualto was teasing; the light in his eyes, so much like Ramón's, was playful, but it was amazing how close to the truth he had struck.

Rualto laughed, giving Sirena a glimpse of how Ramón might look if he would truly laugh instead of presenting her with that sardonic twist of his lips he so often passed off as a smile. "Sirena," he admonished her lightly, "don't look so stricken." He reached out to take her hand, pressing it to his lips in a courtly kiss. "Ah, it's true what they say," he sighed, his breath whispering across the back of her hand, so proper, so much more gentle than Ramón's assault had been earlier. "It's true that one who has cold hands has a warm heart. I know it must be true, for you could have nothing but a warm heart. I can see it there, shining in your eyes."

"Thank you, Rualto." Sirena gently tugged her hand free of Rualto's grip, her fingers feeling suddenly icy in the aftermath of the assault on her senses.

"Anita packed a picnic lunch." Sirena spoke quickly to cover her embarrassment, but she knew in the same painful moment that she was merely emphasizing it. "She always packs far too much, and I can't imagine a nicer place than here to eat it. Why don't you join us, Rualto?"

Ramón stood wordlessly to one side as Sirena extended the invitation, his troubled eyes moving back and forth between them. His gaze was stony, his eyes damning, and Sirena sensed her invitation to Rualto was at the root of it. As soon as his brother was gone, Ramón undoubtedly planned to pick up where they'd left off.

"I'd be delighted." Rualto bestowed a smile upon her that revealed a small dimple in his left cheek. Then he swung gracefully down from his horse, dropping the reins to the ground as Ramón had done with theirs. "I'll even bring the lunch," he offered, and stepping close to Ramón's mount, he undid the ties that secured the saddlebags.

Sirena couldn't help smiling in return. She wondered idly if Ramón, too, had a dimple that would be revealed if he ever truly smiled at her.

Rualto slung the saddlebags into Ramón's hands where he stood on the embankment and lithely climbed up to join them. Sirena noted that while Rualto's clothes were not exactly his Sunday best, neither were they the worn and faded jeans Ramón favored. His pants were of a heavy, tightly woven brown canvas, immaculately tailored to his athletic limbs, and his shirt a startlingly white cotton. His hat, though straw in deference to the burning sun, was of the finest quality, and highly polished boots gleamed through the light layer of dust he had picked up in stepping down from his horse. Whereas Ramón wore his dignity like an old patched cloak tossed casually over one shoulder, Rualto sported his as a perfectly fitted suit of armor. Strange, the pair of them, so different and yet so alike. . . .

Sirena led the way to a towering tree that clutched the side of the embankment. Its roots were exposed where the rush of waters had torn away the anchoring soil, leaving the aging tree standing in mute testimony of its tenacity.

"What brings you out this way?" Ramón asked of his brother as Sirena busied herself spreading the blanket Anita had thoughtfully included in their supplies.

"The bull has been grazing near this pasture, and I wanted to make sure the fencing between our ranch and Rancho Reese was secure," Rualto said easily, his words heavy with the accent

Sirena had come to expect when he spoke. He gave a short laugh. "It seems, though, that I was already too late; a section is down and will have to be repaired. Fortunately the bull was unaware of it, or he would have already been through the fence and a devil to find on Rancho Reese's fine grass."

"I don't think so," Sirena commented. "He would probably have stayed close to the riverbanks. That's where the grass is the most lush."

"Ah! A clever woman," Rualto complimented her. "You're undoubtedly correct, and should he ever make his escape to this side of the wire, I shall follow your advice and search here first." He grinned in his most boyishly charming manner. "So you see," he added, "my second reason for coming here was even more valid than my first." Rualto swept off his hat to Sirena as she began unpacking copious amounts of food from the packs. "And that second reason, of course, is you, my dear Sirena." Rualto was at his most gracious, and the ease of manner that seemed somehow beyond Ramón's capabilities seemed to ooze from his every pore.

"You just saw me yesterday," Sirena reminded him as she took from the saddlebags some pieces of cold chicken, more than half a loaf of fresh bread, cold beef, plenty of raw carrots, green peppers and celery, washed and cut-up, and several apples. As well there were two thermos bottles, the contents of which she had yet to discover.

Rualto, looking genuinely pained, arranged his dark features into a pattern of desolation. His eyes, Sirena suddenly noticed, lacked the golden depths that swirled within Ramón's. Why had she not observed that earlier?

"Ah, Sirena, but now that I've seen you, talked to you, enjoyed your company, a day without such pleasures would be as a day devoid of all the beauty around us . . . a day without sunshine or flowers."

Sirena's eyes sparkled with good humor. "You sound like a courtly lover of the seventeenth century, Rualto," she said lightly, "but I can't help enjoying it."

"My brother is the poet of the family," Ramón informed her dryly as he dropped to his knees at the edge of the blanket. He was careful to keep his distance, almost as if he were aware of the solid mental barrier she had erected between them.

"I'm in the hands of powers beyond my control when confronted by such beauty," Rualto said breezily, then seated himself across from Sirena.

Sirena didn't know Rualto well enough to tell if he was half kidding or all the way serious. She smiled in response to his extravagant compliments but could think of nothing appropriate to say in return.

"You know," she began finally with sincerity and good humor, "you're welcome at Rancho Reese anytime —"

"Is tomorrow too soon?" Rualto broke in eagerly, his words teasing. Yet there was no doubt about the sincerity of his request.

Ramón glared, and Sirena shook her head happily. "No, tomorrow is wonderful, and you'll stay to dinner. I'll tell Anita."

"Only, my dear Sirena, if I may spend the night, as well," Rualto returned firmly, grinning wickedly as Sirena nearly choked on a mouthful of food. "In one of your guest rooms, of course."

"Of course," Sirena managed, her eyes shifting back and forth quickly between the two brothers, noting their expressions — and wondering at the black cloud that seemed to have enveloped Ramón.

Rualto caught the rapid movements of her eyes. "Remarkable, are we not?" he observed bluntly. "So much alike, and yet inside —" he touched his chest with a finger freed from a chicken drumstick "— so very different."

Sirena warmed to Rualto's wry good humor, and Ramón tore viciously at the piece of chicken he held, giving Sirena the distinct impression he imagined it to be his brother.

The simple lunch passed far too speedily for Sirena's liking, and before she realized what was happening, Rualto was cheerfully announcing his departure, rising from his end of the blanket still spread with food. Ramón had eaten in silence, his eyes glittering beneath dark brows, the look in them shuttered from Sirena by lowered lashes.

"Until tomorrow, then, lovely Sirena," Rualto was saying,

his words almost caressing as they fell upon her ears. "My only regret is that I must leave you now to see to the work your beauty has distracted me from." His words were lightly bantering, filled with a genuine warmth, his eyes telling her much more than he was actually saying. A stray breeze rose suddenly and tousled his thick black hair as the dimple she had noticed earlier momentarily appeared again, giving him the look of a naughty little boy.

"Tomorrow," Sirena responded, feeling a pang of regret as Rualto turned away without further preamble. He raised a hand in farewell before riding off astride his magnificent black stallion.

Almost the instant he was gone from sight, Sirena could feel the strange pulsing tension asserting itself between her and Ramón. Tautly masked and restrained during lunch, it once again sprang back to life. She didn't meet Ramon's gaze but instead sipped at the bracing tea that had been in one of the thermos bottles — a blend of herbs and flowers, its taste similar to that of fruit punch.

"I . . . I think we'd better be getting ready to go, too," Sirena ventured. She moved like an automaton, starting to pick up the stray bits of food that could be rewrapped and salvaged for another meal, every joint in her body feeling stiff beneath Ramón's steady gaze.

Abruptly he rose and stood towering above her, the molten gold swirling in the depths of his eyes, dampened, Sirena sensed, only by sheer force of will. She was painfully aware of his darkly tanned countenance, framed by the thick thatch of black hair, longer than Rualto's, silhouetted against the brilliance of the blue sky behind him. An odd expression was on his face, one Sirena had not seen previously.

When Ramón spoke his voice was roughened, his jaw a hard line that set the other angles of his face.

"If what you intimated earlier is true," Ramón said slowly as Sirena finished packing the remains of the picnic in the saddlebags, "then perhaps I owe you an apology."

Sirena's cheeks flamed. Why had she told him? What had possessed her to let him know she was a virgin, even though it was a simple fact? In New York "virgin" was nearly a dirty word. For years, since she had been eighteen, Sirena had been adept at pretending sophistication, and her friends had thought her as experienced and worldly-wise as they. It had not been hard, since that was what they had chosen to believe even without any assistance from her. Why, then, had she lowered her defenses with this man, this stranger who had nearly assaulted her?

"You guess!" Sirena railed, jumping to her feet, counting on her suddenly added height to give her confidence. "You are. . . ." Sirena flung her arms wide in fury. "You're absolutely unbelievable!" As she threw the words at him, she regretted she couldn't think of something much more bitingly witty with which to slash at his inflated manly pride.

Ramón grinned mockingly. "So far I have only your word on this condition you claim. And you were quite willing just a short while ago — of that I am sure. *Querida,* how am I to be certain this is not merely some little game of yours, an attempt to make me feel guilty over what passed between us? Maybe you want to ensure that I'll keep my distance in the future, in spite of all your teasing and tempting. I'm not a monk, Sirena. A man can be pushed too far."

"Pushed!" Sirena flared. "I am what I am, and I don't give a damn what *you* believe or don't believe!"

"Alas," Ramón said smoothly, ignoring her ire, "there is only one way you can prove what you claim." He spread his hands in a helpless gesture, his lips twisting into a wicked grin, eyes gleaming his mockery of her position.

Anger caused Sirena's body to tremble and her tone to turn viperish. "You're insufferable," she breathed, the words threatening to catch in her throat. "I thought I disliked you the moment we met in Tucson, but then I believed I wasn't being fair, wasn't giving you a chance. Now . . . now I find I dislike you more by the minute! Ever since the second we met you've been playing the role of the masterful male, ordering me around, dominating, even threatening. I am, I can most heartily assure you, sick to death of it! Today I was trying to be a little pleasant because we're going to be spending a lot of time together until

95

I learn the workings of the ranch, and you caught me with my defenses down. How could I have resisted? I was too stunned to resist. And *you*," she accused, "you would have been just as pleased as anything to take advantage of that situation if your brother hadn't turned up, wouldn't you have?"

Ramón's eyes went cloudy, amusement touching the darkened contours of his face, the mocking gleam in his eyes fueling Sirena's fury. "Is this some subtle way of trying to tell me you're growing fond of me?"

"No, I am not!" she spat, turning on her heels and stalking off in the direction of the horses. She left Ramón to bring along the heavily laden saddlebags as he chose.

Sirena was moving fast, the heat of her anger coursing through her veins to drive her. Until she reached the horses where they stood patiently waiting the return of their riders, she didn't alter her pace. Snagging one dangling rein, she found herself holding only open space where the other should have been.

"Damn!" she groaned as she stood staring at the raw end of the severed rein, wondering what to do next.

There was no time to fully contemplate the matter. Ramón's footsteps were heavy behind her, and he casually slung both sets of saddlebags over the backs of the saddles before turning to Sirena and her problem. Without a word he pulled a knife from his pocket, unfolded it and began hacking away at one of the leather strips that hung from the saddle. Severing it, he then attached it securely to the dangling piece of short rein. During the entire proceedings Sirena was forced to endure the humiliation of needing and waiting for his assistance.

"I'll have to speak to Mike about this when we get back to the corrals," Sirena said quietly, seeking to turn the conversation away from the subject that had gone on much too long. "It was careless to leave a bridle unrepaired like that." The raw smoothly sliced edge of the leather had not escaped her notice.

"You won't have to speak to Mike," Ramón informed her as he handed the newly spliced rein to her. "He didn't saddle the horses. I did."

Without another word between them, they mounted and

started back for the ranch, Sirena's mind in a turmoil. What had she got herself into, coming thousands of miles to this primitive corner of the world only to find herself — no matter how she tried to argue otherwise — at this man's mercy?

CHAPTER FIVE

"Be wary of the Savedel men," Anita warned as she sipped a mug of steaming coffee. Then, setting the mug on the small courtyard table, she leaned forward to observe more closely as Sirena carefully positioned a dollop of paint on the picture she was near to completing. "They can be ruthless when it suits their purposes, just like their mother."

During the several days that had passed since Sirena's shattering experience with Ramón, she had managed to keep him more or less at arm's length. And lately there was always Rualto. He was becoming a frequent visitor, showing up regularly for dinner and turning up at odd hours in between. He had wasted no time in making it quite clear he was courting her. He was thoughtful and considerate, but his old-fashioned manner was in stark contrast to that of Ramón's, whose more direct approach didn't exactly mean he was wooing her — in fact, far from it. Still, though Sirena was attracted to Rualto, absolute sincerity seemed to be lacking in his courtship. She had the vaguely uncomfortable feeling that something besides her drew him to Rancho Reese.

The two brothers were a puzzle to Sirena. Deep in thought, she frowned as she carefully applied more color to the impossibly blue sky that dominated her picture. With a professional eye she contemplated the towering cottonwoods that stood majestically along the creek, thrusting their mighty limbs into that incredible blueness.

Her thoughts once again strayed to Rualto. There was a studied politeness to his courtship, a lavishing of attention and seductive words. It was all very logical and pleasant. She had no doubt he would be a gentle and considerate lover, and she did enjoy his company and his ready wit. It was easy to spend quiet hours with Rualto, speaking of a wide range of topics, including Rancho Reese and its future. But in spite of all that, there were times when Rualto's thoughts seemed to be elsewhere.

With Ramón it was more like the rushing of the ocean tides. Each time they were alone together, Sirena felt herself being swept away on a cresting wave of emotions she couldn't understand. He was always mocking, and at times he seemed cruel. But there was a power there, a strange magnetism between them that Sirena had to fight with every ounce of her will or risk falling into his arms again. And she admitted to herself just how very much she longed to be held in the circle of those strong arms. But she knew only too well she couldn't risk it. Ramón, Sirena was convinced, would just take from her, and she would be helpless to do anything but give.

"I don't think 'ruthless' is quite a fair word to use," Sirena finally answered Anita, glad they had found this opportunity at last to spend some time together, to talk.

Anita shrugged. "I can see how it must look to you, Señorita Sirena. You see only the charming side of the brothers, and Carlotta was most polite when she was here."

Sirena laughed and turned toward Anita. "You promised to just call me Sirena, remember? And as to Ramón and Rualto showing me only their charming sides . . . well, I wouldn't quite say that." Sirena couldn't help blushing a bit as she vividly remembered Ramón's towering passion, the overwhelming virility of him, the demands he made and that mocking smile that so often twisted the corners of his lips.

Holding her paintbrush poised away from the canvas, Sirena stepped back to get a better perspective on her painting. The ever evolving strength of her work was there, reflecting the graceful wild beauty of this place. The tameness of the lush green courtyard in the foreground, the stark rugged beauty of the mountains beyond — it was there once again, all the life and power that had lingered in her memory as little more than a dream.

"I don't know too much about any of the Savedel family, except what Austin told me the last time I was here," Sirena admitted as she continued to examine the painting on the easel with a critical eye. "He said Carlotta had been widowed when her sons were no more than babies, and he spoke of her as a strong woman to have taken charge of the ranch on top of caring for the two boys." Sirena turned her inquiring gaze on the young woman sitting at the table. "Perhaps you can tell me more about them, Anita."

Anita sipped again from the steaming brew. "Yes," she mused, "that's what Austin would have told you. There was a time when he and Carlotta were like this," she added, twisting one finger around another in a symbolic love knot. "And even when they were no longer so, he would never harm her. He always did everything in his power to protect her."

"Protect?" Sirena's tone was questioning.

Anita nodded. "What Señor Austin told you was not true. Carlotta was not widowed; she was never married. When she was very young, she was very beautiful, and a man from up north forced her away from her village and raped her. Ramón and Rualto are the result of that man's cruel lust. No one knew who he was, and he was not seen after that again. Señor Reese was a young man then," Anita went on. "I was not yet born, but I heard the story when I was growing up in the village. Also, he told me some of it when we talked after I came to work here."

"Raped?" Sirena turned the thought over in her mind. Both Ramón and Rualto were the result of a young woman's violation. How must it have affected her? After all these years, was that, Sirena wondered, what made her seem so cold, so withdrawn? "You said Austin protected her?"

Sirena didn't have to say much to draw Anita out. It was obvious she had been waiting for just such an opportunity to impart what information she had.

"Yes," Anita continued. "It's not the same here as it is in your country."

Sirena could well imagine it was not the same at all!

"When it became known that Carlotta was with child, she was shamed, destroyed. It became impossible for her to find a husband, and the few who would have her, she turned away.

100

She bore her babies alone, and she raised them alone. Except for her brother."

"Brother?" Sirena echoed Anita.

"He was much older. Their parents had died close together when Carlotta had been but a baby herself, and she had been living with her brother when this horrible thing happened. He never had a family of his own, so when he died shortly after the boys were born, he left everything — the *rancho* bordering this one — to Carlotta. She ran the ranch, even improved on it, and alone raised her two sons."

"She *must* be a very strong woman," Sirena mused, "to have undertaken so much alone — and succeeded. She must have been more than capable of taking care of herself. Yet Austin felt he had to protect her?" she puzzled aloud. She could feel a flicker of kinship to Carlotta, so buffeted by life and yet strong enough to go on, and she felt pity for her sons, Ramón and Rualto, who when young must have suffered the taunts of other children. Perhaps in time she could be friends with Carlotta.

Anita shrugged. "People talk. There were those who thought Carlotta must have brought her misfortune upon herself, and there were those who treated her like a leper. So . . . Austin created the story of her unhappy early widowhood. It was mostly for the outsiders, since the villagers knew the truth and few were willing to let her forget it. But through the years it lent a kind of dignity to Carlotta's position, and as the boys grew into men . . . well, few around here would be willing to risk uttering the sort of cruel words Carlotta suffered in her youth anywhere they might reach the ears of the brothers. I told you the Savedel men can be ruthless and very dangerous." There was a note of admiration in Anita's voice for the Savedels' willingness to defend their mother, and a becoming blush rose in her cheeks as she realized the forcefulness of her statement.

"How awful it must have been for them when they were children," Sirena observed, her attention for the moment completely distracted from the painting she'd been working on since just past dawn that morning. "What about Carlotta and Austin?" she asked. "You said they were very close, but it ended. Did Austin ever tell you why?"

Anita nodded slowly, then took up her coffee cup, peering into it as though studying its contents. "We talked once," she answered softly, as if the admission made her feel somehow guilty, "because he needed to talk to someone about his pain. Even before he spoke to me, I understood what was happening. Carlotta is as ruthless as her sons," she added bitterly. "But in a much different way."

"What are you saying?" Sirena prodded.

"Señor Austin had long been friends with Carlotta's older brother. When he died, Austin felt great pity for poor Carlotta at the tragedy that had befallen the family. She had been so young to bear such shame. Señor Austin was good to her, and after her brother died he would help at her *rancho,* always sending his own men to do her work when things were not going well. Carlotta would never admit it, but it's because of Austin Reese that her *rancho* prospered. He helped her when she needed it, and after her brother's death he taught her all she needed to know to run the *rancho.*

"I wasn't working here long," Anita went on, "when Señor Austin began to think more seriously about Carlotta. And he believed she felt the same about him. He, of course, was much older than she, but that didn't seem to make any difference. Much of the time she was here, at Rancho Reese, and Señor Austin treated her with love and kindness, accepting her sons as his own, since he had never married or had a family himself."

"But what happened?" Sirena couldn't help asking, though she knew Anita was going to give her the answer without being prodded.

Anita's bright green eyes, usually filled with humor as if she were sharing an incredible joke with the world, were sad. "Señor Austin discovered that what she felt for him was not love, but greed. She was also aware that he had no real family — at least, as far as she knew. She'd been using him, expecting that one day they would marry and she would gain control of Rancho Reese to add to her own. It would have made her a very powerful *patrona* here, very powerful.

"When Señor Austin discovered her intent, he was very hurt.

102

They had a terrible fight. And that's part of the reason you didn't see the Savedels or hear much about them when you were here, Sirena," Anita revealed. "For a time Carlotta was forbidden to set foot on Rancho Reese. And Rualto was very angry with Señor Austin and refused to come where his mother was no longer welcome." Was there a special note of regret in Anita's voice when she spoke of Rualto's absence, Sirena wondered.

"Ramón," Anita went on, "well, Ramón seemed to be angered, as well. He left his mother's ranch at the time to travel in your country for several months. He didn't return until after your visit here ended."

"Oh," Sirena said thoughtfully, as if all the information Anita was giving her somehow answered the questions she'd had stirring within her since her arrival. But in fact it was leaving her more puzzled than ever.

Rualto's reaction Sirena could understand, but what about Ramón? What had his sudden travels meant? Had he hated Austin so much he had to put thousands of miles between him and the aging owner of Rancho Reese? If that was true, why had Austin still charged him with seeing that she learn to take care of the ranch? It was all very confusing to Sirena. She was beginning to realize just how much digging it was going to take for her to learn not how to run Rancho Reese, but what was simmering beneath its calm beautiful surface.

"Ah, but you, *señorita*," Anita began again, "you were such a joy to Señor Austin in his time of pain. I remember how pleased he was when he received your letter telling him of your intended visit. And —" Anita waved her arms excitedly "— when you came, you brought such happiness."

"I'm glad my coming made Austin happy. I grew to love him while I was here," Sirena replied truthfully. "But I was just being me — I didn't do anything special."

Anita nodded. "I know, but that was what Austin loved about you from the start. You were nothing but yourself. You pretended at nothing, asked nothing of him. It was clear to him you wanted only to drink in the beauty of his beloved Rancho Reese and to put it on canvas. He knew you loved the land,

103

and though it may seem strange, there are few who truly do."

"Then that's why he left the ranch to me?" Sirena conjectured.

"Yes and no." Anita laughed softly. "Señor Austin was a very complicated man. He was old-fashioned. He had an inborn wish to leave his home and holdings to those of his own blood. It was a thing deeply rooted within him. But there was also his consideration of the land. He wanted to put it into the hands of someone who would truly love it, as you did from the moment of your arrival. Anyone who looked could see it shining in your eyes, Sirena," Anita added shyly. "He was always very poetic about the land. He claimed it was a giving thing, alive but far too easily bent to man's will, far too easily destroyed by those who care about only what they can take from it and not what they can give back."

Sirena smiled faintly. She could still remember the joy she and Austin had shared when they'd ridden together over the ranch and in their evening talks beside the crackling fire in the living room. Sirena was a city girl, but she felt as Austin did about the land. Man was basically a destructive creature, and the land was frail indeed. Ever since Sirena could remember she had feared for the land, but never had she experienced the deep-seated love that had struck a chord within her inner being before she'd set foot on Rancho Reese. The wild stark beauty of the place had been powerful and breathtaking to her, and the oasis Austin had created at the heart of such wild country, the hacienda with its comforts and gracious beauty, had been like a balm to a battered soul.

"Austin knew that Ramón and Rualto loved the land," Anita went on, dragging Sirena back from her reveries. "And they were like sons to him. But by the time you arrived here, he also knew of Carlotta's grasping and scheming ways. She doesn't truly love the land as her sons do and as you do. Still, he worried a bit that you were a city girl and wouldn't want to stay here once you had tried it for longer than just a holiday trip. It was a difficult time for Señor Austin. I remember how many nights I would walk past his study and see the light shining under the door far into the early-morning hours. Finally he decided on what you already know. He fixed it so you could try it to see if you could stay without really hurting the *rancho*."

Sirena's brilliant blue eyes turned introspective. "So if I hadn't turned up when I did, Ramón and Rualto would have inherited with no obstacle?" A glimmer of an explanation for Ramón's attitude toward her was beginning to show itself. He and his brother had wanted Rancho Reese, felt they were somehow entitled to it, and she had become a major stumbling block to their ambitions.

Anita nodded. "Yes," she said in a heartfelt voice. "Despite his troubles with Carlotta, Ramón and Rualto were like sons to him, and there was no one else to leave the *rancho* to. And he still cared for Carlotta. He realized that after he had time to let the wounds heal. He wanted her to have the benefits of the *rancho* through her sons, but not the control."

Absently Sirena nodded her head. Her gaze was fixed on the painting she had been working on, staring sightlessly at.

"The Savedel family had known much grief," Sirena ruminated. "And it seems I've become a part of it."

"No, that's not true." Anita, with a deep sigh, sat back from the edge of the chair where she'd been perched. "I can see how they could appear as hurt frightened little boys," she said quickly. "I have seen that side of them, too. But always remember that beneath there is a ruthless man. And as for their coming to grief because of you — the *rancho* was years of Austin Reese's life. It was his to do with as he saw fit, and he saw fit to leave it to you."

Sirena couldn't help grinning ruefully at Anita's astute observation. She had never seen that side of either Savedel brother. The hurt little boy in Ramón would be interesting to see indeed.

"I'll have to invite Carlotta over for a long talk, but tell me," Sirena said naively, "how do you happen to know them so well?" Sirena knew now she was trespassing on private territory, but the story of the Savedels so fascinated her she couldn't stop.

Anita gave a bright laugh, then confided, "I know one of the brothers *very* well, the way any woman knows a man very well." Her eyes glistened with a new depth of meaning, and her lips curved into a sensuous smile.

Somehow Sirena managed not to gape at the young woman seated near her on the patio of Austin's courtyard. The stunning revelation hit her like a not too well-padded blow to the solar plexus.

"We're in love, but there are some problems now." Anita hesitated, as if unsure of exactly how much to tell Sirena. "I'm but a serving girl, and Carlotta. . . ." She trailed off wistfully.

Anita's words sent a shiver of apprehension through Sirena. Ramón? Ramón couldn't be the one! Anita couldn't be his mistress. Sirena's flesh tingled even now with the memory of his caresses. It had to be Rualto. Damn! Why had Anita not just called him by name? Sirena felt her head begin to swim. It was too much to absorb at one time.

"I'd better get back to work," Anita announced, almost bouncing to her feet. "Ramón has been up since even before you and I! He will not want his lunch to be late."

It just *couldn't* be Ramón! Sirena seethed inside. The way Anita catered to him — all the signs were there. Yet it couldn't be. An odd feeling permeated the pit of Sirena's stomach, and a rage was building within her, pulsing through her veins with the rhythm of her heartbeat. That peculiar feeling could most certainly not be jealousy, Sirena decided. But she had to know it was not Ramón Anita was in love with, had to know it from her lips.

"I feel like working in the kitchen today myself," Sirena said lightly, tossing her brush into the small can of cleaning fluid she kept by the side of her easel. "I'll tell you what, Anita." She wiped the tips of her fingers on a small rag that dangled on the other side of the easel. "You fix whatever you planned, but whatever needs to be cleaned, chopped, minced or mashed, give to me."

"You are sure? . . ." Anita hesitated just inside the doorway to the kitchen.

"Of course!" Sirena insisted. "Don't worry, Anita. I don't get inspired often. I just feel as if I'd like to do something in the kitchen today."

"You're the *patrona*," Anita laughed, leading the way into

the spacious, brilliantly lighted and sumptuously supplied kitchen.

The kitchen had always been one of Sirena's favorite parts of the hacienda. It was immense, and one end faced the court-yard in a huge curved bay that overlooked the beauty of the thick green grasses and beautiful flowers. The breakfast room was there, dominated by a beautifully hand-carved table much smaller than the one in the formal dining room. In fact, Sirena far preferred eating there to eating in the dining room. It was cozy and lovely with a pastoral serenity.

Inside the kitchen was just as lovely. Anita kept the place absolutely spotless. Racks of shining pots hung above the island comprising the stove and work center, and huge drawers were set in the work counter. Clumps of herbs were already dried and ready to add to Anita's wide array of dishes, while strings of chilies and garlic dangled on either side of the bay window, putting the condiments at Anita's fingertips and adding charm to the quiet room. A stray soft breeze crept in through an open window, carrying the startlingly fresh scent of the outside air in among Anita's hanging herbs and nose-tickling spices.

"There will be chili for lunch —" Anita indicated the already simmering pot on the stove "— and fresh bread." She pointed to a large bowl filled with rising dough and covered with a clean bit of toweling. "There isn't much work remaining, just the dessert — a fruit salad. Ramón is very partial to fresh fruit," she added in an explanation Sirena could well have done with-out.

"First I must separate the dough into loaves and put it in the oven. The fruit is in the basket," Anita went on, nodding toward a huge basket of freshly washed fruit of every type. There were papayas, mangoes, apples from storage somewhere, peaches Sirena could not even guess the origins of, oranges and grapefruit from the trees in the back courtyard, grapes of several varieties and a large honeydew melon set to one side.

"If you wish to begin peeling and slicing, I'll join you in a few minutes. Then we can grate the coconut and chop the nuts before I mix the cinnamon and nutmeg. The knives are in the drawer beside you," Anita added almost as an afterthought.

107

Then she turned to examine the mound of swiftly rising dough she had left lying submissively in the bottom of the bowl. Expertly she tumbled the dough out onto the breadboard for separating into loaves that would fill the black cast-iron pans.

Sirena slid the drawer open and grasped the smooth wooden handle of a carefully sharpened knife. Tension filled her as she hastily began to slice the fruit. She would draw Anita out; she would have her answer. Distracted, she wielded the razor-sharp knife.

An audible gasp escaped her and jerked Anita around to stare in horror. Sirena pulled her hand abruptly from the knife as if she'd been bitten by a rattler. Blood surged from an ugly gash.

"Por Dios!" Anita exclaimed, grabbing a handy towel and rushing to Sirena's side. She mopped ineffectually at the blood that spilled with alarming volume from the long deep cut.

"Stupid, stupid!" Sirena muttered, dragging herself from her momentary shock of the sight.

"I'm so sorry, *señorita!*" Anita accepted full blame immediately for the mishap as she tried to staunch the blood with the hopeless dish towel.

"It wasn't you I was calling stupid, Anita!" Sirena gasped. "It was me. It would never have happened if I'd been watching what I was doing."

The blood ran in a crimson flood that stained the towel. Sirena could feel pain now, the sting of abused flesh. The length of the wound appalled her. Never before had she cut herself this badly.

"We must do something!" Anita was first to voice their rising concern.

"About what?" Ramón had strolled into the kitchen from the dining room, hearing Anita's frightened wail before he could see what was happening. *"Perdición!"* he exclaimed, and then his long strides carried him the length of the room to Sirena. "Do you plan to stand there and watch her bleed to death?" he cried, his tone harsh, rasping.

Sirena felt the urge to make a cutting remark in reply — something to the effect that they were perfectly capable of handling the situation without his help. But suddenly the world started to spin, making her dizzy and sapping her of all will.

"Quickly!" The voice had the timbre of authority as Ramón's eyes locked momentarily with Anita's. His hand, strong and sinewy, wrapped around Sirena's wrist. "Get the first-aid kit. I'll stop the bleeding."

Without waiting to see if his command was being obeyed, Ramón dragged Sirena over to the sink, turned on the water and pulled her wounded hand and wrist beneath the cool water, washing the blood away at least momentarily so that he could see the extent of the damage.

"It hurts," Sirena murmured, tugging against his iron grip, her eyes glazed with shock.

"I don't doubt that it does." The words sounded almost impersonal. Ramón pulled her hand and arm out from under the water, grabbed a fresh towel and dabbed roughly at the profusely bleeding wound. *"Por Dios,* what a lot of blood!" Harshly he jerked her away from the sink, drawing her up closer against him, wrapping one hand around her slender wrist below the end of the cut like a tourniquet. With his other hand he encircled her slight frame and at the same time managed to bind the towel tightly around her hand, now elevated to slow the flow of blood.

"Here." He drew her back across the room to a stool by the work counter. "Sit down!" His words brooked no disobedience — and Sirena had no will to disobey him in the first place.

Anita's sandals beat a whispery tattoo against the tiled floor as she hurried back with the first-aid kit Ramón had demanded. Sirena allowed herself to lean back against the strong support of his arm.

"What a lovely way to die," she murmured, feeling a bit giddy. "Is that what you're going to do, Ramón?" Sirena couldn't suppress the small giggle that caught in her throat. "Are you going to let me die? I'll bet if you did you could somehow get this whole ranch for yourself." Sirena knew she was babbling, but she couldn't seem to stop the words. "Then you and Anita could live happily ever after!" Now why had she said that? It couldn't be Ramón; it simply couldn't be! Oh, couldn't it, the devil inside her slyly questioned.

"What's she saying?" Anita's face was creased into lines of shock and disbelief.

Ramón frowned in disgust. "She doesn't know *what* she's saying," he shot at Anita. "Just ignore it and give me what I need from that box."

Anita nodded briskly and handed him, in the order he requested, the iodine, a thick pad of bandage and the gauze with which to wrap the wound.

"I think you'd better lie down," he warned Sirena. "I'll get you back to your room." He still held her wrist within the iron grasp of his curled fingers. "Anita, fix a rich broth for her to drink and clean up this mess. This bandage should hold until I can get some stitches in that cut."

Nodding, the color drained from her cheeks, Anita immediately began moving about the huge kitchen to carry out Ramón's instructions.

"Don't order her around. I'm the *patrona*, remember?" Sirena attempted to put strength into her words as Ramón swung her easily into the circle of his heavily muscled arms. "Anita, do whatever you like!" Sirena gave a cavalier wave of her good hand as Ramón turned on his heel and carried her from the room.

"I can walk," Sirena protested a bit belatedly, even as she felt a thrill at being held in his enveloping arms.

With one of his arms beneath her knees, the other around her slim shoulders, Sirena was pressed tightly up against Ramón's chest. The strong beat of his heart as he carried her easily toward her room made her feel a bit giddy. The rich male scent of him created a heady aphrodisiac that fogged her brain. Light-headed, she felt as if she were being carried along on the foam of a surging wave.

Sirena could feel a flush of embarrassment rising in her cheeks, and she began to tremble in his arms. "I don't need to be carried." Her words, though blunt, were lacking the usual barb that Ramón so often drew from her. "And what did you mean when you said something back there about stitches?"

Ramón's concern expressed itself in anger. "That's no little cut. It looks as if you tried to slice your hand off. What the hell were you doing?" The words grated against Sirena's ears.

"I was going to cut up some fruit for *your* dessert — that's what I was doing!" Sirena snapped back. Her response made it seem as if no one else was going to partake of Anita's special fruit salad. "It . . . it was just an accident."

Ramón bent low to grasp the knob of Sirena's door with the hand that passed under her knees and pushed it open. "I'll have to talk to Anita about helpless city girls and sharp knives."

"You don't have to talk to Anita about anything. As you yourself have pointed out, *I* am the new *patrona,* and I can manage very nicely from here, if you don't mind!"

Sirena squirmed within the grip of his unyielding arms — but to no avail. Ramón strode purposefully across the broad expanse of what had once been Austin Reese's bedroom and deposited Sirena on the new bed she'd had brought in from one of the guest rooms.

The entire look of the room had been changed according to her instructions, though she still managed to convey the rough-hewn rustic charm that made the house so warm and attractive. The bed was a massive four-poster, each of its aged wooden posts deeply carved. A large woven rug had been laid down at her request; Austin had apparently preferred bare tile. Also at her request, Mike and a stable boy had carried in a pair of beautifully matched chests for her considerably larger wardrobe. She had discovered them in storage at the far end of the house and was taken with them immediately, for they were magnificently carved with birds and intertwining vines. She had retained Austin's large bedside table, stout and serviceable, containing a drawer below as well as an extra narrow shelf above. She now had plenty of room at her bedside for the stack of books and magazines she always seemed to accumulate. Despite the new additions, however, the room still looked immense.

Ramón sat down on the edge of the bed beside Sirena, and she shifted quickly to the far side, barely able to avoid body contact with him. With some surprise she noticed that he had tucked the first-aid box under his arm when they left the kitchen

111

and brought it along.

"You didn't really mean . . . ?" Sirena's blue eyes were large and round as she stared at Ramón.

"That's not a small cut you've got there — that's the Grand Canyon," Ramón informed her. "If you don't let me take some stitches, it will never heal smoothly and you'll have a scar for the rest of your life." His expression softened a bit as he gazed into Sirena's panicked eyes. "I told you a doctor would be a long way off down here," he reminded her. "But there's nothing to a few stitches. Besides, I've had some basic medical training for emergencies. Barbed wire can do a much nastier job than that," he added. His eyes moved to her tightly bandaged hand.

From the box with the red cross painted upon its lid, Ramón deftly removed what he needed: a long slender needle from a sealed packet, already looped with clear thread; some sort of liquid in a bottle; a sterile bit of cotton and a supply of fresh bandages. Swiftly he unwrapped her wounded hand.

"It's not bleeding so much anymore." Sirena's tone was apprehensive, her words quavering. She had always been terrified of needles. A shot in the doctor's office had been enough to make her faint a time or two, and she couldn't see much of a difference here. Though she hated her own weakness, there was no help for it, at least not enough to get her through this. "Maybe you shouldn't disturb it now," she suggested hopefully.

"Shut up and close your eyes," Ramón ordered gruffly.

"Do you *always* have to be so damnably rude and overbearing?" Having spoken the words, Sirena turned her head away, closing her eyes as Ramón positioned himself with her hand in his lap so that she couldn't see what he was doing if she happened to peek.

Biting her lip, Sirena waited for the expected pain. Instead she felt a cool liquid brush across the wound, and almost instantly the skin started to tingle and feel fuzzy, as if it had gone to sleep like a foot or a hand held in one position too long. Ramón worked carefully and with a surprising gentleness. Sirena could feel the light tug of the flesh at the raw edges of the wound but nothing else. She didn't experience the pain of

112

the needle. When Ramón finished, he applied more disinfectant and rewrapped the wound. Sirena heard him put his instruments away and close the lid of the metal box, but still she didn't open her eyes.

Then she felt something. Something warm was fluttering along the outside of the bandage that covered the jagged cut. Ramón was kissing her injured hand. Fiercely she kept her eyes tightly closed. Her mouth and throat went suddenly dry.

"My poor Sirena." The voice was Ramón's and yet so unlike his; it was caressing, somehow tender and at the same time rough. The words had the texture of a new saddle blanket, the underlying tone that of smooth well-worn leather.

His fingers, long and work hardened, turned gentle, as well, touching a strand of sparkling auburn hair that had childishly curled down into the corner of her lips. For a moment the fingers lingered there, strong hard fingers she knew could be hotly demanding, even cruel. But for the moment their touch was light and sensitive. Delicately they brushed her lips and smoothed back the stray strands of gleaming reddish brown hair from her face.

"Sirena . . ." the voice came again. Ramón's voice . . . and yet not Ramón's voice.

Sirena's nerve endings were alive and tingling. She could feel strange unbidden sensations beginning to rise with an intense heat within her, and she was all too aware of the deepening of Ramón's breathing. She forced herself to remain as she was, lying limp upon the coverlet, her head turned away, eyes tightly closed.

There was warmth in those fingertips as they hovered about her face, touching first the smooth surface of her forehead, then the soft planes of her cheeks, flushed beneath his caresses. She could feel his eyes fixed on her, waiting for some small movement that would indicate the response she felt building within her, surging and boiling like floodwaters against a dam that couldn't hold forever.

"Sirena. Sirena, look at me!" The voice was louder now, though still barely above a whisper. Ramón's breath fanned the smooth flesh of her cheek.

He was leaning over her now — Sirena could feel the shift in his weight — and suddenly his hands were no longer merely stroking her hair and face. With a sudden show of the strength Sirena had come to recognize only too well, his hands were gripping her shoulders, gently but firmly turning her body toward him, drawing her into his embrace.

Sirena's eyes sprang open in surprise to find Ramón's piercing ones lying in wait for her. The gold smoldered in their depths, swirling, mesmerizing her and bothering her limbs with the same enervation that had plagued her before when they'd been together on the bank of the arroyo.

The gold in the depths of his eyes seemed to move and grow, to sway like the plants at the ocean's bottom, and the glint there reflected passions barely leashed. Scarcely breathing, Sirena sighed and waited, eyes large and round, for what would happen, what must happen.

But it did not happen. Ramón's mouth, poised scant inches above hers, remained there, and he drew her injured hand to his lips once again. He continued to gaze into her eyes as if seeking something there. Sirena had neither the strength nor the will to resist, and she stared back as his lips tasted and teased the flesh of her hand.

Stiff and mute, yet trembling inside, Sirena lay tensely within Ramón's embrace, strangely incapable of movement, unable to draw a sustaining breath. She was aware of him with every fiber of her being as she had never been aware of a man. He drew himself up beside her on the bed, his elbows keeping his weight from her body though one leg moved possessively across hers.

A soft thrumming ache deep inside her matched the pulse of Ramón's body poised above hers, and Sirena felt a psyche-shaking dizziness flood her with an intensity that left her light-headed and flushed. Second by second she became more and more aware of her own vulnerable womanhood.

Long supple fingers wandered to the crisp collar of Sirena's red-checked shirt and slid along it, following the vee downward to the first button. With a quick movement they opened it, then the second and third. The hand slipped inside the shirt, brushing the cloth back to capture the curve of her breast where it swelled against the fragile lace of her bra. There was fire in Ramón's fingertips as they continued to explore, circling the exposed flesh, descending to the satin rosebud clasp that nestled between her breasts.

"Oh, God, Sirena," Ramón groaned from some untapped interior well, his voice sounding strange and unnatural. His lips swooped down, his mouth overpowering hers easily, forcing her lips apart, allowing him to invade the softer inner recesses of her mouth at will.

Sirena gasped as she suddenly realized Ramón's shirt had been freed, as well. The crisp little hairs of his chest were brushing maddeningly across her breasts, turning their tips to fire.

"So beautiful, Sirena," Ramón murmured roughly between kisses that continually sapped her of any will that threatened to return to her. "So very beautiful. You're like a drug, Sirena," he groaned. "I shouldn't want you, but I do. I can't help myself."

Sirena felt the honeyed glow of surrender threatening to engulf her as Ramón's hands glided smoothly over the flesh of her back, leaving behind a trail of goose bumps and shivers that ran up and down her spine. Then they trailed over her denim-clad hips, stroking and soothing as they went. He gently rubbed his knuckles over the flat surface of her stomach as his lips clung to hers, scarcely allowing her to breathe. She felt herself drowning in a warm and sensuous ocean, with waveless of chilled surprise alternately touching here, then there on the suddenly tingling surface of her skin.

There was a hollowness deep within Sirena, a peculiar aching want. Warmth flooded through her as Ramón's long strong fingers played, teased and tempted, until instinctively she reached for him, trembling in her need, a soft moan escaping from her like some sweet essence Ramón had tapped within her. A momentary thought raced through her mind. It wasn't Ramón Anita had been referring to earlier. The warm earnestness of his embrace reassured her and swept her along on a tide of unstoppable emotions.

Above her Ramón smiled tenderly, the stark angularity of his features softening for just a moment in the midst of his passion. Then all of a sudden — Sirena wasn't sure just how — her jeans fell in an untidy blue heap at the foot of the bed, and the cooler air brushing over her thighs sent shivers of anticipation through her. Ramón wound a hand through the silkiness of her bountiful auburn hair fanning out around her like the glow of a western sunset. She was warmed by the heat of his body and quickly losing herself in satin folds of forgetfulness as her body was awakened to one new sensation after another. She found herself caught in a whirlpool that was pulling her ever downward into its spirals.

At that moment Sirena didn't care about time or place or even Anita. Ramón's lips sought the long slender column of her throat in a warm moist caress that enveloped her head in fog. The heated masculine presence of him was all that filled her world — filled it to overflowing. She was acutely aware of every part of his body, of every surge of his pulse where he lay pressed up against her.

A soft buzzing in her ears was all Sirena heard until the rapid whisper of sandals sounded on the tile floor outside the door. A sharp knock on the solid wooden floor followed. Anita!

"I have some broth for Señorita Sirena," she called softly from the other side of the thick barrier.

Sirena went as stiff as a board in Ramón's grasp, her breathing hushed as if she were a schoolgirl caught in the utility closet with a boy. Anita! Her scattered thoughts began to reassemble themselves into a frenzied sort of sanity. What had she been doing? How could *he* do it to her? He who only desired her but didn't love her.

Ramón laid a finger across Sirena's lips for silence. "You had better keep it warm," Ramón called quietly, demonstrating remarkable control over the husky passion-warmed timbre of his voice. "The *señorita* is resting."

"*Bueno,*" Anita acknowledged. "I will look in on her later."

Sirena felt a chill of another sort suddenly creep over her at what she had almost allowed to happen. Shame sent a rosy flush high into her cheeks. Outside the door the sandals moved

116

off down the hall, and Sirena wished that she could miraculously just disappear, that she could just vanish into oblivion, or — better yet — that Ramón would do so instead.

Ramón returned his lips to hers, warm, persuasive, gently probing, but her own had turned stiff and cold. All of a sudden she was pushing against the encroaching weight of his body, trying to squirm away from his embrace.

"No!" Sirena pleaded. "No, stop! You have to stop!"

Bruisingly his lips sought hers yet again, but Sirena wrenched free, turning her head away as shame burned through her. She wanted only to be free of him.

"It's all right." Ramón's words were gentle, quieting, a tickle of breath against her ear. "I'm not going to hurt you. I know you might be a little afraid now, but —"

Sirena didn't wait for him to finish. "Oh! Oh . . . damn you! Damn you, Ramón Savedel! I am *not* afraid. I want you to stop! Let me go!" But she *was* afraid, a damning little voice inside her accused maliciously. She was afraid of the feelings he ignited within her, of the weakness it brought, of *loving* him.

For a while longer, for what seemed an eternity, Ramón's grip on her didn't loosen. He stared down at her, the passion-darkened depths of his eyes in turmoil, questioning. Sirena averted her eyes and tried to drag her shirt across her breasts to cover her nakedness . . . to restore some decency, if not self-respect.

"Just go — get out!" Sirena demanded when Ramón stopped his assault on her senses and merely held her.

"Why?" he breathed. "I don't understand."

Sirena nursed a fury to shield herself from the shame and frustration that filled her at the sudden absence of Ramón's caress. "You wouldn't understand, would you?" she snapped in response to his pained expression.

Cursing, Ramón levered himself away from Sirena with an abruptness that left her feeling bereft and unaccountably drained. Her dignity in shreds, she drew herself into a sitting position in the middle of the bed, long legs tucked beneath her, shirt clutched about herself, the tails draping mercifully over her hips.

All six feet two inches of Ramón's dark handsomeness towered over the bed as he raked a hand through the raven hair that grew so abundantly. He stared down at Sirena, the fires of passion barely banked, still burning in the surge of molten gold that lighted the depths of his smoky gray green eyes. It seemed to Sirena he was making an extreme effort to hold himself back from touching her, or his passions would rage out of control and there would be no way of stopping him at all.

The virile imprint of his body upon hers was a burning memory, and Sirena instinctively cringed inside. She somehow managed to maintain a good front for his benefit, joking with herself that if this series of charades kept up, she would soon be a consummate actress. Her exterior she consciously managed to keep cool and aloof, frigid, as immovable as a block of granite, while inside her heart beat like a wild creature's after a panicked run for its life. Her lips felt stiff and cold, as though the blood no longer flowed through them, and her eyes stung with the tears that threatened to burst forth.

For a few moments longer Ramón continued to regard her silently as bit by bit he struggled to regain control of his body. Shirt still unbuttoned, shirttails flapping outside his jeans, he shook his head in disbelief.

"Damn, Sirena," he said, his words rasping, the Americanized English a stinging slap in the wake of the soft Spanish love words he had been whispering in her ear, "if you did this to the men you knew in New York, I don't know how the hell you managed to hang on to that damn virginity of yours for so long. Every last one of them must have been a saint!"

"*You* think I let a football team of men do this?" Sirena demanded. "But of course, I keep forgetting: *you* would think that! Get out of here, Ramón. Just go!"

"Do you know what that does to a man, Sirena, being stopped halfway?" Ramón was ignoring her sharp-tongued demand to leave. "Why, Sirena? Just tell me why. You wanted it as much as I did. Even now I can still see it in your eyes. Don't try to lie that away," he cautioned her, "or I'll be tempted to prove my point."

"That's just sex talking," Sirena returned bitterly. "We're

attracted to each other like a couple of animals in mating season. Thank God you did stop — I'm grateful you were gentleman enough for that."

"Gentleman!" Ramón threw his head back and laughed. "My God, Sirena, don't you know yet that I —" Ramón cut off his words before he finished, eyeing her with a new hesitation, almost a wariness that Sirena could not begin to understand.

The harsh unnatural laughter died in the silence of the bedroom. Ramón sighed deeply, his eyes inexplicably withdrawn, emotion shuttered behind lowered lids and the sweep of his thick black lashes.

"It's there, Sirena, between us, and you can't deny it." Ramón bit off the words. "It will happen, mark my words, *querida*," he said more gently. "But I promise you one thing: I won't touch you again without your consent or your encouragement. Next time you'll have to come to me."

His words sent an icy dart of regret through Sirena's already anguished heart. She knew deep inside she was falling hopelessly in love with Ramón Savedel, and there was nothing she could do about it. How could she love such a man — one who spoke of desire but not of love. It was over then, even before it had started, for she would never allow herself to go to Ramón.

Sirena gathered herself into a small ball of misery in the middle of the bed.

"Then our problem is ended," she announced lightly, reflecting not the least bit of concern. "I admit to the sexual attraction between us." Sirena could feel a sob building at the back of her throat, but she managed to suppress it, though her words thickened. "I admit, too, that you turn me weak, that I can't fight you. Is that what you wanted to hear? Does that help your masculine pride?" She found it impossible to meet Ramón's eyes as she spoke the words that threatened to lodge in her throat. "But now," she stammered, "now that you've said you won't touch me again, that problem will be solved . . . for both of us."

Ramón gave a scornful laugh. "You may think so now if you

119

wish, *mi amada,* but sooner or later you'll learn that it isn't me you're fighting."

Without another word, his angular face arranged into an expressionless mask, Ramón stepped through the door, silently drawing it closed behind him.

"I didn't see anyone else in here with me," Sirena flung at him. "And I'm not your lover!"

She knew Ramón had hesitated on the far side of the door, that he'd heard her words, but there was no reply. After a moment she could hear his footsteps moving off down the hall, and the sound of them made her feel more alone than she could remember being in her life.

Sirena's lips had begun trembling even before Ramón left the room, and though her chest ached from the effort, she continued to try to hold back the hot tears. But it was no use: the misery she had sown for herself demanded release. Tears coursed down her cheeks in twin rivers to splatter on her hands, in which she still so fiercely clenched the red-and-white-checked material of her shirt.

CHAPTER SIX

Beyond the study window, which was open to admit the balmy air, Sirena could see sunshine spilling like liquid gold across the land. The ranch corrals were starkly outlined in the distance, tiny figures moving about them. With no difficulty Sirena was able to pick out Mike's silhouette, spry and quick moving, from the others. The stable boy was also there, helping with whatever project Mike had lined up for the day, and although Sirena didn't see Ramón, she was sure he was down there somewhere with the horses. At any rate, she knew he was nowhere within the walls of the hacienda.

A week had passed since her last encounter with Ramón, after she'd cut her hand; at least, it had been a week since they'd had that sort of encounter. Since then they had certainly spent enough time together, but Ramón, true to his word, had made no attempt to touch her. The week had passed with a special kind of agonizing slowness and a succession of restless nights.

Leaning back in the comfortable swivel chair, Sirena continued to let her gaze wander beyond the ranch corrals and tack rooms to the far horizon where earth and trees met the dazzling blue of the clear sky. The hills rolled green into the distance, and stunted trees studded their crests, spreading dwarfed limbs beneath the blazing heat of the water-sapping sun. In the far distance the glowing mountain peaks intruded upon the scene.

Sirena glanced at the easel that stood to one side of her desk, a painting half completed quietly awaiting her return. The study window had a northern exposure, and the strange play of light that came with each evening was what she was attempting to capture in the painting. The setting of the sun in the west invariably colored the now majestically purple mountains an almost bloodred and the sky often an orange-streaked gold. It

121

was never exactly the same twice, but it was the magnificent essence of the event Sirena was trying to catch. Her own critical eye told her she was succeeding.

Her painting, though, much as she loved it, was not all that daily occupied her thoughts. In fact, it was the painting that helped her to sort things out, to relax and let her brain absorb all that she'd experienced that day. And Ramón made sure she experienced plenty. The books for Rancho Reese were complicated. For his own information, Austin had kept separate accounts of ranch and household expenses. Periodic cattle counts were made and a harvest tab kept on fields of feed grown for the winter. Then there were the horses, bred for more than merely riding about the ranch. Under Austin's instructions, Mike had years before instituted an entire breeding program, and the horses at Rancho Reese were acquiring a wide reputation as good solid stock. Records were kept of the mares' bloodlines and of the stallion that stood at stud, including those instances where Austin had chosen to pay for the services of a special stallion to broaden the bloodline base of his stock. In addition, the foals' bloodlines and inoculations were strictly recorded, as well as any illnesses that struck the horses. Austin Reese had been a meticulous man, and his ranch remained strong because of him.

Yet in spite of it all, Rancho Reese was only barely in the black. Each year it was at the mercy of nature's whims. Sirena realized the ranch was a sprawling operation, but she had never seriously considered its breadth. Now more than ever she was grateful Austin had also been an excellent employer, choosing his people carefully and making it worth their while to stay on. The ranch almost ran on its own momentum, and this is what gave Sirena the encouragement to formulate an idea for Rancho Reese that would be her very own.

She intended to build on the sturdy foundation Austin had seen fit to leave her. Oh, she was going to stay all right. She was gong to stay and build on her inheritance — build something of her very own to be proud of as well as to add to the value of the beautiful ranch. She was going to build with the land, make it her partner and prove she was not the grasping fortune-hunting defiler Ramón believed her to be.

For days she and Ramón had pored over the books and stacks of records that were the paper heart and soul of Rancho Reese. He had stood over her shoulder or sat beside her for hours, explaining, answering questions and challenging her to be sure she understood all he was telling her.

Then he had tried to get her to ride out with him to inspect the fencing and check the windmill that had been giving trouble. He wanted her to ride with him *everywhere* and see firsthand *everything*. Exhausted by all she'd absorbed, Sirena had refused. She'd have to do it later; she just didn't have the energy to do it all at once. She needed time to be alone, to paint and to formulate the plan growing stronger in her by the moment. Her refusal had drawn Ramón's most condescending look of scornful patience.

"You cannot run a ranch from behind a desk," he had said scathingly. "You must see what's happening on the land for yourself." Ramón, when speaking of the land, became almost poetic. "You must see it, feel it change with the seasons, know it as you know yourself. If you cannot become one with the land, know its moods as you know your own, then you don't belong here. It's like being in love, *mi amada*," he'd added softly, then spun on his heel and left her sitting in a daze, staring after him.

Through it all Sirena had been very much aware of the tension that existed and was building between her and Ramón. It arced between them like an electrical current, creating sparks at every encounter. Ramón kept his promise; he hadn't touched her again. But his eyes spoke volumes, and Sirena knew that somewhere in the depths of her own eyes was the mirror of his desire.

Sirena sighed as the knot that had become a familiar companion in the past week formed again in her chest. She desired him as she had no other man, but reason strove to assure her it was no more than that. It could not be love . . . *would* not be love. It was an impossible unthinkable situation that she should love a man who didn't love her, a man who even now, for all she knew, might be counting on her leaving Rancho

123

Reese for good . . . planning for the day he and his brother, at her default, would be able to take over as Austin Reese's will specified. Since Ramón considered Sirena to be no more than a fortune hunter, would he not consider himself within his rights to use her?

Sirena knew Anita was right. She'd read the will in detail. Austin had been very plain and specific in outlining his decisions and his reasons for them. He had wanted to leave his life's work to a blood relative and had hoped she would love the land as he had. In her he had seen that love. At least *someone* had seen it, Sirena noted ruefully. If she couldn't live that life, if she chose to leave, then the vast ranch would go to Ramón and Rualto. In Austin's eyes they had always been adopted sons, in spite of his difficulties with Carlotta. Rualto had said nothing about the uncomfortable situation during his visits; he seemed merely to accept the fact she would be staying on. But Ramón questioned and prodded at every turn. Could it be, she wondered, that he wanted the ranch badly enough to try to push her out?

With considerable effort Sirena forced the painful thoughts from her mind. She had her painting — that had always been enough in the past — and now she also had Rancho Reese. There was no reason to believe she would have any part of her left over to give attention to anything or anyone else. And if by chance she did . . . well, there was always Rualto, who was becoming a more and more frequent visitor to the ranch. Rualto, who was with great enthusiasm and quite gallantly courting her, despite the heated look that arose in Ramón's eyes at his attentions. Jealousy? Sirena pondered the possibility almost without realizing it, forbidden thoughts once again surfacing. Ramón couldn't possibly be jealous of his brother, for to be jealous he had to love her, and that without a doubt was not the case.

Besides, Sirena, by simply observing, had seen Rualto's gaze following Anita wherever she went. After her accident with the knife in the kitchen, there had been no reason for Sirena to bring up the topic of Anita's boyfriend, but Sirena's eyes told her it was Rualto who was Anita's lover. And yet he came to see Sirena, ostensibly to court her. Why? Sirena was afraid to probe too deeply, afraid she already knew the answer.

She would have a talk with Carlotta soon. Anita had mentioned the cool aloof matriarch as being the problem. Maybe she could find answers to the questions that bothered her and help Anita at the same time.

Her thoughts threatening to scatter, Sirena marshaled them and forced them back to the matter at hand. She had spent much of the past week prowling the far reaches of the hacienda — that is, when she and Ramón hadn't been skirting each other tensely like a pair of cats with their backs up. What Sirena had discovered had been a revelation and had sparked an idea.

There were rooms in the hacienda at Rancho Reese that even the help had not really explored, rooms that had been closed off for years — storage areas off the wing where the house help lived and extra bedrooms. In the living wing were extra rooms, as well, some the size of suites, with alcoves adjacent. And in the rear was a staircase that seemed to lead to nowhere. At its top lay an almost complete apartment — or what could be one with a few adjustments. Sirena wondered if Austin had ever even bothered to go up there — and seriously doubted it. Dust, inches thick, had billowed into small choking clouds when she'd explored the extra rooms, her idea coming more clearly into focus as she went. Now Sirena decided she would have to speak to the help, to Anita and Mike in particular, since they would be the most heavily affected should she resolve to go ahead with her project.

As if in answer to a mental summons, a soft knock sounded at the door. It lacked the demanding authority Ramón's knock usually carried, so Sirena knew immediately it had to be Anita. "Come in!" she called out brightly.

Anita slipped into the room as if she were fearful of disturbing Sirena, but it was obvious she bore important news. Before she could get the words out, however, her eyes fixed on the half-finished painting standing near the window.

"Oh, it's beautiful!" she gasped, almost in reverence.

"Thank you, Anita, but I'm glad you came right now. I have something I want to discuss with you."

"Is anything wrong?"

"Of course not!" Sirena instantly assured her. "Everything has been perfect." It was only a little lie, and the problems she'd had at Rancho Reese since her arrival had been far from Anita's fault.

"Then — excuse me, Señorita Sirena, but there's something I must tell you first."

Sirena smiled. "When are you going to drop the *señorita*? But go ahead, Anita — what is it?"

"Ramón asked me to tell you that a call just came in on the radio phone." The expression on Anita's face showed her displeasure with the new situation. "Rualto just called. Carlotta wishes to pay a social visit to her new neighbor now that you've had a chance to get settled, and Ramón told Rualto they were welcome. They'll be here for lunch."

Sirena sighed. Why had Ramón, without consulting her, invited them to visit? She didn't feel up to having guests right now. She did want to have a talk with Carlotta soon, but not yet. Rualto had already become a regular visitor at Rancho Reese in the past days, so his presence didn't bother her.

"Oh, nuts! Well, do your best, Anita, and don't worry about Carlotta. This is certainly short notice." She shrugged. "But maybe now I'll have a chance to have a serious talk with her."

Anita looked immediately relieved. "Don't worry — I won't let the *rancho* look bad before Carlotta."

With a smile Sirena shook her head. "I'm not worried, Anita. Quite frankly, I don't care *what* Carlotta thinks of the ranch, me, or the way things are run here. Such matters are of concern only to me and those who work for me. Now sit down for a moment. I have a matter of much more importance to discuss with you."

Taking a chair, Anita perched on its edge, not leaning back against its high back. She didn't appear very comfortable, but then Anita wasn't very tall, and had she leaned back into the overstuffed vastness of the chair, her feet wouldn't have reached the floor. Anita frowned, assuming the countenance she thought was expected of her for a serious discussion.

Tapping the pencil she'd been holding on the desk before

126

her, Sirena gave Anita an impish grin. The grin immediately brought the beaming smile back to Anita's round face, her emerald eyes sparkling with good humor.

"That's better," Sirena remarked. "What I have to discuss with you is not the end of the world; it's simply an idea that I think will help Rancho Reese. Perhaps it will eventually mean a bit more money and a better life for all of us here."

"If it's an idea to help Rancho Reese, should you not talk to Ramón about it?" Anita broke in. "He knows everything about the *rancho*."

"Yes," Sirena agreed with a nod. "I'll tell him about it as soon as I get the chance. I see no reason to discuss it with him first. He's helping me learn, but the decisions regarding the ranch are mine to make." Sirena's tone was forceful. It was time everyone around here knew she was taking her ownership seriously.

Anita looked a bit puzzled, but she didn't question Sirena or challenge her authority.

"Besides," Sirena went on, "Ramón won't be here too much longer. Then the burden of extra work from this idea of mine would fall mainly on you, Mike and me anyway, so I feel you and he are really the people I should be talking to. Austin used to discuss new ideas and problems with you, didn't he?"

Anita blushed, her embarrassment becoming to her. "Yes, he did, but most of the time Señor Austin had no one else to talk to, and you have. . . ."

"Ramón?" Sirena filled in for her. "No, Anita, I don't have anyone to talk to, either. And I feel you're my friend."

Sirena's last remark had a sobering effect on Anita. Her usually sparkling green eyes turned suddenly opaque.

"Now here's the idea." Sirena waved her still bandaged hand in her eagerness. The cut was healing quickly, but she was very cautiously keeping it scrupulously clean to avoid even the smallest possibility of infection.

"I thought I'd like to try having Rancho Reese take in guests . . . people who would be glad to pay for a short stay in this beautiful country, who would love the opportunity to ride out into the wilds to fish and camp. Of course that would mean more people to cook for and more cleaning duties inside the hacienda. I've discovered some closed-off rooms and some that are being used only for storage. They could be cleared out and cleaned up for the guests, and some on the kitchen side of the house could be converted for extra help."

Anita didn't say much. She was deep in thought, considering all Sirena was telling her.

"Initially we'd be short of actual cash for the project, although I'm sure my new paintings will be bringing in some soon. But the main problem is that it would mean a lot of extra work here and down at the corrals. You, Mike and I would have to take on all the additional work in the beginning. We'd be forced to cut corners anywhere we could for a while, because as soon as we were near ready to have our first guests, we'd be obliged to hire a young woman to help with the house. At the same time, we'd need a young man to help Mike out at the corrals — someone to lead the guests on long rides and camping and fishing trips. Altogether it would mean more money for the ranch and more jobs for the people living nearby. Of course, I'd leave you and Mike in charge of hiring whomever you thought best for the jobs. And we could shift some of the rooms around until everyone is happy."

"It sounds to me like a wonderful idea!" Anita bubbled effusively. "But you must tell Ramón — he'll like it, too." The words were sincere. "He wants only for the *rancho* to prosper. You'll see — he'll like it!"

"I'll talk to him, Anita," Sirena promised with a lighthearted laugh, feeling better than she had since her arrival at Rancho Reese, "but I'll still talk to Mike about it, as well. If he agrees, I'll get some figures together and we'll find out exactly what this project would cost to get launched."

"But —" Anita began.

"No buts," Sirena cut her off. "Don't mention anything about this to Ramón yet. I'll tell him after I've lined up facts and figures so that it looks like more than just some harebrained scheme I've hatched up."

With the look of a coconspirator, Anita rose from her chair, the familiar mischievous light dancing in her eloquent eyes.

"Ah, you wish to impress him!" She gave a knowing nod and slipped out the door before Sirena had a chance to deny it.

Impress Ramón? That was silly. Sirena didn't care one fig what Ramón thought about her or anything else. And yet it was true this idea could make her look less the fortune hunter in Ramón's eyes. It would prove she was at least thinking of the ranch and not only of herself.

The thoughts were irritating, and Sirena brushed them from her. She had to get hold of herself. Everything she did or thought didn't revolve around what Ramón might think of her. Her future here was what mattered.

Sirena glanced at the small gold-faced clock that sat on the corner of her desk. It was still early — plenty of time for her to get down to the stable and have her little talk with Mike. Then she'd have to return and get cleaned up to play the hostess when Rualto arrived with Carlotta — another little treat she had Ramón to thank for.

Her legs swinging in the long stride that came so naturally to her here, Sirena left the imposing hacienda behind and strode purposefully toward the corrals. She'd caught a glimpse of Ramón there and skirted broadly around him, her face turned as if she were totally unaware of his presence. She could feel his eyes following her as she ducked into the stable in search of Mike.

With his usual cheery good humor Mike came forward on a rolling gait to greet her. Black eyes peered from the crags and crevices of his deeply lined, darkly tanned face, wreathed in smiles at her approach.

"You wish to ride, *señorita?*" Mike urged and questioned in the same sentence. "The horses are glad to see you! They are full of vinegar today. They need the exercise. Have you chosen a favorite yet?"

"I'm afraid I can't ride just now." Sirena's voice was filled with real regret when her eyes fell on the line of beautiful rambunctious horses. "Unfortunately I have to play the part of hostess in just a short while. But there is something I wanted to discuss with you."

"Certainly." Mike gave a sweeping gesture toward the tack

room behind them. "Would the *señorita* care to join me in my office?"

In high spirits Sirena preceded him into the tack room, the scent of leather and saddle soap tweaking her nostrils. He offered her a saddle slung across a sawhorse to sit on, and she smiled and accepted, admiring the softly glowing palomino-colored leather as she did so.

It took only a few minutes for Sirena to outline her idea to Mike. Once again she met with an enthusiastic reaction.

"It's true," Mike observed, "it'll take a lot of work, but it's a magnificent idea! Many people would want to come here, wouldn't they?"

Sirena grinned. "I think so, but we'll keep the number we accept very small." She hesitated. "There's one small problem."

Mike raised a graying eyebrow questioningly.

"It's a very long drive by Jeep," Sirena went on. "Is there somewhere we could have a landing strip? It would be best if there were one so that people with their own planes could fly in. Or a charter company from Tucson could ferry in guests."

Mike's face broke into an answering grin, his teeth gleaming whitely. "There's an open meadow — there beyond the corrals. It might work." He pointed out a spot through the tack-room window.

Sirena's eyes followed his finger, and after a moment she realized she was gazing out across a wide open meadow lying on the far edge of the fenced pasture adjoining the stable and corrals.

"I don't think it would take long to make it a useful landing strip," Mike said in his low gravelly voice. "But Ramón would know better."

"Oh, Mike!" Sirena bounced to her feet and threw her arms around him in elation. "That's wonderful! I'll talk to him right away," she promised.

Sirena's logical side quietly reminded her this didn't mean her idea would come to fruition, but it was another door opened that carried her forward just that much farther. It made all the other hundreds of little things she would have to investigate before she went on just that much more worthwhile.

130

Mike chuckled softly at her enthusiasm. "You're what Señor Austin wanted for this ranch," he said with open admiration molding the lines of his creased weathered face. "Full of life and fire. We'll keep Rancho Reese together and even make it better, so Señor Austin would have been proud! And we'll all be proud, too!"

"Thank you, Mike. It's sweet of you to say that." Sirena felt suddenly shy and awkward as she stepped back from her impulsive embrace of the older foreman. "There's still a lot I have to check on before I'll know if the idea can work," she cautioned. "But I really think it will if we all pull together."

Moving to the door, she lifted the latch. "I have to get back to the house now. I'll talk to you more later after I've worked out some of the details and spoken to Ramón."

With long sure strides Sirena swept the length of the stable and stepped into the brilliant sunlight that splashed down from the azure sky. Rounding the corner at full tilt to head back to the hacienda, she walked right into Ramón's arms.

With a squeak of surprise Sirena leaped back as if she'd been scalded, her heart beating a furious tattoo in her throat.

"It would be nice to think I had something to do with that radiant smile." Ramón looked as if he longed to reach for her, and Sirena thought she could detect a slightly wistful note in his voice, but mostly his words had that old sarcastic edge, and she immediately dismissed the possibility.

"Let's see . . . what could be so wonderful and what could you want to talk to me about? It couldn't be my mother coming to visit." He grinned wickedly, knowing the discomfit that such a visit would bring to Sirena. "Perhaps my brother —"

"It has nothing to do with you or your family," Sirena cut him off. "My happiness is *not* dependent on you and what you or your family might do."

"I see," Ramón said softly, as if he really did see, and that thought made Sirena want to flee from his presence. It would be unbearable to have him know how much his opinion did affect her, how much she had to fight his influence over her — which seemed to be growing instead of dissipating with time.

"It's just an idea," Sirena offered, wondering how much of

her conversation with Mike he'd managed to overhear. She hesitated. "I want to open Rancho Reese as a guest ranch for about half the year . . . transport people in by air, offer riding, fishing and camping." Sirena hurried on. "It would bring in money, employ more people and support the ranch in bad times."

Ramón frowned for a moment, but it was not disapproval she read in his face. Quirking one eyebrow, he appeared to be turning the idea over in his mind. Something new sparked in his eyes as he regarded her, something that looked almost like admiration or a glimmer of respect.

"It's a good idea, Sirena," Ramón said in an odd tone she had never heard him use. "A damn good idea," he repeated, obviously warming to it. "And I doubt anyone around here would have come up with it."

After all the criticism Ramón had tossed her way, Sirena enjoyed the small crumb of praise from him. Cautiously she savored it. But she couldn't afford to bask in it. Instead she rushed on. "As for Carlotta's and Rualto's visit, I'm sure I'll find it quite enjoyable."

"Quite the little diplomat, aren't you?" Ramón teased. "You *could* use a bit of it where I'm concerned, you know. Why have you been so studiously avoiding me these days, Sirena?"

With an effort Sirena managed to avoid meeting his smoky green eyes. "I'm not avoiding you," she denied. "I see you every day!"

Ramón laughed. "Yes, in the study when Anita is conveniently cleaning, or perhaps at a meal when Anita is scurrying about serving or cleaning up behind us. When I show you some papers you should know about, you instantly disappear for hours to study them more closely. But when I suggest a ride to see more of your holdings and discuss the future of them in a businesslike way, you refuse, using your injured hand as an excuse not to come with me."

Sirena blushed, the warmth rising rapidly in her cheeks, staining her fair skin with color. The mere mention of her injured hand instantly brought back vivid images of that day and the intimacy they'd shared. Keeping her head slightly bowed, Sirena attempted to hide the flush in her cheeks, evidence of the embarrassment he was causing her.

"If I wasn't aware of your independent nature —" Ramón's smile had turned into a wry twist of his lips "— I'd swear you were afraid of me and thought you needed a chaperon."

"I'm not afraid of you!" Sirena's blood boiled at the suggestion, but deep inside a tiny voice sneered at her. No, it told her, she wasn't afraid of Ramón; she was afraid of herself. She was afraid of what she might allow him to do to her life if she for one moment let down her defenses. His strange influence over her was a frightening thing.

"You're not afraid of me." Ramón echoed her words with a patience that made Sirena want to scream at him.

"No, I'm not," Sirena snapped angrily. "You yourself said there was a lot to learn about Rancho Reese and how it's run, much more than just riding around the countryside and surveying my acres! So I decided I'd better get down to it and learn what you're here to teach me." Why was she explaining herself to him? How had they got off on this track after that brief moment of warmth and approval only minutes earlier?

"And you've been learning a lot?"

"Yes . . . yes, as a matter of fact, I have."

"Good." Ramón caught her eyes with his, and because there was no avoiding it, Sirena met his gaze for the first time. "At least I'm accomplishing what I'm here for." Ramón sighed wearily. "Sirena, look, I'm going to be here awhile longer, and I really think we should make an effort to be friends."

Sirena gaped at him. "Friends?" She uttered the word as if tasting it, not quite sure what Ramón was getting at. She tore her eyes away from his, sensing this conversation might be easier if she were not aware of the compelling gold glittering in their depths. At the same time she felt an odd distracted sort of disappointment.

"Yes, friends," Ramón repeated. "Sirena, can we talk a bit? I have to talk to you."

"I . . . I really should get back to the hacienda." She gave a nervous laugh. "Remember those guests I have coming."

"All right, then. I'll walk you back," Ramón offered.

Sirena couldn't refuse, though she could feel the old familiar tension rising up between them. If Ramón was aware of it, he didn't show it.

"Was there something special you wanted to talk to me about?" Sirena ventured as they strolled toward the hacienda. She managed to keep her voice strong and full of authority, with a slight condescending edge.

Ramón frowned, his eyes lost in the shadows of his darkened brow. "There's something wrong on Rancho Reese," he said without preamble.

With a derisive laugh Sirena tossed her head, her auburn hair flashing with red highlights in the brilliant morning sunshine. "That something wouldn't happen to be connected with my being here, would it?" she asked acidly. "You don't suppose," she added sweetly, "that this problem could be cured by my returning to New York, do you? Send the city girl home before she destroys the *rancho* single-handed. Turn it nobly over to someone who *really* cares. *You,* Ramón?"

Why was she talking to him this way when he'd just made the first peace overtures since her arrival? Because she didn't know how to react to him when he wasn't being sarcastic and deprecating was her answer.

Before Sirena could absorb what was happening, Ramón spun around to face her, his hands settling on her shoulders. His fingers digging into her soft flesh mirrored the sudden anger she saw in the depths of his eyes.

"Damn it, Sirena!" Ramón's grip tightened on her upper arms. "I know we got off to a bad start back there in Tucson, but I'm not fooling around now. I'm telling you something's wrong here. So far I don't know if it's partly coincidence or if the ranch is just into a run of bad luck. Look, Sirena, that rein that broke when you were riding didn't just break — it was cut almost all the way through!"

For long seconds Sirena stared at him round-eyed, speechless. What was he saying?

"You're hurting me," she uttered at last in little more than a breathless whisper once she found her voice.

"I'm sorry," Ramón apologized, instantly contrite. "I don't

mean to hurt you, Sirena. But I do think someone may be out to frighten you, and that could be dangerous."

Sirena gave a strained laugh. "If someone is out to do that, they've really missed their mark. I've been too busy even to think about it." She tried to brush off the possibility. "Who could be doing such a thing? Only Anita and Mike are close enough to try anything like what you're suggesting, and I can't believe. . . ." Sirena pulled herself up short.

"Neither can I." Ramón raked one hand through his thick black hair and gazed down at her, an unreadable expression on his face. His other hand still rested warmly on Sirena's arm where he'd first grabbed her.

"It was probably just a misunderstanding," Sirena suggested. "Some bad feelings that have been ironed out by now. It's been more than a week since the rein broke. There hasn't been anything else, has there?"

Not answering her question, Ramón went on seriously, "I'm worried, Sirena. There's nothing I can put my finger on right now, but I do think you ought to look out for yourself." A tense look traced the lines on his darkly tanned face.

"I see." Sirena felt obliged to make some sort of reply, but she really didn't see at all. "So what are you trying to tell me? That it would be better if I went back to New York?" Sirena felt a heavy lump in her stomach and a piercing in her heart at the thought of that, but her words weren't bitter or biting.

"It would probably be safer for you," Ramón admitted. "But no, I'm not telling you to leave. Just be careful."

"I'll bear that in mind," Sirena observed dryly, trying to extricate herself from his grasp.

Ramón sighed and released her. "Sirena, I meant what I said a while ago about wanting to be friends. If we become friends, maybe it'll be possible for us to spend time together without fighting like a pair of ill-matched cats."

Sirena couldn't restrain the smile that crept across her full lips, even if it was a bit strained. She didn't want to fight anymore. God, she was tired of fighting. Maybe Ramón was right; maybe if they became friends the tension would pass.

"Friends?" Ramón asked at length.

"Friends," Sirena agreed, feeling better for it already.

"Good!" Ramón rested one hand beneath her elbow, guiding her briskly now in the direction of the hacienda. "I'd better get cleaned up. If I smell like a horse, Carlotta will be the first to complain."

Sirena laughed, for the first time feeling comfort, not antagonism, in his touch.

CHAPTER SEVEN

"You do seem a bit young to have taken on such an enormous . . . undertaking." Carlotta sipped from her wineglass, setting it back on the table before her with an aristocratic air. "Still, I imagine my Ramón has been a very large help to you."

Sirena smiled graciously, not missing the emphasis in Carlotta's words. She undeniably was giving Ramón all the credit for Rancho Reese's mere two-week survival under her hand. And the tone in her voice was not one of approval.

"Ramón has made it all seem very easy," Sirena agreed lightly, stepping out of character. She could feel Ramón's smoldering gaze upon her and lifted her eyes to meet his.

Laughter was dancing in those disturbing eyes of his, though his expression was somber. He was clearly enjoying Sirena's discomfit in his mother's presence. Then, in another swift switch in character, he seemed almost supportive, giving her an encouraging wink when he saw he'd caught her eye.

Knowing what she did now about Carlotta and Austin, Sirena could sense the frustration within the other woman and could understand the jealousy Carlotta harbored for her. For years the proud woman had angled to possess for herself what Sirena had inherited. Each time she met Carlotta's dark burning gaze, focused on her from that flawlessly smooth alabaster face, Sirena could feel hostility in the air.

"I take it, then," Carlotta continued, "that you're planning to adhere to the terms of the will? That you'll be staying on at Rancho Reese?" It was more of a statement than a question, but the implication in her tone was one Sirena didn't relish.

"Yes," Sirena returned smartly. "Yes, I'm definitely staying." If Ramón was right, if someone was trying to frighten her off the ranch or fate itself was trying to force her to give in, she might as well make it evident to the world that she had absolutely no intention of leaving. Just vocalizing her aims made her feel stronger and more sure of herself in the face of the formidable Carlotta.

"Ramón will not always be here," Carlotta reminded her, taking another sip from her wineglass.

The luncheon party consisted of just the four of them: Carlotta, Ramón, Rualto and Sirena. Sirena let her eyes slide toward Rualto, trying to read the expression on his face. So much like his brother and yet so unlike. Rualto's moods were far easier to read than Ramón's. Now he was obviously annoyed by his mother's juggernaut tactics. Her total disapproval of Sirena — and in her own home — was as plain as the sun shining outside the windows. Rualto was uncomfortable with her attitude, Sirena decided, and that in itself made her feel an emotion closely akin to pity for Carlotta.

By any standards Carlotta had had a most difficult life, and now she seemed determined to keep it that way — perhaps make it even worse, driving away even the possibility of friendship between them and raising the ire of her two sons.

"I know Ramón will not always be here," Sirena replied tightly, "I've read the terms of the will closely many times. I believe I know what to expect."

"Do you?"

Sirena let her gaze wander from Ramón to Rualto. Suddenly, for no particular reason, she noted that Carlotta's two handsome sons had the same long aristocratic nose, the same high smooth forehead, the same black hair that shone with midnight blue highlights and the same piercing eyes as she.

"You're a brave young woman, then," Carlotta complimented her with a definite lack of sincerity. "Many things can go wrong on a *rancho* of this size. It can destroy you, make you old long before your time."

"It doesn't appear to have hurt *you*." Sirena's retort was a honeyed sweetness that concealed a sharp edge, referring pointedly to Carlotta's past.

"I was born in this country." Carlotta let her soft accent fill her words to overflowing. "I love it and I understand it. You, though, are a stranger to it. It wouldn't be a great dishonor to

138

you if you decided to give it up and return to what you know."

Sirena could feel her outrage building at the new direction Carlotta's conversation had taken, but she managed to smile tolerantly in front of the overbearing aristocratic matriarch. All through lunch there had been an undercurrent of antagonism, but Carlotta had kept her claws dutifully sheathed until now.

Twirling the delicate wineglass by its fragile stem, watching for the moment the faintly golden-colored liquid slide along the bottom of the nearly empty glass, Sirena gave an elegant shrug of unconcern.

"Honor isn't a very big issue with me, Carlotta," Sirena lied. It *was* a bit part of Sirena's life. It was just that she didn't interpret it the same way as Carlotta. "To be perfectly blunt," she went on, "I don't really care much what people think of me — or don't think of me, for that matter. I have my own life to live, and I intend to do it in my own way."

Carlotta's black eyes glowed with a malevolent light, almost causing Sirena to shudder. With an effort she smiled without blanching and met the nakedly hateful gaze of the older woman. Sirena's veiled eyes frosted over, telegraphing a warning of her own from beneath long curved lashes.

As though talking with an old friend, Sirena went on smoothly, "As a matter of fact, I've already come up with a few ideas for changes to make here. Perhaps," she suggested, "you'd like to walk with me in the garden and hear about them?"

Ramón was quiet, finishing his wine, then refilling his glass from a carafe that sat on the table between them. The expression on Carlotta's face, her stiffly erect spine, told Sirena the imposingly proud woman would in other circumstances have spit like an enraged cat at Sirena's mere suggestion of change.

"A young woman wise beyond her years," Carlotta remarked dryly, her surface geniality barely maintained. "Yes, I will enjoy the gardens. If the gentlemen will excuse us?"

With polished manners Ramón and Rualto nodded their acquiescence, and Carlotta rose gracefully to accompany Sirena from the room.

In silence they strolled away from the house, across the sprawling courtyard down the rolling slope of the sweet meadow grasses, toward the great cottonwoods that towered on the banks of the stream. The early-afternoon sunshine was brilliant, splashing down through the leaves of the cottonwoods, describing intricate patterns of light and shade upon the grasses that grew in lush abundance, even more so close to the stream.

Sirena loved the venerable old trees whose stately presence filled the courtyard. To her they resembled wild elusive creatures that Austin had seen fit to tame and domesticate. The wind whispered delicately through their leaves with a rustling sound that was softly peaceful in a starkly beautiful land.

Carlotta paused a moment beside Sirena's easel set up on the flagstones near the kitchen door. With an appraising eye she regarded the painting that stood upon it; then, without comment, she moved on. "You wished to talk," Carlotta said flatly as they approached the stream.

"Yes," Sirena acknowledged, readily seeing there was going to be no delicate way to approach matters. "There have been a few problems here since my arrival," she began awkwardly.

"Ramón will take care of them." Carlotta's reply was prompt and uninterested.

Sirena sighed, then plunged ahead, discarding entirely her wish to be tactful. "What I'm trying to say is that I know about everything, Carlotta — about Austin and you, your sons, everything. None of that matters. What I really want is for us to be good neighbors and, I hope, friends."

Her eyes as cold as a January frost, Carlotta settled her unwavering gaze on Sirena. "How do you think you know everything?" she snapped waspishly. "How? From that little cat Anita?" Her hands clenched at her sides, she glared at Sirena. "Well, let me inform you that half of what that slut tells you is a lie, and the other half is none of your business!"

"Carlotta, I just meant —" Sirena tried.

"What you meant is of no concern to me — nor is what you think you know about me. If there's been trouble here —" Carlotta's cold black eyes remained locked with Sirena's, her slim aristocratic frame held erect, her face a mask of frozen fury "— then let me assure you there will be more! You don't belong here, and your pretty speech to us all inside means nothing.

140

You *will not* stay here! My sons will inherit Rancho Reese after you're gone! The *rancho* should have been mine, but at least I shall see it become theirs!"

Sirena stared at the older woman, taken aback by her outburst. Through her sons Carlotta very obviously planned on control. It was all too clear that the only things that meant anything in her life were power and money.

"Friends!" Carlotta bit off the word as though she found its taste as bitter as the most vile of medicines. "You wish to be friends?" she hissed. "You stand there attempting to steal what is rightfully mine, and you wish to be friends? You won't succeed. Go back to New York. *Then* we can be friends!"

"No," Sirena said flatly, the chill in her tone coming close to matching Carlotta's. "I won't go back. I'm staying. I want *you* to understand *that*. No matter what it takes, I'm staying."

Carlotta's eyes held hers with the malevolence of a poisonous snake, but Sirena didn't flinch. She was regarding her adversary from her own position of strength. Her nerves stretched as taut as the strings on a violin, Sirena didn't even notice Ramón's and Rualto's quiet approach through the thick grasses until Rualto laid a hand on her shoulder.

"I hate to break this up," Rualto lied with suave gentility, "but it's such a beautiful day outside we thought we would join you. *Madre*," Rualto added firmly, "you and Ramón haven't seen much of each other these past weeks. Perhaps you'd like to talk."

Hastily Carlotta rearranged her features into the expression of a gracious guest. "Yes, of course," she agreed, smiling stiffly and attaching herself possessively to Ramón's arm.

Sirena was aware of Rualto's light touch on her arm, but she was even more aware of Ramón's stony gaze. The warmth of friendship that had existed between them such a short time ago was lacking now in his eyes as he moved off with his mother. What could Ramón be thinking? Sirena didn't have time to ponder the question. Almost without realizing what she was doing, she complied willingly with Rualto's gentle persuasive touch guiding her in the opposite direction. She looked up into his face, so much like Ramón's.

141

"My brother doesn't seem to want to share you," Rualto observed with a lighthearted chuckle. Then he drew Sirena's hand into his and brought it to rest on the crook of his left arm as they walked across the quiet of the courtyard. "Forgive me," he added, his words silken, "for taking you away, but it appeared things weren't going well with you and my mother. This will give mother a bit of time to compose herself."

Gazing up into his darkly handsome face, Sirena returned Rualto's smile a bit timorously. "There's nothing to forgive," she said simply.

Rualto's expression was warm and open, without the touch of mockery that stained his brother's features. Sirena was aware of his hard athletic build, his aristocratic bearing and his impeccable manners. All the surface things that set her nerves to tingling whenever Ramón was near were there, and yet she marveled at the fact that Rualto didn't affect her in the same way. Still, there was a certain endearing quality about him, a gentleness that Ramón definitely lacked.

"You must forgive my mother," Rualto persisted. "She's a bit . . . unbending. Change of any kind disturbs her, and of course she was quite fond of Señor Reese." Rualto measured his stride to fit comfortably with Sirena's — something Ramón never bothered to do, usually leaving her far behind him. "In time she'll adjust," he went on, "and I have high hopes that you'll eventually become friends." Lightly he squeezed Sirena's captured hand for emphasis.

"I don't hold a grudge, Rualto." In truth, Sirena felt mostly pity where Carlotta was concerned. The woman with her spiteful eyes and proud bearing could flare Sirena's temper momentarily, but deep down was that feeling of pity. And now she doubted, after her past altercation with Carlotta, that they could ever be friends.

"I feel you and I are already friends," Sirena said to Rualto with sincerity.

"Ah!" Rualto's smoky eyes twinkled down at Sirena. "But you and I are destined to be much more than friends — do you not feel it also?" He squeezed her hands and gently stroked her forearm, a small gesture that in some way seemed to be one of piercing intimacy. "I wish to make you my wife."

Sirena was speechless, and Rualto pressed her, "You have nothing to say?" He caressingly placed his hands on her shoulders, turning her to face him as he drew her nearer. At the look of unfeigned astonishment on her face he laughed lightly.

"Surely you aren't as surprised as all that, *mi adorada*," he teased softly, his eyes gazing into the depths of hers. "You're a beautiful woman. I've been courting you, my naive little innocent," he went on with a warm chuckle. "Did you think I've been making all these long rides to Rancho Reese for my health?"

"Rualto, I —"

"Ah," Rualto interrupted, laying a finger softly across her lips, "now is not the time to say anything."

Smoothly, with consideration, he drew her down to sit on the bank of the small stream that bubbled merrily within its banks.

"I wished to be very patient," Rualto informed her with a shrug that bespoke the predicament he had found himself in. "But Ramón is at your elbow every day, and you'll have to forgive my saying so, but my brother is like an alley cat. He has charm, that one; few women can resist him. But he never stays with one woman — he's always off after new conquests. I don't wish to see you have your heart broken, little one." Rualto raised her hands to his mouth and kissed each one in turn, his lips feathery light against her skin. "I wish to marry you, Sirena," he declared openly, "but I can see already that you're infatuated with my brother."

Sirena started to protest, to tell him she knew about him and Anita, but Rualto, it seemed, was bent on finishing what he'd started.

"Shhh, I know. I've seen it before." His hand moved to her face, fingers lightly caressing the skin, bringing a flood of color to her cheeks. "I want you to know I understand. To exorcise this thing from your heart you must pass all the way through it, just as iron is made strong by passing it through the fire. I'll be here often, and I'll wait until you have him out of your system and are ready to marry me."

Teasingly Rualto's fingers continued their gentle journey of discovery, touching Sirena's cheekbones, sliding over her silky hair, tugging loose a tangle they discovered and stroking her brow to brush away the lines that had formed there at his unexpected words. His caresses soothed her, lulled her into a state of sensuous languor, but the explosive tension she felt with Ramón was lacking. Her body responded passively to Rualto's practiced touch; missing was the spark of arousal, the tingling excitement of the spirit, that his brother seemed so easily to ignite. In their every encounter Ramón seemed to draw from her an intense physical response that almost made her dizzy.

This shouldn't be happening, part of her protested. Rualto loved Anita, or so it appeared. Why was he proposing marriage to her . . . trying to seduce her? What was his motive?

"We're like day and night, my brother and I," Rualto murmured in her ear, his breath tickling her neck and sending a chilled wave racing the length of her spine. His thumb idly traced the outline of her delicate chin, following the strong angle of it with appreciation. "So very different and yet the same."

Sirena regarded Rualto through bright eyes burning with the tears she withheld at his unexpected declaration. Here was a good man, a solid man, one Sirena believed would be thoughtful and considerate, yet he was saying things he couldn't mean. Asking her to marry him with no words spoken of love. How could he . . . ?

Carlotta. The stinging realization hit Sirena with a slap. Carlotta was manipulating him, playing on her strong maternal influence over him. There could be no other reason. Her last line of defense, no doubt. If she couldn't force Sirena to leave, the next best thing was to absorb her. Through marriage the ranches would be joined.

Staring up into Rualto's unfathomable eyes, Sirena thought she read many things in their misty depths, but she could be sure of none of them.

It was damnably unfair, she decided, sitting there on the soft grassy bank with Rualto, that she should have managed to avoid affairs of the heart for so many years only to be ensnared now. Always, for the sake of her work, her future, she had managed to remain aloof, removed from it all. Or maybe, she pondered in reflection, it had merely been that the right man had not come along. *The right man.* The thought brought an unbidden smile to her lips. She had been at Rancho Reese for a little more than two weeks. In that time she had managed to fall in love with a man who would happily bed her for his own convenience but who felt nothing for her, and have a second man, Rualto, declare not his love but his desire for marriage. Which, then, was the right man? Neither, a perverse inner voice warned her.

Rualto, as if reading Sirena's mind, wasn't about to allow her thoughts to continue in such a direction. Cradling her face between his large palms, thumbs softly caressing her high cheekbones, he placed a gentle kiss upon her lips while Sirena marveled that such powerful hands could be so gentle.

His lips moved softly, persuasively, against hers, delicately luring her into a response. A kiss, a simple kiss, could not be a terrible thing. Sirena let her eyes droop closed and did not pull away, savoring the moment in hopeful anticipation of the surge of passion Ramón had ignited within her more than once. A pang of guilt touched her for allowing it, but she had to know whether it was her own inexperience that fanned the flame of passion at a virile man's touch, that it was not a magical spell that Ramón alone held over her.

Rualto's kiss deepened, his tongue teasing her lips, his breath mingling with hers as one hand shifted, moving to embrace her and draw her nearer. Sirena could feel the warmth of physical desire stirring within her veins, but the flame she sought did not spark. The feelings Ramón aroused within her were not duplicated with Rualto, even though, when Sirena opened her eyes, the face of this twin was hauntingly the same.

Squirming a bit, Sirena began to push gently at Rualto, seeking to end the embrace. But he didn't budge. Forcefully she tore her lips from his plundering kiss and braced her hands against his chest.

"No! Rualto, please —"

Rualto froze, though he still held one arm possessively about her. He gazed ardently down into her brilliant blue eyes.

"I'm sorry, little one. Did I hurt you?" He was instantly

contrite; then, seeing Sirena's faint shake of the head, he gave a wicked grin faintly reminiscent of his brother. "It seems I have difficulty controlling myself where you're concerned."

Sirena stared up at him, her eyes wide, her breathing no more than short gasps. He had stopped. She searched his eyes darkened with passion and read in them his desire to go on, to fulfill his manhood; yet he had stopped almost instantly at her cry.

"Forgive me, Rualto." Sirena shivered and let her hands drop into her lap, shifting her eyes away from his all-enveloping gaze.

"It's all right, Sirena." Rualto reached over and took one of her hands in his, pressing a light kiss into the palm. "I understand. You're not yet ready. Haven't I also told you," he added with a seductive smile, "that I can wait?"

Weakly Sirena attempted to return his smile. An infinite sadness was descending upon her.

"I know about you and Anita, Rualto," she blurted. "I can see the love in your eyes when you watch her. I shouldn't have let this go so far."

Rualto's face darkened at Sirena's words, his arm falling away from her. His gaze shifted off into the distance.

"You said nothing to me of love in your offer of marriage," Sirena pointed out to him. "It's Anita you love. Marry her!" she urged. "We could have the wedding here."

Rualto sighed deeply. "You're as kind as you are beautiful," he said sincerely. "But Anita and I, we can never be. Carlotta —"

"Is your *mother,* not your dictator! It's your life, Rualto. You love Anita!"

"And you love Ramón," Rualto said softly. "You're not the only one with eyes, *querida.*"

Footsteps muffled in the thick grass behind them drew Sirena's and Rualto's attention from each other. Rualto still held her hand lightly, but there was no further discussion.

Ramón walked with long strides toward them, his mother's hand tucked into the crook of his arm.

At Ramón's approach, embarrassment suddenly infused

146

Sirena's cheeks with color. With an apologetic half smile she withdrew her hand from Rualto's gentle clasp. Why did Ramón's wicked grin, his appraising eyes, make her feel so damned guilty?

"I envy you, brother." Rualto bestowed a devastating grin upon Ramón and his mother, effectively drawing attention from Sirena. "To be in the company of such a beautiful, charming and intelligent woman much of each day is not a gift to be taken lightly."

The two brothers locked eyes, tightly controlled anger swirling in the molten gold depths of Ramón's and the sadness of the unattainable lurking in the smoky shadows of Rualto's. Carlotta's gaze was fixedly cold and leveled unswervingly in Sirena's direction. Sirena resolved to show no weakness before Carlotta, and a small smile froze on her lips. She could feel the undercurrent of conspiracy between Carlotta and Rualto as she continued to meet the woman's withering gaze.

"It's been an enlightening visit." Carlotta's words dripped acid, but she could find no chinks in Sirena's psychological armor. "Now, Rualto, I believe we should be returning to our *rancho*."

The afternoon was waning in spite of the still brilliant sun overhead. Though it wouldn't grieve her to see her guests leave, Sirena was a bit surprised by the announcement.

"It would be no trouble for you to stay the night," she offered graciously as convention demanded, the frozen smile remaining fixed on her face.

"That's most kind of you." Carlotta mouthed the appropriate phrase, although Sirena felt sure the older woman wouldn't know what kindness was if it leaped up and bit her on her aristocratic nose. "On our *rancho* there's much work that needs to be tended to, just as there is here." Carlotta's eyes slid suggestively toward Ramón where he stood insolently to one side, his set face revealing nothing. Had he been recruited into this farce, as well? It was hard to believe — no, impossible to believe — that Ramón would bend to anyone's will, even to someone with such overpowering strength as his mother.

Sirena was sure she detected more of a slap in the face than a polite refusal in Carlotta's tone, but she continued to smile amiably. Gracefully she climbed to her feet as Rualto reached out a hand to assist her. Carlotta could interpret the gesture any way she chose.

"It's been lovely having you," Sirena lied smoothly, recalling manners with an effort. "You're welcome here anytime," she added, but omitted the usually obligatory, "Hope it will be soon." There was only so far, Sirena decided, that one could extend insincere hospitality.

Ramón, looking over the top of his mother's head, winked at Sirena conspiratorially when Rualto's attention was directed solely toward his mother. Seeing the wink, Sirena wished she were somewhere other than Rancho Reese at that particular moment. She never had been good at games of this sort.

"Very well, mother," Rualto agreed, "we'll go." Then, turning to Sirena, he captured one of her small hands in his and raised it to his lips to place a feathery kiss upon her palm. "I'll be seeing you again very soon, Sirena," he promised with caressing sensuality, completely ignoring the presence of his mother and brother. "Our friendship will endure," he added softly, and his knowing look told Sirena that all had been set right between them.

"Let me walk you to your car," Sirena offered a bit stiffly.

Rualto gave a courtly bow, and Carlotta returned Sirena's painfully tight smile. "You must visit my *rancho* one day," she murmured, the sting in her words emphasizing exactly who was in control of the Savedel ranch.

"I will — very soon." They were neighbors after all, and Sirena knew she'd have to hold to her word. Maybe with a bit of time and exposure they would at least learn to tolerate each other; perhaps even respect would eventually grow between them.

Quickly they walked back through the lush courtyard, retracing their steps through the grand entrance hall of the hacienda to where Rualto had parked the Jeep on the broad expanse of the sweeping drive. In spite of the clean-lined black twill slacks and starkly contrasting white ruffled shirt Carlotta had worn in deference to the uncomfortable Jeep ride, their short walk seemed like a royal procession. As the woman strolled with a possessive regal air through the halls of the magnificent hacienda, Sirena wondered if Carlotta would ever truly be able to forget the loss of what she believed was meant to be hers. Before Austin's death, Carlotta had no doubt assumed he could be made to change his mind about the inheritance. Such a woman could never accept that she would have no recourse, that she wouldn't be able to work her way back into his affections and confidence. She felt that Rancho Reese was her due, and she was obviously convinced that if Sirena had never turned up for that visit, Austin would have turned again to her. Then, upon his death, the ranch would have been hers.

And now the only alternative was to gain control of the ranch through her sons. To Carlotta, Sirena was sure, that would be the same as total control.

But Sirena had no intention of leaving, and with that decision came only more confusion and uncertainty where the Savedel family was concerned. What could she believe? Whom could she trust? Realizing she was falling hopelessly in love with Ramón, how could she ever be sure he wasn't using her, maneuvering for control of the sprawling ranch? He made no secret of his eagerness to run the ranch, and he certainly didn't love her.

Rualto smiled encouragingly in Sirena's direction as he helped his mother into the Jeep, obviously pleased by Sirena's declaration that she would visit — and soon. Sirena wished she felt half as pleased as he looked.

Before climbing into the driver's seat, Rualto again took Sirena's hands in his, lifting both close together to bring first one, then the other, into soft contact with his lips. "I'll think about what you said," he promised.

Sirena felt a hot flush envelop her body as she became aware of Ramón's burning eyes upon them, and a chill went racing up her spine. She had emotionally held Rualto at arm's length even before she'd known of his love for Anita, while Ramón stormed in where no man had trespassed previously. It worried her a bit that her love for Ramón was so obvious . . . that Rualto could read it in her face.

Reluctantly Rualto released her hands and jumped into the Jeep where Carlotta waited wordlessly.

"Thank you." Carlotta intoned the words politely in her coolest, most pleasant voice, though she deigned not to meet Sirena's eyes. "It was a most enjoyable lunch. It's gratifying to see that the hospitality of Rancho Reese has not suffered since the loss of Austin." She used his name with familiarity.

Rualto brought the Jeep's engine to life with a metallic roar. Once more, before he slipped the Jeep into gear and drove smoothly away from the hacienda, his eyes met Sirena's in a knowing glance. They were both in love . . . but not with each other.

Sirena stood motionless, watching the Jeep move off in a cloud of dust that obscured its two occupants from view. As the Jeep grew smaller in the distance, Ramón came up close beside her so quietly that Sirena was hardly aware of his presence.

"My brother has a lot of charm, don't you agree?" he remarked softly.

Startled, Sirena jumped and hastily stepped back, putting distance between the two of them. It took only an instant to compose herself, and then a genuine smile at last curved her full lips.

"Funny," she mused, "he said much the same thing about you."

Ramón laughed. "That's because it runs in the Savedel blood."

Sirena bit back the spiteful question that came to mind. Considering his origins, how could Ramón know *what* flowed in the Savedel veins?

"I, uh, have some work to do," Sirena excused herself. Actually, it wasn't an excuse. There was plenty of daylight, and if she hurried, she could still ride out to a spot she remembered and get some painting in before sunset.

"Ah, your painting," Ramón anticipated her. "You're very good, Sirena." He paid her the compliment somewhat awkwardly. "They reveal much about you, your paintings. There's a special beauty in them that speaks of your feelings for the

150

land." He seemed to be formulating his thoughts as he spoke, and his eyes explored her face intently.

"Thank you," Sirena responded graciously. Then, suddenly uncomfortable at the intimate way he was gazing at her, she announced, "Now if you'll excuse me, I have work to do."

Ramón smiled enigmatically, obviously aware of the strange magnetism between them, the tension that was always there. His mouth took on a suggestive curve that spoke volumes, and his piercing eyes seemed to plunder the depths of hers. Ramón's dark angular good looks served to disarm her as he towered over her, proudly arrogant and sure of what he wanted, as well as his ability to get it. There was something of the sensual predator about him.

"Still fighting the battle?" Ramón was implacable, the truth of his words ringing in Sirena's ears. He looked more relaxed than Sirena could remember seeing him, and she felt more than saw his overwhelming desire to reach out and touch her, to enfold her within his strong embrace.

And yet he didn't move toward her. He'd given his word. He wouldn't touch her again unless she invited it. The longing for her was there in his eyes, and she wanted so much to believe it was more than just desire.

Sirena raised her chin in a defiant gesture. "There's nothing to fight," she said sharply in spite of the tingling she felt all through herself at his presence and suggestions.

The best defense, she decided at that moment, was attack. She couldn't risk the flood of feelings welling within her, ready to surge precipitously to the surface with little encouragement. Deep within Sirena there quivered the fear that she would give him the encouragement he sought and which his eyes so eloquently requested of her.

"Maybe there's more of your father in you than you know," she mused softly, unthinkingly.

Ramón's silky demeanor of only moments earlier changed instantly. A dark shadow passed over his probing eyes, coldness settling around him like a protective mantle.

"What exactly do you mean by that?" Stiffly the words were forced from lips that, uninvited, stirred in Sirena the wildest flame of passion, opening the door to desires only Ramón had been able to make her realize she possessed. Mutely she stared at those lips, at the suddenly hard set of Ramón's face, feeling a hunger she didn't fully understand.

"It's just that I think I have the right to know something about you, about your family, since Austin saw fit to throw us together this way," she replied huskily.

"And you started checking into it on your own?" Ramón's voice was bitter. "Is that it?"

Dumbly Sirena nodded, appalled by the cold fury that had surfaced in an instant. "I . . . I wanted to know. I still do," she stammered lamely by way of explanation. "But it would be better if I heard it from you."

Sirena caught her breath. She had only herself to blame for this sudden turn in Ramón's temper. Anita had warned her. Ruthless and dangerous — that was the reputation of the Savedel brothers.

"Yes," Ramón growled acidly. "Yes, I can see where *you* would think such a thing — that it would be better to get the whole vilifying story from me! Well, my sweet —" he ground the words out "— I'm here to teach you to run this ranch, not to relate my family history. So you just run along and listen to any bits of gossip you can pick up with my blessings!"

"You're not being fair!" Sirena shot back, managing to conceal the hurt at Ramón's sudden attack, knowing she was at least partly at fault. She should have held her tongue.

"Not being fair!" The anger was deep-seated now, flashing sparks in Ramón's eyes. "Because I don't want to discuss with you something that's none of your business?"

"I thought we were going to be friends," Sirena tried tentatively. "Friends talk about things."

"We aren't good friends yet." Ramón's eyes gleamed with seductive suggestion.

"That's not what I meant!" Sirena said hotly. "You're talking about lovers, not friends!"

"Ah, *mi amada,* but lovers can be friends, and friends can fight," Ramón pointed out artlessly, his tone softening abruptly. "Do you know why we fight, Sirena . . . even now that we're friends?" he asked mockingly, his lips twisting into the sardonic smile she had come to know so well.

"No!" Sirena returned defensively. "No, I don't!"

Ramón shook his head. "Why do you fight it so, *querida?*"

"Why do you think you're so irresistible?" Sirena questioned airily, denying all the feelings welling up inside her at his closeness.

"Why do *you* think I am?" Ramón's words were cool and scorching at the same time. His eyes were twin pools of desire that reached out to caress her, though his hands remained, with great restraint, at his sides.

"You — you're insufferable!"

Ramón shrugged. "Just truthful. Sirena, we want each other. Can that be so bad?"

Sirena felt her heart begin to pound like a wild thing at this new restrained approach of Ramón's. But there was no doubt in her mind as to his motives: she was a handy female to him, and then, too, there was the ranch. . . .

It was impossible for Sirena to deny to herself that she was strangely, powerfully, attracted to Ramón, but she was determined to remain strong. He had promised not to touch her, and as long as he held to his promise, she would be able to cling to her own resolve.

"We both have urges, Sirena. You're a very beautiful woman, and I've never denied I want to take you to bed. You'll find, too, once you've been here awhile, that this isn't New York. There are no nightclubs for you to display your charms and seek out candidates for your affections."

"Oh!" Sirena sputtered. Deep in her heart she knew how very much she did want him, but he would never know, for he would never love her. She could never give herself to a man who didn't return her love. She had turned to face Ramón fully, and her eyes absorbed the restless maleness of his tall long-legged frame. His dark brows were knit together in a studied frown, the angular features frozen into a finely chiseled mask, while his eyes glittered in a combination of banked passions and rising temper.

"Your licentious suggestions don't interest me!" Sirena gave

153

a laugh that sounded like broken glass, hoping it would hide the painful emptiness that gnawed at her insides. "And just so there is no misunderstanding, I've never displayed my charms, as you put it so sensitively, nor have I ever sought out candidates for my affections. I've done just fine without a man to this point, and no doubt I shall continue to do so!"

Would she? The thought plagued Sirena even as she mouthed her contemptuous statements so blithely. Could she go on this way, so close to him, and yet not give in?

"I thought we had a truce, Sirena." Ramón spoke so quietly his words were barely above a whisper.

"We did! We do!" she stammered, floundering for the right phrases.

"Well," Ramón said dryly, "when you figure it out, you let me know what you decide." He leaned extremely close to her, but through a supreme effort of will he refrained from touching her.

Sirena could sense the battle raging inside Ramón, the tension that filled his whipcord body, those strong athletic limbs. That same tension made his words seem suddenly cold and flat, devoid of feeling other than contempt. "Until then I have things to do myself," he said pointedly. And turning on his heel, he moved off before she could say anything more.

For a few moments Sirena stared venomously at Ramón's broad retreating back. Her mouth felt dry, and the back of her throat ached with raw emotions her intellect could analyze and understand but her heart could only feel. Ramón didn't look back.

Anger, frustration and actual pain bubbled inside Sirena like a witches' brew in a caldron. Not bothering to turn again, she didn't see that Ramón had stopped and turned to gaze thoughtfully in her direction. With purposeful strides she headed back inside the hacienda.

The cooling shadows of the hacienda were a soothing balm to Sirena's nerves as she stepped out of the afternoon sun and turned toward the kitchen. She could use a cup of coffee to revive her energy level. If she knew Anita, there would be some left over from lunch, probably being kept warm for her even now. The thought lifted the corners of Sirena's lips in an almost unwilling smile as her feet whispered along the hall, through the formal dining room and into the kitchen.

Even before she reached the connecting door between the dining room and the kitchen, she thought she caught the muffled sounds of crying. Hastily swinging the door inward and striding through it, she was just in time to see Anita turn away and grab frantically for a dish towel, dabbing at her eyes.

"Oh! Oh . . . I'm sorry, *señorita*," Anita sniffed before Sirena could say anything. "I didn't mean for you to see me like this."

"Don't be ridiculous," Sirena returned, swiftly crossing the distance between them, her own turmoil for the moment forgotten in the face of Anita's obvious distress. "Tell me what's wrong." Sirena's tone was insistent. She raised a hand to head off Anita's protests, accurately reading the hesitation and apprehensions on the housekeeper's troubled face. "We're friends, Anita, and I want to know what has you so upset."

A tremulous smile tried to peek out through the steady flow of tears, and though Anita was none too successful, her round face brightened a bit. "You have enough problems to worry about, Sirena," she protested feebly. "You don't wish to hear about my troubles, as well."

"Anita, what is it?"

"Oh, *señorita*, it is terrible!" Anita hiccuped, unable to keep the words from spilling out. "It's as if Carlotta has passed her misery on through her son! My life's a disgrace! I'm . . . I'm going to have a baby!"

155

CHAPTER EIGHT

"You should tell the baby's father right away, Anita."

Sirena absently guided her horse down the gentle slope of the hill as she reflected on the conversation of four days earlier. Her hands were light on the reins; her soul absorbed the vast beauty of the day while her mind toyed with the exchange she and Anita had shared. She had thought instantly of Rualto, convinced he should know immediately.

"No!" Anita had looked horrified at the idea of confronting the father of her child.

"But it's possible he loves you even more than *you* believe," Sirena had encouraged her. "He may wish to be married immediately."

"No!" Anita had repeated. "I don't wish to be married that way! I want him to ask me himself, to decide for himself. Please don't say anything! I'll tell him — but later. Maybe he'll ask me soon, and then I can tell him." Anita had brightened hopefully at the thought.

It was, after all, Anita's life, yet Sirena couldn't help identifying with the plight of the young woman. Rualto seemed pretty much under Carlotta's thumb, hesitating to marry Anita against her will. But this was different. When he found out, he would have to do something.

"Whatever happens, Anita," Sirena had assured her, "I just want you to know there'll always be a home here at Rancho Reese for you and your baby. It's a wonderful place for a child to grow up," she'd added, attempting to lighten the mood.

"*Gracias,* Sirena." Anita's eyes had grown large and round at the suggestion. "You're very kind."

Those last words still rang in Sirena's ears as she moved over the rough countryside on horseback, keeping the pace slow in consideration of the painting paraphernalia she carried, along with the hearty lunch packed for her outing. Time and again the conversation passed through her mind together with the numerous other disturbing incidents that had occurred since her arrival on Rancho Reese. The one bright light in an increasingly dark picture was the physical beauty of the ranch itself and Sirena's exciting plans for it.

Mike and Anita had taken to the idea of receiving guests like doves homing in on water in the middle of the desert. Sirena had barely broached the subject and already Mike had managed to get a rough landing strip cleared in the meadow. Anita, using all the spare time she could muster, had thrown herself with great enthusiasm into the project, beginning to clean out the closed-off storage rooms at the back of the hacienda as well as the upstairs suite Sirena had discovered. Signs of change had become obvious throughout the ranch in only a few days' time.

Sirena had contacted several travel agencies in Mexico City, Phoenix and New York. All were receptive to the idea of the isolated guest ranch opening its doors to visitors. Two charter services were willing to fly in patrons from Phoenix and Tucson as soon as the landing strip was completed and approved.

Ramón was handling the bureaucracy. He knew the right people and understood the maze of paperwork necessary to get permits and licenses. In his hands the whole operation seemed mere child's play. He was also assisting Mike with the stock, helping to train the horses, taking off the rough edges for the less experienced riders.

Rualto had been over to see Sirena twice more in the few days that had passed since he and his mother had visited. It seemed he was always around now. Anita had not yet told him of her condition — of that much Sirena was sure. And Rualto, though always considerate and polite, appeared suddenly distant and withdrawn. There was pain reflected in his sad eyes. Odd that he should suddenly seem so contemplative, but then perhaps not so odd. After all, the only thing she herself could think of was Ramón. Always Ramón.

Maybe it was that way with Rualto where Anita was concerned. Yet Sirena doubted it was entirely the same. Rualto and Anita had their troubles, but they loved each other. Sirena hated to feel like this. The fire Ramón always seemed to stir in her blood wasn't welcome. She sighed deeply. If only Ramón loved her. She had little doubt that he viewed her more as a skittish filly that had still to be soothed and cajoled into submission. Love had nothing to do with it.

Under her steady guiding hand, Sirena's horse, the little mare Chispa, moved down the side of one hill and began the easy climb up the next. Sirena moved smoothly with the animal, aware of her burden strapped to the saddle — the paints and canvas and the folded easel. She was going to find the small catch basin below the diminutive waterfall she remembered visiting long ago with Austin. It was a particularly beautiful place to paint and a lovely spot for a solitary picnic. Sirena smiled slightly in anticipation.

Already she'd completed two paintings, crating them with Ramón's help to ship to her gallery in New York. Curiously he had not made any of his usual remarks about her city background then, and Sirena had caught him staring at the paintings before they'd disappeared into the crates, his eyes glowing with a strange inexplicable light. His gaze had rested upon her with a softness she couldn't define. If she hadn't experienced the bite of his words and the piercing anger of his eyes more than once when sparks had flown between them, she might have been tempted to read affection, or something even deeper, in their glittering depths.

"Good girl, Chispa." Sirena stroked the mare's silky mane and heaped praise upon her performance. Her smooth gait continued to carry them on, increasing to a slow trot as easy to bear as rocking a rocking chair.

A genuinely involuntary smile tugged at the corners of Sirena's lips and finally brought sunshine to her face as she remembered the first uncertainties that had plagued her since her arrival at Rancho Reese. It had not been so very long ago — a matter of weeks really — but those uncertainties had turned into certainties. When exactly, she wondered, had that happened? Or had there ever *really* been any doubts? Despite her excuses to herself even as she'd flown to Tucson, her reservations had been just so much smoke thrown up for cover. Sirena now realized the seed of Rancho Reese had been planted in her more than two years earlier when she visited Austin. He had purposely shown her the entire ranch, with well-concealed ulterior motives. If he'd suggested it then — a New York city girl moving to a wild and raw country, even with the finest trappings of civilization available — how would she have reacted? Sirena was not sure. But she was certain of one thing: it had taken time for that fragile seed to root and begin to grow. Austin had recognized in Sirena that delicate core of love for the land, and he had carefully nurtured it.

There was no doubt now of Austin's motives in Sirena's mind. Her lips quirked a bit as she came to understand that what she felt was much more than nostalgic memories shared with a wily old man who was now gone. It was a fierce protective love; a sense of belonging somewhere, really belonging, which she had never felt before in her life.

New York had always been Sirena's home, but the sense of belonging there had been lacking. True, the museums and art galleries were very much a part of her life, yet she never felt truly alive in the city. And until now she'd never found the nerve or the motivation to try someplace new. Reflecting on her life in New York, Sirena recognized that she'd lacked a sense of adventure; and worse, the lack had been reflected in her paintings. Oh, her work had been good, the colors lovely, blending in a symphony of movement on the canvas; her technique, her instructors had told her, was almost flawless. But until that first visit to Rancho Reese, a certain power, a vibrancy, had been missing from her work. Never before then had her paintings sold as quickly.

Now, in the past weeks, it had all come flooding back to her — the wonderful strength of the land, the power that had filled her paintings for those few short months she'd stayed at the ranch. Sirena felt herself growing with the passing of each day, discovering new and untapped wells of creativity and even determination within herself.

Determination and strength were very desirable traits out here. No matter how tame the hacienda appeared on the inside, life here was not a study in simplicity. In fact, Sirena often reflected in wonderment on how her simple orderly life had become so suddenly complicated. The land gave abundantly to Sirena, but it and all that was upon it — the people, the animals, the rocks and even the trees — took something in return. It was a remarkable balance, and Sirena would gladly pay the price.

A schedule was taking form in her mind, and Sirena saw clearly that if they continued to work at the pace they'd set at the ranch, they would be in a position to welcome their first guests in a few short months. It was a staggering thought and yet at the same time an exhilarating one. There was so much to be done: insurance to be checked into, simple tasteful brochures to be printed, the rooms to be freshly painted and furnished. It was almost midsummer now; the time was passing quickly. But if they all pitched in and worked hard, they'd be ready for an opening sometime in November.

A beautiful time of the year, that was. It was a time when people from the northern climates would undoubtedly be thinking of vacations away from the snow and freezing temperatures. Rancho Reese was protected by the towering bulk of the Sierra Madre, and winters, from Austin's descriptions, were usually mild with little snow. Most of the snow usually fell around Christmastime; a more perfect situation Sirena could not have wished for. Yes, she would set an opening date for sometime in November, and somehow they would rise to it.

"Just a little farther, girl," Sirena encouraged the small energetic mare moving smoothly beneath her, carrying them into the sandy dip of an arroyo. "We're going to have a lovely quiet day together, just you and me." She reached out to stroke the horse's mane again, and Chispa tossed her head in response as she kept up her spirited gait. The mare's small ears delicately twitched and turned in the direction of Sirena's softly modulated tones.

Sirena was pleasantly surprised by her own sense of direction. It had been more than two years since she'd come to the lovely waterfall with Austin. She had vaguely supposed she could find it, but everything was becoming clear to her now, and she knew she was heading directly for it. She was glad of that, since the sun, though it was only ten o'clock in the morning, was already burning fiercely into her skin right through the protective long sleeves of her yellow cotton shirt. The old straw hat Anita had found for her provided welcome shade from the blazing sun, and visions of the beautifully cool and green oasis of water and desert grasses beckoned her on.

Early that morning, preparing to leave, Sirena had not revealed her ultimate destination to anyone. She had just wanted to be alone and did everything to ensure she would have her wish. The incident with the sliced rein had taught her caution, and she had carefully checked Chispa's tack before mounting. Riding alone, she didn't care for a repeat of that experience.

Ramón had not been anywhere in evidence that morning; presumably he'd got up earlier than Sirena, breakfasted alone and disappeared, no doubt checking on something to do with their new guest-ranch plans. Could her heart be deceiving her, or had he in fact mellowed in recent days? Ramón had looked at her differently when he saw her paintings of the ranch, and he really put himself into the work of making her idea a paying reality.

Sirena was learning about Rancho Reese and quickly, but it was an insulated sort of learning, with Ramón keeping various problems from her until they were solved and he could report them as such. She sighed. She and Ramón were going to have to get together on these matters. They should each have full knowledge of what the other was doing. He had a way of awakening a ready anger within her, but if they continued this way, it was possible they would end up hurting the ranch, and Sirena was willing to bury some of her pride to keep that from happening.

Her resolve brightened Sirena as she rode. Already the outing had proved to be of benefit. The learning process demanded her sharing in the problem solving, not just hearing about it after the fact. She and Ramón had their share of problems, but he was an intelligent man. They were working together as a team much better now.

Chispa tugged lightly at the reins, mouthing the bit in her eagerness to quicken the pace. Sirena laughed softly at the mare's persistence and patted her sleek arched neck fondly, marveling at the brilliant red highlights that wove their way through her chestnut coat, picked up by the intense morning sun.

"All right, Chispa," she said lightly, "we've time for a short lope; we're almost there." She shifted her weight slightly in the saddle, leaning forward just a bit, and that was all it took.

Chispa leaned forward into an easy rocking-chair canter that skimmed along the surface of the soft stream bed with ease. Experienced with the mare now, Sirena kept a firm grip on the reins, holding Chispa to the gait she had chosen. The mare, though all fire and grace, galloped obediently, her long smooth strides whisking them along.

A warm dry breeze blew against Sirena's face as she guided her horse up a low slope of the streambed and into the hills that rose on the east side of it. Skirting their tops, she made her way quickly along the bottom slope, following the natural contour of the land. Today Sirena preferred this route to the hillcrests. She liked the feeling of being embraced by the land, of being cradled within that benign embrace. Other days she longed for the hilltops, the highest peaks, reveling in the feeling that she was at the top of the world, experiencing the unbridled power of the earth.

Before her the tiny canyon she remembered opened up in a startling green sweep that took her breath away. She drew Chispa to a halt at its mouth, drinking in its sweet beauty. The small mare tossed her head impatiently, but Sirena lingered a bit longer, feeling the shifting of the horse's weight on her small hooves. In the distance Sirena could hear the soothing rush of running water. Pressing on, she worked her way back into the canyon, and a bit farther up she again found the spot she so vividly remembered for its fresh beauty. She sighed contentedly. Here she would unpack her supplies and paint. The whole day spread out deliciously before her.

The canyon was green and lush. Deep grasses grew on each side of the tiny stream trickling from the outer lip of the stone basin that cupped the spill from the waterfall above. The sheer rock wall that made up the end of the hot canyon glistened and gleamed with the moisture thrown up in the mists from the high waterfall. Coming off the stone lip, the water was almost bluish in color as it cascaded into the rock catch basin about the size of a swimming pool, though much deeper. Huge ancient trees towered in a proud guard to either side of the sparkling waters, their roots reaching deep beneath the porous rock to partake of the flowing water's bounty. In odd contrast, the canyon walls to either side of the waterfall rose up stark and devoid of vegetation, forming a dusty backdrop to the lush canyon floor. The air within the confining walls of the canyon was full of moisture, a refreshing balm to Sirena's skin.

"Come on, Chispa." Sirena dismounted and led the mare forward, the sound of her hooves muffled in the springy lushness of the vegetation. "Do you want to eat some fresh green grass?"

Captivated by the scene around her, Sirena was unaware of the dark eyes that watched her from high above the canyon lip. Her senses were too filled with the wonder of her own miniature Eden. Oblivious to the intense gaze that remained fixed on her, she walked up the canyon with an easy stride, leading Chispa at the end of her reins like a large obedient dog. And if some instinct had caused her to turn her head toward the top of the canyon's high walls, all she would have seen was the dark shadow of a tall slender rider astride a dark horse, silhouetted against the brilliant glare of the late-morning sun. There would have been no way for her to know that the rider had positioned himself just so. His body was held as taut as that of an eagle searching the land below for its prey. The difference was, he didn't have to search for his prey: he had already spotted it.

Quickly Sirena stripped her supplies and her lunch from Chispa's back and loosened the saddle cinch. They were going to be there for quite a while. The sky was clear and cloudless, and there would be plenty of good light in the canyon for hours. It was oriented almost perfectly toward the path of the sun, the benevolent ball of fire overhead remaining between the canyon walls throughout most of the day. Sirena didn't bother to stake the little mare; her reins trailing along the ground would have the same effect. Mike Vargo had trained his horses well. Chispa would wander enough to graze but not go very far.

Humming softly, Sirena set up her easel and canvas and got out her paints. She had chosen to bring along her palette of water-based acrylics, since they would be easier to handle here than the oils she usually preferred to paint with. Eagerly she set to work, putting on canvas the beauty of the hidden little canyon, the stark contrast and yet harmonious blend of rock, trees and earth. Swiftly she recreated the blues of the sky, the lush greens of the trees and grasses and the slate gray of the towering rock walls.

Time fled on the wings of the creative impulses sweeping Sirena along, her mind momentarily cleared of all the complications that had so recently descended upon her life. She was alone. The paint flowed from her brush with a smooth gliding power that sent a thrill rushing through her blood. Rapidly the painting took form as the hours slipped past, and Sirena forgot completely about lunch, though her stomach began to growl impatiently.

The small waterfall sparkled on the canvas while towering trees crowded in from either side against the brilliant cloudless sky. Sunbeams cascaded down the canvas, bringing the scene to intense throbbing life, exuding a power Sirena had experienced only briefly a few times previously in her work. In the process of painting this picture, she had suffused it with a life of its own, a moment captured in time.

With a sigh Sirena put the last few touches on the still damp painting. Then, carefully laying her paints and brushes aside, she let herself fall into the moist embrace of the sweet-smelling grasses at her feet. Though she'd taken little notice of it until now, the day had been a hot one, and her cotton shirt stuck uncomfortably to her skin.

It was the middle of the afternoon, and the sun's rays were still intense, shining down through the outspread limbs of the trees that provided shade almost everywhere but where Sirena had chosen to drop down in the grass. She smiled lazily and languorously, reveled in the heated kiss of the sun upon her skin. From beneath the shade of her sweeping lashes she gazed in satisfaction up at her painting.

The waterfall and pool beckoned to her from the canvas and

across the distance that separated her from its cool reality, and abruptly Sirena sat up from her sprawl. Why not? It had been years since she'd even contemplated doing such a thing, and that had been in the much more public setting of the Great Smoky Mountains. But that was a lifetime ago, a different world. She was here and this was now, and she was wonderfully, completely alone. So why not? Sirena giggled in the grass like a small girl. Was it possible she'd truly found paradise? Logically she knew she hadn't, but for now this would do!

Rolling to her feet, Sirena kicked off her boots and bolted for the inviting pool on the rise above her, her fingers working on the buttons of her shirt as the soft grass tickled the bottoms of her feet. A refreshing dip *au naturel* in the mountain pool, some nourishment from the carefully packed food Anita had supplied, and then she would be ready to return to the hacienda.

Hastily she disrobed, tossing her clothes over a convenient bush growing close beside the pool. Then, without testing the temperature of the water with so much as a toe, she dived in. Cleanly she knifed into the water, barely a ripple breaking the smooth surface. The chill of the mountain water sent goose bumps racing along the surface of her skin, washing away the clinging perspiration and flushing the faint traces of tiredness from her long, silken limbs.

Sirena surfaced, the icy water making her feel as if she might pop right out of its embrace. Treading water for a moment, she remained where she was, then turned and swam the length of the rock basin with rapid warming strokes. Once again she dived beneath the surface, feeling the cool caress of the water along her scalp as it rippled through her long auburn hair. The shock of her initial entry was leaving her, and she savored the delicious weightlessness of the water's soothing grip. It was almost, she fantasized, like being cradled in the arms of a lover. Enjoying the soft caresses of the water all over her body, she floated for a few moments . . . a sudden sensation of coolness here, a tightening of the flesh there as she drifted lazily upon the surface, her mind drifting to wherever it willed.

Ramón. Her mind focused on Ramón, as it was wont to do when she allowed herself a few minutes off guard. Sirena sighed as she felt the familiar quivering within her. She loved him. It was silly — incomprehensible, really — and it had been difficult to admit it to herself. But it was the truth. She loved him. Hiding from it would not change the reality. Yet facing it had solved nothing, had helped nothing. In fact, she admitted to herself, it made matters even worse. Sirena was almost certain Ramón felt nothing for her other than a sense of duty and a frequently surfacing anger. Or did he? The devilish question rose in her mind to plague her, but she found no answer.

Unbidden, Ramón wandered the corridors of Sirena's mind and heart. Ramón, strong and virile, almost overwhelming in his presence. His smile, when it was not sarcastic, could be a soft beckoning of his sensuously full lips. Behind closed lids, as Sirena drifted on the cool surface of the water, she could easily visualize that darkly tanned, proud and aristocratic face. She could actually *feel* that probing gaze fastened on her, the glittering gold reaching out from the depths of his unusual eyes to entrap her. And she could feel the power of his warmth when he had looked from her paintings to meet her questioning gaze.

Sirena knew her lips were quirking. The irony of it — to have waited so long for the right man and then to have it turn out like this. She sighed, turned over in the silken grip of the cool water and knifed downward toward the smoothly polished rock bottom. Holding her breath as long as she could, she relished the weightless feeling of being submerged, relished the gentle stroking of the moving water across the quivering surface of her skin, caressing every square inch of her body. As her breath began to run out, she gave a powerful kick and shot toward the surface, where she could see the sunlight streaming down through the water above her. It seemed almost primeval, a stretching, reaching out of the womb toward the beckoning sunlight.

With an erupting splash the surface of the water broke as Sirena lunged through it, head tipped back to keep her flowing hair from her eyes, arms automatically extended to stabilize herself again on the surface. The sun was an instant flood of warmth on her upturned face.

"Thought you were going to need rescuing there for a minute." A voice drifted in a mellow caress to her ears, a voice only too familiar. Ramón!

Instinctively she wrapped her arms around herself for modesty's sake, and her eyes snapped open. Through the droplets of water that still clung to her long eyelashes, she saw Ramón standing on the lip of the rocky basin. The view presented a somewhat blurred picture, but not so blurred that Sirena couldn't see Ramón had already removed his boots and shirt and was standing there with that mocking smile on his face, clad only in his jeans.

"What — what are you doing here?" she spluttered. "How did you find me?"

"Why shouldn't I find you? Were you hiding?" Ramón challenged teasingly, completely at ease with the situation.

How much of her could he see? Sirena's mind formulated the question even before she quite realized what was happening. Was the sun's reflection on the water enough to block his burning gaze? From the way he was staring at her, open appraisal in his eyes, Sirena doubted it.

"Yes, I was!" she snapped. "I told Anita I wanted to spend the day alone. I didn't even tell *her* where I was going, so how did *you* find me? No, wait . . . don't answer that. Just go away, Ramón!" Sirena stammered, feeling the chill of the water in full now that she'd stopped moving around. She clamped her teeth shut against their chattering.

"I'm getting cold," she persisted. "Please go away so I can get out and put on my clothes."

"I found you quite simply, *querida,* by following your tracks." Ramón answered her original question, ignoring her present plight. "And, my sweet, I'm not stopping you from coming out of that pool, although I think it would be much more fun —" his fingers went to the button at the top of his jeans "— if I joined you. . . ."

Rapidly Sirena backpedaled in the water. Her jaw dropped in disbelief as Ramón jerked the zipper down its length in one swift movement, hooking his thumbs inside his waistband to remove his jeans.

"What's the matter, Sirena?" he chided in that damnably

167

soft voice he reserved for such occasions. He hesitated as his unfastened jeans hovered around his lean hips, exposing a band of white skin that had rarely, if ever, felt the kiss of the sun. "Haven't you ever seen a naked man?"

Sirena's eyes were fastened on the thick mat of curly black hair that covered his chest. Her mouth felt suddenly dry and her heart fluttered away at a trip-hammer beat. The beauty of the male animal in Ramón was impossible to deny. He had an aristocratic bearing, and his near nakedness revealed the graceful lines of a powerful untamed lord of the land. There was something of the conqueror in his stance, as well, and Sirena felt a sudden ripple of apprehension.

"No!" Sirena answered somewhat shakily, covering up the real reason for her discomfort. Naturally she'd seen plenty of nude bodies in her art classes, but never a man as imposing as Ramón — and never in a situation as suggestive as this! "And now if you don't mind," she went on, "I'll save that experience for another time." She couldn't even begin to imagine Ramón's intent. The man was totally unpredictable.

Ramón threw his head back and laughed. "I'm sorry, Sirena. I forgot about your, er, sensibilities. I must say, though, that you're very attractive when you blush. Besides, I'm very hot and dusty from my long ride and do need a dip in the lovely cool waters. Regrettably I neglected to bring along suitable swimming garb, so like you I'll have to make do!"

"Ramón!" Sirena blurted out her protest, but it was already too late.

As the huge splash erupted behind her, she turned in the water with frantic movements of her hands and feet, then struck out for the far side of the rock pool. She didn't know what she was going to do. She doubted she would have the courage to emerge naked from the opposite side of the pool and dash back around to the side where she'd left her clothes draped over a brush. She knew only that she had to get away, to put as much water between herself and Ramón as was possible in those few short seconds.

Her feet touching rock in the shallows, Sirena tucked her legs beneath her to keep from rising out of the water and watched apprehensively as Ramón surfaced in the center of the pool. Water dripped off his hair in streams as he turned with an easy languor and began swimming lazily in her direction.

Brilliant blue eyes widening in alarm, Sirena breathlessly watched Ramón's mesmerizingly slow approach. His lean hard-muscled body cut a clean line through the mirrorlike surface of the pool, a miniature wake moving out to either side of his quiet passage.

"You look just like a water nymph," Ramón said to her in low vibrant tones. "Your hair all wet and streaming down your back, floating in the water all around you. . . ."

He hovered there in the water directly before her, and Sirena imagined she could feel the heat of his body through the cool water that still separated them. And that was all that separated them. The hard realization shook her reserve. He was so very near — so near she could reach out and touch him. Her hands, crossed protectively over her breasts, twitched with the desire to do so.

"Why," she finally choked out, "why did you follow me out here?"

"Don't get all huffy on me," Ramón cut off her accusations. "I wasn't sure you knew the ranch well enough to be able to find your way around through this country alone. You could get lost out here. And —" he breathed the words as if they really meant something to him "— I wouldn't want to lose you, Sirena."

Openmouthed, Sirena stared. She couldn't help it; it seemed with Ramón that staring was what she found herself doing most. He hung easily in the deeper water before her, his face mere inches away from hers, and held her eyes in the magnetic grip of his own.

"I . . . I'm not mad." Hearing the uncertain stammers that fell from her lips, Sirena was disgusted with herself. "I just want to be alone. I've been painting —"

"So I saw when I came up here." Ramón's voice had the silken caress of the finest satin. "I must tell you again: your paintings are much more than just pictures. There's a depth to them, a life that could only come from a deep feeling for the

169

land. You have that feeling, Sirena." His hand was drifting in the water, bobbing on the surface, moving slowly toward her. "I was blind not to have recognized it sooner. I hope you can forgive me for that."

The words echoed hollowly in Sirena's head as, entranced by Ramón's hand, she watched its steady progress. The sun-browned work-roughened hand drifted lazily toward her with the soft motion of the water. Her brain clamored an alarm. She should be moving back, sliding away from that steadily approaching hand, but there was nowhere to go that wouldn't severely strain her modesty. Sirena touched her tongue to lips gone dry and swayed slightly forward on the insidious, almost undetectable currents of the water. Some irresistible force seemed to be drawing them together. She could scarcely breathe as her eyes remained fixed on Ramón, his mocking smile tugging at the corners of those lips so full and tempting.

"To hell with promises, Sirena — God knows I've tried! I want you. . . ." The words were such a shock to Sirena's ears that she was uncertain she had heard them at all.

"No!" she squeaked, denying the stirrings that raced hotly through her veins as her senses returned to her in a flood. The emotions that whirled through her were all too bewildering. Vaguely it registered that he had said he knew she loved the land. But did he know she loved him?

Sirena cringed. How could her simple arrival at the ranch to take possession of what had been left to her have resulted in putting her in this position? How could she ever have imagined falling in love with the mocking arrogant man who'd been assigned to pick her up in Tucson and escort her to Rancho Reese? She loved him . . . oh, God, how she loved him! Perhaps she had from the very beginning. But it was wrong — it was all wrong! Even now he spoke no words of love to her, only desire. It would be so easy to give in to the feelings that made her heart seem ready to burst, so easy to fall into Ramón's strong and warm embrace. But what of later? Without love there was nothing.

"You promised!" Sirena wailed, throwing herself sideways in the water as Ramón's hand lightly brushed the length of her silky thigh. With a strength she didn't know she possessed, she stroked feverishly for the opposite end of the pool where her clothes, her defenses, fluttered from the branches of the bush.

Without hesitating, she pulled herself out, snatched up her clothes and darted for the privacy the thick brush below the pool offered. It no longer mattered what Ramón saw; it mattered more what he might do. And how could Sirena fight him when her knees turned to jelly at his touch? She could only pray that he wouldn't follow, because if he did — if he took her into the embrace of his strong captivating arms, if he made her a prisoner of his sweet demanding lips — all was lost.

Breathless, Sirena stumbled through the grass, clutching her clothes to her bosom until she reached the thicket. She didn't hear footsteps following, and she let nothing distract her from dressing with uncommon speed, jerking her clothes roughly onto her dripping body, fingers trembling as they fastened her jeans and buttoned her shirt. There was no time to tuck her shirttail in, and her hair was soaking wet, the water running down her back, seeping through her shirt. But the air was warm, the sun drying, and Sirena felt once more in control.

Her heart was pounding wildly after the mad dash, and, annoyingly, her stomach was growling with hunger. Collecting herself, she turned back toward the pool.

Ramón, clad only in jeans and carrying both boots and shirt, was striding easily through the soft grass toward the blanket Sirena had laid out before she'd begun painting that morning. Dropping his boots beside the blanket, he grinned as though nothing unusual had happened in the pool. "Care to join me?" he offered easily, gesturing toward the bag of food, as if the entire outing had been his idea.

For an instant Sirena stood rooted to the spot, clutching her boots before her as though they were a kind of armor. How she wished she could turn and go the other direction, but her paints, her painting, even her horse were beyond Ramón. She had to pass him to reach them.

Sirena took a deep breath and started forward.

"What?" Ramón teased, "no picnic for Rualto?"

Moving up a bit unsteadily, the apprehensive quiverings of

her body refusing to subside, she smiled faintly. "Why, Ramón," she taunted, trying to divert attention from her body's traitorous behavior, "are you jealous?"

Ramón sprawled in the sweet grasses and threw back his head to laugh. It was a genuine laugh, a wondrous sound that tugged at Sirena's heart. Why did he laugh so infrequently?

"I don't have to be jealous," he shot back. "I'm here and Rualto is nowhere to be seen!"

"That doesn't mean he isn't planning to meet me here," Sirena retorted. "Perhaps that's why I brought along so much food and why I haven't eaten yet."

"You brought so much food simply because Anita packed it," Ramón countered with a laugh. "And as for Rualto, I don't believe I'll be seeing him here this afternoon. But come, little one," he coaxed. "Are you going to join me and eat, or are you going to stand there glowering at me until the sun sets?"

Grudgingly, her body tensed into a wary knot, Sirena lowered herself to the edge of the blanket, as far from Ramón as she could manage, keeping the food and miscellaneous tools of her trade between them. Putting her boots aside, she crossed her legs beneath her, Indian style, regarding Ramón from behind a coolness she forced into her frank blue eyes.

"Come, you're like a delicate little bird, timid and ready to fly away. You must be very hungry if you haven't eaten since breakfast. I'm not going to hurt you. Relax, *querida*."

Sirena didn't doubt that Ramón had no intention of hurting her; what worried her were his other intentions. And how could she relax when he was sitting there clad only in jeans that damply outlined the hard muscles of his thighs and hips, with no shirt to hide the soft springy mat of hair that covered his broad bronzed chest?

Briskly she set about doling out the food that crammed the canvas sack. There was freshly baked bread, cheese, cold roast beef, carrot sticks and fresh spring onions, not to mention the usual fresh fruit — several apples and a couple of oranges — as well as some of Anita's freshly baked spice cookies and a tightly capped thermos of the wonderfully fruity tea Anita prepared for every outing. It was the most refreshing drink Sirena had ever tasted, perfectly suited to this dry environment, with just the right amount of tartness to banish a thirst.

Sirena carefully avoided encountering Ramón's eyes as she gingerly placed the various foods between them. Without looking up, she began studiously to build her own sandwich. Ramón could take care of his own hunger problem.

Sirena was uncomfortably aware of Ramón's half-smothered chuckle, but still she wouldn't meet his eyes. She didn't need the added indignity of enduring his mocking laughter. She sensed movement from his side of the blanket; he was no doubt helping himself to the bounty of food Anita had provided.

Ramón bit into his sandwich and regarded Sirena from beneath dark brows. "I think your guest-ranch idea is going to work," he said unexpectedly. "I've heard from the authorities, and all is in order. You may open as soon as you're ready. We have a good string of ridable horses, and the airstrip is coming along very well.

"There's the money Austin left for the *rancho*," Ramón went on. "That should help considerably. If it isn't enough, you could get a loan from the bank using the property as collateral." He paused a moment, then cautiously broached another idea. "As an alternative, there's always me, *querida.*"

"You?" Sirena's eyes glittered with apprehension at what Ramón might be suggesting.

"Yes, me." Ramón was firm. "I could be persuaded to give you a loan — say, twenty-five percent of what you need in exchange for a partnership."

"A partnership?" The dubious note in Sirena's voice must have been even more obvious than she'd intended, for Ramón burst out laughing. He rolled back to rest on one elbow on the edge of the blanket, still holding his haphazardly made sandwich, having taken only a few bites out of it.

"Only in the guest-ranch profits," he assured her. "We could have an arrangement of honor between us. If I loaned you twenty-five percent, you could pay me twenty-five percent of the profits until a time when you could pay back the loan. That way, if there was no profit, you would pay me nothing. We would share the risk, and you wouldn't have to worry about a

173

bank and payments and the interest you'd be forced to pay whether you had good times or bad."

"But why?" Sirena felt a tug at her heart. Ramón was offering to back her with more than the hard work he'd promised Austin. He really believed in this venture, in her idea; believed it would be good for the ranch.

"Because, as I told you, I think it's a good idea. I don't believe I'll be risking anything. I'll get a good return on my money." His tone said much more than his words.

Sirena thought she recognized a soft glimmer of caring within the depths of his eyes, but she was afraid of the heartbreak that was inevitable if she read his expression incorrectly. Determinedly she put the brief impression from her.

"You would want nothing more?" she probed.

"My lovely Sirena, you know what I want, and that won't change whether you accept my offer or not."

Instantly Sirena regretted bringing his attention back to his desires . . . and her own, as well. Ramón was a deep and complex man. He was capable of intense anger, such as she'd witnessed upon her arrival, and sarcasm, which she'd borne the brunt of more often than she cared to recall. But, she had discovered, there was also within him a keen sense of humor and insight. Apart from the love for him that ached within her heart, Sirena found there were many times when she could actually like him.

"Do . . . do you think you'll ever marry, have children?" she inquired abruptly, changing the subject. Now why had she asked that, she silently cursed herself.

"I don't know . . . I doubt it." Ramón eyed her speculatively. "It's a strange question, Sirena. Do you ask it," he went on lightly, "because you brought a small problem along from New York and now seek to find a father for it?"

Sirena stiffened but chose not to answer him immediately. Ramón frowned, his eyes suddenly becoming fathomless, his face a mask revealing none of his feelings. Only the quick anger that seemed too much a part of him was visible.

"Sirena?" Ramón had assumed the air of an inquisitor. A flicker of expression slipped past his graven mask of a face, and for an instant Sirena glimpsed some shred of emotion — concern, perhaps, or sadness, or even jealousy. But as quickly as it had appeared, it was gone.

"No!" Sirena snapped, even before she realized the word was out of her mouth. "And even if I had, what would *you* do about it?"

"I might marry you," Ramón suggested sardonically, his old self once more.

"No, thank you!" She unfolded her legs to ease the cramping that had suddenly pinched her. "I don't need you, and I don't want you!" *Liar,* her heart accused her. But at the same time she quivered with outrage at his offhanded suggestion; a solution to a problem, as he so casually put it.

"Liar!" So quietly she could barely hear the word, Ramón was repeating her heart's denial.

The word echoed throughout her brain, and suddenly Sirena was aware of Ramón's hand encircling her bare ankle, his thumb softly caressing her foot near the sensitive arch. She tried to pull it from his grasp, but in another instant he was across the debris that had been their lunch, drawing her to him, his lips descending with amazing speed to smother any protests she might have.

Sirena's head swam at the suddenness of Ramón's attack. There was no time to prepare a defense, no time to let her anger build. For a moment she pressed her hands against his chest, trying to push him away, but then her resistance crumbled. She could feel the shuddering tingle of surrender coursing through her veins, the curve of his smiling lips against hers as his body blanketed her with warmth. Her hands relaxed their pressure against his chest as she lay back within the circle of his arms and relished the slow gentle way in which he lowered her onto the rough fabric of the picnic blanket. With a deep sigh she abandoned herself to the inevitable, to what surely must be.

A sweet languor touched her, and Sirena gave herself up to it. Her arms moved sinuously to encircle Ramón's neck as he bent over her, and the silky curls at his nape beneath her fingers tantalized her. She could feel his body molded against hers, the intensity of his desire for her, and her bones felt as if they had dissolved within her body.

Ramón withdrew slightly, dropping tiny kisses at the corners of her mouth teasingly, drawing her on. He leaned on his elbows above her, his eyes filled with laughter.

"You don't want me," he reminded her in a whisper that tickled her ear. "You don't need me. Liar," he repeated softly.

"You're being cruel!" Sirena felt suddenly ashamed, the mood of the moment instantly evaporating. Now the only thing in the world that seemed to matter was getting away from here, away from Ramón. She began to squirm, but Ramón held her easily in place, smiling wickedly down at her. He seemed to be enjoying her helpless struggles to be free of him.

"I'm not the one who's cruel, Sirena." Ramón held her easily with the weight of his body upon hers, the strength of his hands upon her soft shoulders. "You've tortured and tormented me. I saw something in your eyes for me the day we met at the airport. Haven't you returned my kisses? My caresses? Then you withdraw, jump back like a frightened cat. Why, Sirena? Why do you fight what's between us so?"

"You're blaming *me* for your insufferable unforgivable behavior?" Sirena flared, honest anger kindling the flames that threatened to sear her heart. "And how many others have there been?"

"I've never claimed to be a hermit, *mi amada*," Ramón countered, missing the thrust of Sirena's remark. "There have been other women, yes, but at the moment I'll be content with just one." He chuckled softly, gathering her closer to him. "You're a mature woman, Sirena, and yet at the same time you're a ruthless selfish child. You're so closed within yourself I don't think you know how to give." His words were like iced barbs, finding their way into her heart. "Or is it," he accused, pulling away from her, a hard glint in his eyes, "that you've given too much? Is it my brother? Have you been with Rualto for more than just quiet walks in the garden?"

Ramón laughed shortly, a bitter tone insinuating itself into his colorless mirth. "Is that truly it, Sirena? Do you respond to Rualto as you do to me? Do we look so much alike that you have no difficulty transferring this fire in your blood from one brother to the other?"

Sirena gaped at Ramón, eyes burning with tears she refused to shed, feeling as though he had dealt her heart a mortal blow. How could he say such things to her? Only moments earlier he'd been so different. She'd read something in his eyes that had warmed her, thrilled her, caused her to hope.

"Yes," Sirena hissed in retaliation. "It's the same with you and your brother. It's the same with all men! You're not so very special, Ramón," she added scathingly, her throat aching from the lies she forced herself to tell. "It's my weakness. I told you before I wouldn't have the strength to fight you."

"Fight me?" Ramón's face had gone as still as the air that surrounded them, darkening somehow. Anger was swimming within the depths of his gray green eyes, and there was something else, something that resembled pain. But that wasn't possible, Sirena told herself. Ramón Savedel gave pain; he didn't feel it.

"You can't win, Sirena," his voice broke into her thoughts, "when the one you fight is yourself. I know — I've already fought the battle. You throw words like stones. How many of them are true? You say it's my touch, my kiss that steals away your will?" The arrogant planes and angles of his chiseled features seemed harder, more forbidding than ever. "I say it's more!"

Mutely Sirena stared at him. Ramón could see through her as clearly as if she were only tissue paper. In some inexplicable way he knew no man stirred the fire in her blood as he did. But Sirena didn't know whether to welcome the wild primitive surge that he called up within her.

She had no more time to think. Ramón was rising, drawing her to her feet along with him. Then he faced her, hands falling away from her slim shoulders, leaving her to stand with bare inches between them.

"Now it's up to you, my sweet," he said huskily. "Kiss me, Sirena," he commanded in low vibrant tones, his eyes molten.

Sirena swayed toward him, feeling the strange magnetic force that was always there between them. She absorbed the satiny caress of his roughened words, the warmth of his breath upon her cheek. Somehow, though, she steeled herself. She couldn't give in, wouldn't let him see how sick her heart was with love for him. Where was the joy and exhilaration of love so many others had spoken of? To Sirena, it was a wild uncontrollable monster.

Ramón's eyes mesmerized her, and the heat of his body reached out, drawing her toward him. Despite her resolve, Sirena felt helpless before the onslaught of feelings that his nearness sent coursing through her. Ramón was waiting, standing as still as a statue, only his eyes alive . . . devouring, his sensuous lips beckoning.

Desperately Sirena fought her desire for him, knowing that to give in now would reveal every lie and half-truth she'd told; that to submit to him, to let herself cross those sparse few inches, would be tantamount to admitting surrender, and then Ramón would know. Without a doubt he would know. Her nerve endings tingled wildly. Love and its cousin, desire, sapped from Sirena her last reserve of resistance. A wrenching sob formed in her chest, threatening to tear her apart, and as if in a dream she felt herself moving forward, seeking his embrace.

She could feel the deep rhythmic movement of his chest, hear the thud of his heart beneath her ear as his strong arms encircled her, pressing the length of her body against his.

"Mi amada, mi adorada." Ramón's breath ruffled her hair as he drank in the sweetness of its scent. His hands described gentle wondrous circles of exploration across her back. "I love you, Sirena," he breathed the words into the silken mass of her hair.

Love. Sirena thought she heard the word, but it was like a dream, unreal, as his lips moved to tantalize a delicate ear. Her arms crept around his waist, and as she lifted her head to gaze up adoringly into his face, knowing he would see all the love she had for him there, wanting him to know, a flash of movement caught her eye. What was it?

"Dear God," Sirena gasped as her eyes focused clearly on the riders only a few yards away. "Rualto!" And worse, "Carlotta!"

CHAPTER NINE

Still astride his horse, Rualto looked down on Sirena, an expression closely akin to pity softening his gaze. Then those same eyes turned to flint when they rested on his twin brother.

"A touching scene, Ramón." Rualto's words carried a frigid bite that sent a shock wave of apprehension up Sirena's spine.

Carlotta silently sat upon her magnificently proportioned horse with the proud bearing of a goddess. She wore trim-fitting jeans, high boots over the pant legs and a loosely clinging shirt that fluttered gently in the soft breezes wandering the length of the canyon. Her raven hair was severely bound for riding, starkly emphasizing the patrician lines of her delicately boned face. The broad-brimmed black felt hat she wore was undeniably Spanish in origin, the dip of the brim making her piercing eyes seem upturned at the corners, catlike in their gripping gaze.

"I wouldn't have thought your many duties at the *rancho* would allow time for an afternoon's dalliance," Carlotta observed coolly. Though her comment had been directed at Ramón, her eyes were fastened on Sirena, and her words carried a viperish sting.

Sirena became acutely aware of the coolness of the grass between her toes. With only her boots removed, she felt nonetheless that she was standing naked before them. To her it seemed that her bare feet and Ramón's broad bronzed chest, his shirt carelessly tossed atop the sweet-smelling grasses, told the lie of what had happened. She could see it in Rualto's worried eyes, and in Carlotta's icy gaze.

"What are you doing here?" Ramón turned to face his mother and brother, putting himself between them and Sirena in an instinctively protective gesture.

"Mother wished to go riding; she hasn't done so in quite some time. And I remembered this spot was very beautiful."

On the surface at least, Rualto seemed in a much better humor than Ramón.

"And you?" Rualto spoke past his brother, directing his question at Sirena. A question of concern, not accusation.

"I . . . I came here alone." Sirena felt the need to explain. "I spent most of the day painting until Ramón arrived just a short while ago." She forced a laugh that sounded hollow even to her ears. "It seems no one wants to give me much credit yet for being able to find my way around alone in this country."

The whole situation was ridiculous, Sirena stormed to herself. Rualto and his mother were the intruders here. All of them were standing on her land, but she felt at a disadvantage, embarrassed, as if she owed them some sort of explanation. Her jaw tightened in defiance. She owed them nothing, but they owed her courtesy. Sirena was not going to tolerate being put in the role of the awkward helpless female.

"Did you enjoy the ride, Carlotta?" she asked sweetly, forcing her lips to curve into a welcoming smile. "It certainly has been a lovely day to be outdoors — a real inspiration for my painting. Would you care to see it?"

Carlotta clearly recognized Sirena's about-face tactics, her determined changing of the subject. "Of course, I'd love to see your work." She spat out the last word as if it were of the foul four-lettered variety.

"And so would I." Rualto's words were silken, his gaze constantly flicking back and forth between Sirena, his brother and his mother's cool countenance. There was an odd glint in the depths of his eyes that Sirena couldn't fathom. To her it spoke pain mixed with a look of humble pleading, as if he sought understanding for what he was about to do. "But of course if you were painting most of the day and Ramón only just arrived shortly before we did, that explains the embrace. You haven't as yet had time to tell him about *us*. . . ."

"Us?" Sirena's tone was dubious. What was Rualto leading up to?

She could feel Ramón's attention shift instantly, suspicion showing in his smoldering eyes fixed so intently upon her. Had he truly spoken soft words of love to her only moments earlier?

"I'm sorry, my flower. Of course you haven't had time to tell him." Rualto's voice was filled with remorse. "I shouldn't have asked it now. I trust you. Forgive me."

Ramón's gaze became clouded, his feelings shuttered from Sirena by the sweep of his long black lashes.

"What *are* you talking about, Rualto?" Sirena demanded, feeling the hot prickle of anger beginning to rise in her. She noted the satisfied expression settling on Carlotta's features. What the hell was Rualto trying to do to her?

"If you need a road map, Sirena, let me assure you I do not. So," Ramón declared harshly, "what you told me before they arrived was true. All men are the same to you, my sweet."

It was as if a door had been suddenly slammed shut on Sirena. Ramón had passed judgment on her with no more than his brother's passing comment to confirm his own exceedingly low opinion of her.

Dismayed, Sirena shook her head, emotion choking her throat. But Ramón had already turned on his heel and was making his way toward his horse. "I'm sure," he tossed over his shoulder, "that since you know this country so well, it will be an easy matter for you to find your way back to the hacienda. Or if you're feeling helpless, Rualto will be more than pleased to escort you."

Sirena took a step in Ramón's direction, but Rualto's hand moved to restrain her. Glancing up into Rualto's face, she saw that it was deeply lined in contrition. "I'm truly sorry, Sirena." His gaze slid to Carlotta, hesitation and uncertainty filling his eyes. "It's just — just that," he stammered, "I cannot stand to see my brother hurt you, and Ramón being Ramón, that's what he'll do." He shook his head sadly; then, seeing the anger in Sirena's eyes, he sighed, "I'll go after him and tell him the truth."

Using the reins to turn his mount, Rualto started to move away from her. It would take only a few seconds to catch up with his brother's retreating form. But a stubborn streak Sirena constantly fought to control rose instantly to the surface.

"No!" she said vehemently. "No, Rualto, there's no need for you to do that." No, her heart cried out, if Ramón did love her, he wouldn't have leaped to such wild conclusions.

As she gazed at Ramón's retreating broad shoulders, his athletic form, pain pierced Sirena's heart. How could he so easily believe a lie? The mere intimation that she'd given Rualto what she withheld from him was enough to turn him from her. Her estimation had been correct all along: he didn't love her. The sole reason he was angry now was that he didn't like the idea of being beaten to the prize.

Sirena seethed in anger. The hope that had dared to rise the smallest fraction in her heart only a short time earlier had been crushed as a delicate cactus flower might be crushed beneath the hooves of a passing horse.

Carlotta retained a stony silence throughout the entire exchange. She wore her aloofness as a cloak against such indelicate scenes as the one she'd been forced to witness.

"Come on," Sirena suggested airily, the tautness of her voice the only sign of her distress. "Let me show you my painting before we go our separate ways." She hoped her last comment would make it abundantly clear to Rualto that she wished to ride home alone and he was free to accompany his mother back to their ranch. At the back of Sirena's mind was the niggling feeling that Carlotta was behind what Rualto had done, that the timeliness of their arrival had been all too convenient.

Dismounting, both Carlotta and Rualto trailed along behind Sirena to where the painting stood on its easel in silent testimony to her day of hard work.

"It's truly beautiful," Rualto complimented her immediately, and the color of his voice was enough to tell her he was sincere.

"Lovely!" Carlotta agreed with more than a faint note of surprise tinging her words. "Is it finished?"

Sirena sighed. "I believe it is, although once I return to the hacienda, I might add a few small touches."

But would she add those touches? Only a short time earlier, locked within the warm circle of Ramón's embrace, she had fleetingly thought of painting a small figure swimming in the pool — a dark-haired man; a man with powerful shoulders; a vibrant man, virile and natural as nature had created him. And perhaps, on the far side of the pool, his Eve — a romantically blurred figure of a woman serenely sitting in the water, yet somehow giving the impression of a delicate nymph of the mountain pool, soon to emerge from it. How very beautiful and ethereal it could have been. Yet now the fragile dream had dissolved. Sirena was sorely afraid the figures would never find their way onto her canvas.

"But what touches could you add to such a beautiful painting?" Carlotta asked curiously. Her gaze rested lightly on Sirena but at the same time seemed to pass directly through her.

"Just detail," Sirena said lightly, knowing the words rang false.

"But what sort of detail?" Carlotta pressed, her voice possessed of its usual well-modulated and softly accented tones. "It looks complete as it is."

"Mostly just touches of light or dark." Sirena was purposely sketchy in her explanation. She didn't propose to tell anyone the detail she'd hoped to add to the bright and almost fantastic painting.

"*Madre* —" Rualto spoke gently to his mother, but his words were meant to quiet her questions "— an artist isn't a technician. Sirena undoubtedly intends to live with it awhile as it is and decide for herself then what's needed."

Sirena was surprised at his perceptiveness. Rualto had a deeply ingrained sensitivity.

"Now come," Rualto urged, sweeping his broad-brimmed hat from his head and running a hand through the unruly black hair. "I've seen some storm clouds over the mountains. I'll help Sirena get her things packed and then we'll all start for home."

Carlotta nodded, and Sirena stared thoughtfully at the older woman. The exchange that had passed between them only a few days earlier hung in the air, but neither she nor Carlotta mentioned it. Carlotta's seeming meekness with Rualto, her agreeability, was entirely out of character with the viper Sirena had met face to face in her garden. What was it that had brought out the lighter side of Carlotta's nature, such as it was? She certainly had taken on a more friendly air after Ramón's departure.

Sirena couldn't stop the frown that moved fleetingly across

her face. Ramón. Carlotta's mood had lightened immediately when Ramón had walked away, and now a calculating light shone from her dark eyes. Her face, though icily beautiful, was etched with lines of unbending authority. Carlotta was a woman accustomed to having her word taken as law. Could it be that she decidedly favored one son over the other? Or was it possible that she disapproved of Ramón, her roguish son? Perhaps she saw in him too much of the man who had been their father . . . the aggressiveness, the dominance. Maybe it was simply that he couldn't be manipulated by Carlotta as Rualto could? And what of Rualto, Sirena wondered. How far could he be pushed . . . how easily could he be made to dance by Carlotta like a puppet on a string?

"This waterfall can become like a thunderous cascade," Rualto was going on in a mellow voice. Perhaps he still felt a bit guilty about what he'd done to cause Ramón to leave. "This small stream can turn into a raging torrent within minutes when it storms in the mountains. In the past the entire floor of the canyon has been flooded." Rualto's enveloping eyes, so much like his brother's and yet so unique unto themselves, held hers in a soft embrace. His tones were more clipped than Ramón's and now quietly commanding of attention by their inflection. There were dangers here, his attitude telegraphed. "But," he went on, "a man wise in the ways of nature knows how to avoid what he can and handle the rest."

What was Rualto trying to say?

Observing the sun dipping toward the west, Sirena knew it was best for her to leave, to return to the hacienda before it got dark.

"This country may resemble a scene described in one of your adventure stories," Carlotta said with steely tartness, "but it can very easily kill." She laid out the words as if they were bricks in a wall, locking Sirena beyond understanding of this wild country. Did she imagine it, or was there a dark threat staining Carlotta's cool remarks?

Carlotta could make all the threats she wanted; she could try all the manipulations at her disposal. Sooner or later, Sirena resolved, the grand lady was going to have to realize her scheming simply wouldn't work.

It took only minutes, with Rualto's help, to gather up the things she'd brought with her to the hidden canyon. Carlotta remounted her horse as Sirena and Rualto worked swiftly together beneath the gathering clouds. Carefully they tied the painting, safely stored in its special case, on the back of her saddle, along with her paints and the few remnants of the picnic she and Ramón had so briefly shared.

"You've forgiven me for what I said earlier to Ramón?" Rualto's words were soft, for Sirena's ears only.

"Of course I forgive you, Rualto." Sirena could feel Carlotta's eyes burning into her back, and she sensed that Rualto was equally ill at ease in his mother's presence. His eyes flickered constantly to where she sat on her magnificent horse, towering above them like a queen surveying her lowly subjects, at least one of whom she would have cheerfully seen beheaded.

Sirena knew Rualto cared about her feelings. He was thoughtful and considerate of her — almost the total antithesis of Ramón. "You're a wonderful friend, Rualto," she reassured him. "I know you thought you were doing it to protect me."

She missed the quick darkening, the fleeting frown lines that crossed Rualto's angular face. And as she turned to pick up Chispa's reins from the ground, she didn't see the agitation in his eyes or the swift compressing of his lips when he glanced in Carlotta's direction.

"I'm pretty resilient," Sirena added quietly. "You don't have to worry about me so much. I can do a good job of taking care of myself. Anita needs much more of your attention now." Sirena kept her voice low, the words not traveling to Carlotta's ears. She had momentarily forgotten that Anita hadn't yet apprised Rualto of her condition.

"What do you mean, *now?*" Rualto asked with an intensity Sirena hadn't seen him display previously. "Is there something wrong? Something Anita hasn't told me?"

"I only meant that you love each other." Sirena sidestepped Rualto's question hastily but was sure he wasn't totally convinced that was all she had meant.

Carlotta, patiently waiting for Rualto to join her, had a very

185

faint smile touching her lips. The expression on her face was that of a contented cat, which with Carlotta could not bode anything good.

"Come — we shall ride part of the way back to the hacienda with you," Rualto murmured softly.

Sirena opened her mouth to protest, but Rualto raised a hand to silence her.

"It can be dangerous for you to ride alone," Carlotta spoke up, overhearing the gist of Sirena's and Rualto's last exchange as they brought the horses nearer.

"There's enough light for us to make sure you're indeed headed in the right direction and then still return home before dark," Rualto assured her, anticipating her objection.

The smile Rualto bestowed on Sirena was genuine, touched by a softness that tugged at her heart. And yet she sensed that beneath it lay a will of steel — and something more. Despite his courtesy and gentle ways, Sirena had no doubt that Rualto was a strong man, seemingly in all ways except where his mother was concerned.

For a fleeting moment she looked up into Rualto's face, and for the space of a heartbeat all she could see was Ramón. Ramón, who had brought her nothing but pain from the moment they'd met. He raised her ire and battered her heart, and when he was through, he gave her not so much as a backward glance. Why was he always in her thoughts, even hidden behind the face of his twin?

"That's very kind . . ." Sirena thanked them, stepping to the side of her horse. Slipping her booted foot into the stirrup while Rualto stood close beside Chispa, one hand resting on the bridle, she swung up into the saddle.

Sirena's eyes fastened on Carlotta as the elegant older woman pulled on a dainty pair of black-leather gloves.

"It's a small thing to do for a neighbor," Carlotta intoned before Rualto had a chance to say anything. "Accidents in this country occur all too frequently," she went on in her usual sugar-coated heavy-handed manner. "Ramón has told me there have been difficulties at Rancho Reese," she purred sweetly. "We would not want an accident to befall you."

"Nothing *will* happen to me," Sirena returned crisply. "You can depend on that." Her piercing gaze pinned Carlotta for a moment before she turned her horse down the canyon.

They covered ground quickly, the horses moving along in a smooth trot. Rualto and Carlotta parted from Sirena atop a rise that was just behind a hill that would bring the hacienda into view. Dark clouds were still building over the mountains, threatening to encompass the entire sky. Sirena was relieved they'd left the canyon when they had. Just a bit later and she might have got caught by the storm before she could reach the hacienda. Now, despite the thunder that rumbled threateningly in the distance, she was sure she would make it in before the rain hit.

Once more alone, Sirena hurried Chispa along, conscious of the sudden cooling of the air as the sun was devoured by the thick black clouds. She rode parallel to the wash, heeding Rualto's advice to keep clear of it now that rain was visibly falling in the mountains. If the rain was heavy, the wash could fill within seconds as a wall of water came thundering down out of the mountains. If that should happen, Chispa would find herself suddenly floundering in swirling water and mud. Such a dramatic scene Sirena had witnessed only in films, but she had no desire to tempt the fates.

As she rode, Sirena's thoughts strayed back to Ramón. She was going to have a lot to say to him over dinner. How could he behave the way he had? How could he be ready to make love to her one moment and believe any lie concocted about her the next? She loved Ramón, and she feared she had let him glimpse the deep feelings she had for him. For a brief instant she had lowered her defenses, believed they could share something beautiful together. But that fragile bubble had burst all too easily, and she would not continue to allow him to drag her heart around in the dust. She *could* not allow it. Somehow, Sirena resolved, she was going to set him from her and make it quite clear that from this time forward theirs was only a business relationship. Their association would be terminated as soon as she could assume complete control of the ranch — in her estimation, very soon indeed. In fact, she would make sure of it.

187

Sirena repeated the litany of her resolve over and over to herself as Chispa's spirited gait brought them to the stable just before the gathering clouds and setting sun could conspire to bring on total darkness. Mike was there to meet her and relieve her of the responsibility of unsaddling and rubbing down the mare. She made a dash for the house, carrying the painting, her paints and the leftovers from the picnic.

Sirena didn't dally, for according to her stomach, the hour was late. In spite of the lateness of her lunch, she hadn't eaten much, and after the long ride she was more than ready for one of Anita's deliciously cooked meals. Delightful aromas drifted throughout the house, and Sirena changed out of her dirty riding clothes in haste, reaching the kitchen almost before Anita was aware that she'd returned.

"Oh, Señorita Sirena, it's truly beautiful!" Anita stood admiring the painting Sirena had taken from the case upon her entry, to allow the air to begin drying the acrylics.

"Why, thank you, Anita." Sirena was always warmed by the young housekeeper's sincere compliments.

There was no need to set the formal dining table for just herself and Ramón, who was almost always around for the dinner hour, but tonight the table that occupied the place before the generous bay window in the kitchen was even more sparsely set than usual. Her single place setting looked lonely at the end of the table. Sirena felt an odd catch in her throat but managed to conceal it from Anita. It was ridiculous anyway, she berated herself; she should be glad to have Ramón off elsewhere for a change. He was insufferable, and she certainly didn't need his dazzling conversation to make her meal enjoyable.

"Isn't Ramón going to have dinner here?" Sirena made the question light, as if she already knew the answer.

Anita shook her head. "He was here just a short time ago and told me not to set a place for him. He didn't give a reason, but he did seem upset about something," she added a bit uncomfortably.

Sirena could well imagine that Ramón's being upset would give Anita cause for worry. With Ramón one could never be completely sure who or what was the cause of his ill temper.

"Have you eaten yet?" Sirena steered the conversation away from Ramón.

Anita shook her head again.

"Well, then," Sirena enjoined her brightly, "bring another place setting and join me. There's no reason for each of us to eat alone."

Anita was bright and chirpy throughout the meal, flitting effortlessly from one subject to another, chatting merrily away, her green eyes sparkling with good humor. As always, and in spite of her own problems, she was content to leave no one depressed or distracted.

With a sigh Sirena continued to poke at her food, eating little, though she'd arrived back at the hacienda ravenous. She hoped Anita would not be able to recognize her own unhappiness. Both women did an amazing job of concealing their inner turmoil. Ruefully Sirena decided the two of them were fine actresses.

Exchanging mild gibes and laughing, they sat there talking while the lovely meal before them tasted to Sirena like straw. She wondered if Anita, too, was having difficulty eating. Or did Anita face love differently? Did she nurture complete faith that everything would work out in the end, that Rualto would ask her to marry him very soon? Did she draw her endless good humor from that?

All of Sirena's decisions of the past afternoon had somehow fled. No matter which way she turned it, the inescapable fact was that she was hopelessly, mindlessly and miserably in love. What was she going to do? She knew she couldn't keep on this way, her moods rising and falling with all the speed and predictability of a child's rubber ball.

There were only two choices as far as she could see. She could give up Rancho Reese and return to New York, or she could submerge herself so thoroughly in the work on the ranch, preparing it for the new role she planned for it, that she would not be able to think of Ramón or her love for him. She would have to encase her heart in steel, make herself inviolate. Ramón could hold her to the letter of the will, but she could do the same. She would keep him at arm's length, giving him no opportunity to touch her — both physically and emotionally — again.

Leaving the chore of cleaning up after dinner to Anita, Sirena retired to her room. She had a lot of thinking and planning to do to implement her plans. Maybe what had happened that day at the waterfall had not been so terrible after all. Perhaps now that she was resolute where Ramón was concerned, she could begin to work out the future of *her* ranch.

A nagging thought about Ramón could not help creeping in, though. It was true that Austin had left Rancho Reese to her, and yet he had appointed Ramón as her guide and protector, leaving it entirely up to Ramón as to when she would be prepared to take over completely. How long, Sirena wondered, would that take? How long would he remain there on Rancho Reese?

"Oh, Austin," Sirena whispered upon entering the study, feeling its comfort and warmth envelop her as she closed the door behind her. "Whatever were you thinking of when you created this mess?"

With a gliding grace she crossed the room to the big windows overlooking the distant stable, casting a sidelong glance in the direction of the jar occupying a prominent spot on her desk. As her own joke on herself, she'd taken Austin's cryptic letter and tucked it into the clear glass jar, sealing the lid with glue. Across its front she had taped the message IN CASE OF EMERGENCY BREAK GLASS. Austin, Sirena suspected, would have appreciated the wry humor of it. More than once she'd been tempted to hurl the fragile glass bottle at Ramón.

Sirena moved to the window that looked out over the stable. There was a light burning, glowing softly in the distance. Mike would have left that on. Some of Rancho Reese's finest were there within the walls of the stable. A few of the better mares were nearing their time for foaling, and Mike preferred to keep a close eye on them. The corrals that sprawled out from the stable gave each animal access to the outside and plenty of freedom of movement, but at night Mike was careful to see them safely back inside. Also, there was a lively young filly that had cut herself badly on some wire, and until he could be sure she was completely on the mend, Mike was keeping her confined. Chispa was there, as well, unsaddled, rubbed down and fed her evening ration of grain.

The distant light softly glowing in the all-encompassing darkness was somehow restful, a quiet balm for Sirena's troubled spirit. She turned from the window, making her way into the adjoining bedroom. She would change into her nightclothes and then come back to the desk to work. She had done little paperwork this day.

"I wonder if, after all," Sirena mused, "I would be a disappointment to you, Austin."

Moving to the drawer of her beautiful old chest, she drew out the filmy length of her sea-green nightgown and laid it across the bed. Absently she began undoing the buttons of her shirt.

"No," she said into the quiet dimness of the room, "I don't think you'd be ashamed of me, Austin, because it's just as you told me when I visited. It was only the fools and sluggards who did nothing whom you couldn't abide. I don't know how right I am, but I *am* doing something."

Unbuttoning the cuffs of the striped shirt, Sirena removed it and laid it across the bed, then unzipped her jeans, and finished undressing. The air of the room was cool and bracing against her bare flesh, instantly sending a flood of goose bumps up her arms and thighs. With a swift movement she snatched up the full filmy gown and let it drift into place, sliding easily over her slim white shoulders, catching momentarily on the peaks of her firm young breasts and floating down over her trim hips to the floor.

Catching sight of herself in the mirror, Sirena grinned at her strange silly weakness for feminine nightgowns. The green was one of her favorites. The neck was cut in a low square and trimmed with multicolored braid of a color so rich it fairly glowed against the pale whiteness of her skin. The sleeves were long and full, and with the hem of the gown falling to the floor, her toes peeping shyly out from under it, she seemed to be adrift on a sea of the filmy material. The long gathers that fell from the tailored square cut of the neck were a contrast in hard

191

and soft, and the fullness of the billowing sleeves were caught in a soft cuff of braid that matched the trim of the neck.

A delightful sensuous fantasy — but whom did she have to share it with? Sirena sighed ruefully and couldn't help twirling once before the mirror. The yards of fragile green silk spun out away from her legs, revealing her slim calves and making her appear as if she were a sort of rare wild flower. It was a gown for seduction, and yet she had only her dreams of a someday when the right man would come into her life.

A bit wistfully Sirena reached for her more practical velour dressing gown, drawing it on over the softness of the nightgown and tying the belt securely around her. With a purposeful stride she returned to the study adjoining her bedroom. Her dreams would have to wait for that someday. For now there was a lot of work that needed doing.

CHAPTER TEN

Sirena awoke all at once and felt a small dart of pain between her shoulder blades.

Somehow during the late hours, hard at work, she had fallen asleep at her desk while poring over the details of the guest-ranch plan. She'd been in the midst of writing letters to more travel agencies after setting a firm opening date of November 25, one month before Christmas. The permits and a health license lay in a neat stack on the corner of her desk. She'd written a letter to the charter companies, one in Phoenix and one in Tucson, that would be handling the transportation of many of their guests. Then there were the sources she'd made contact with for food supplies, much of which would be available locally. A number of staples would be brought in, probably by the charter flying in guests.

Sirena blinked and stared about the room. Something had awakened her. What was it? A sound? A feeling? She didn't know. She felt none of the groggy disorientation that usually accompanied her early-morning awakening. Aside from stiff muscles from falling asleep upright in a chair, there were no lingering traces of her slumber.

The light still burned on the corner of her desk. Absently Sirena glanced at the little gold clock that sat under the glow of the lamplight. It was nearly two-thirty in the morning. She doubted there was another creature stirring in the house, but a vague uneasiness assailed her. Some half-formed awareness was trying to make its way into her consciousness. The room was enfolded within an unnatural marshmallowing silence, and the grand old house itself gave the impression of holding its breath.

Swiveling in her chair, Sirena peered out the window into the darkness. The storm still lingered in the mountains around them; not a star twinkled in the heavens, and the moon was completely obscured by clouds. A light glowed dimly down at the stable. No doubt Mike had left it on in case he had to attend a mare in labor during the night.

Sirena's eyes remained fixed on the stable. There was something else — a small flickering twin to the glow of the electric light. For a moment her mind couldn't grasp what she was seeing. A clap of thunder ripped through the silence that had hung so heavily in the room, and a bolt of lightning tore across the blackened heavens — a brilliant light that flared, flickered, then died away, leaving behind only the faint glow from the stable. Sirena climbed to her feet, knees suddenly feeling like water, eyes narrowing as a horrible certainty washed through her.

Fire!

"Dear God!" Sirena whispered, clasping a hand to her mouth. Her mind raced to find an explanation even as she turned and flew into her bedroom, her feet finding the slippers of their own volition before she spun around and dashed out of the room into the long hall. The lightning had to have started it. For the moment her mind chose to ignore the fact that she'd seen the faint flickering glow even before the lightning had ripped through the quiet darkness.

There was no alarm system at Rancho Reese, no way to let the others know of the danger. They had to get the horses out of the stable or all would be lost. Her feet fairly flew over the carpeting of the hall, and she employed the only tool at her disposal to give warning: her voice.

"Anita!" Sirena yelled, feeling anguish tearing at her chest as she bolted for the kitchen and Anita's private rooms beyond. "Fire! There's a fire in the stable. Wake up, Anita!"

Robe and gown billowing out around her, Sirena sailed through the length of the gallery that ran alongside the living room, past the dining room and through the kitchen.

"Anita!" she repeated her frantic call, her voice taking on a piercing note of panic.

Like a wraith, dressed in a flimsy nightgown of white batiste, Anita appeared in the doorway of the kitchen, her black hair falling in a disheveled cascade about her narrow shoulders. Her eyes were wide with fear and darkly circled with sleep.

"Fire? Where? What are we going to do?"

"The stable!" Sirena was nearly breathless from her run. "Use the phone. Quickly! Call Mike and try to find Ramón and the stable boy. We have to get the horses out!" And she spun again and dashed for the front door.

"Wait!" Anita protested.

"No!" Sirena shot back. "Call them! I'm going after the horses!"

The small stones bruising her feet through the thin soles of her slippers went unnoticed as Sirena skimmed over the rough ground through the chilled darkness. She ran for the stable as she had never run before. Flames licking up the side of one wall were visible to her as she drew nearer. Growing rapidly larger, the hungry fingers of searing fire enveloped the wall, crackling and popping in their eagerness to move on.

Sirena kept to her swift pace, one hand lifting the flowing skirts of her nightclothes to keep from stumbling over them as her eyes remained glued on the scene of the fire. Thin tendrils of flame shot out from the superheated center of the fast-burning fire, racing out in all directions along the wall.

Coming from within the stable, Sirena could hear the agitated snorts and short whinnies of the frightened horses as their delicate nostrils caught the smell of smoke. How far had the flames already spread inside? She gaped at the sight of the fire slipping over the top of the wall. It was beginning to eat away at the dry timbers of the roof!

For an instant she hesitated, swaying on her feet, staring at the raging holocaust that now engulfed one entire end of the stable. The heat from the flames grew more intense with each passing moment, competing with the bone-chilling cold of the wee-morning hours. It was then that she spotted the figure dashing through the strange dancing shadows created by the fire, leaving the stable with a pair of terrified horses.

There was no more time for hesitation. It had to be Mike. In her agitation, Sirena was too stunned to realize the figure she had so quickly and dimly observed was much too tall to be

Mike and moved with an athletic grace that the older man had left behind with his youth.

Flames threatening, towering now into the stormy night sky, Sirena made a run for the entrance. Her ears were alive to the growing sounds of panic within the walls — the horses stamping in their stalls, the alarmed nickers of animal terror. Smoke billowed through the length of the building, which seemed to act like a large chimney and suck the smoke out on the draft. The roar and crackle of the flames, the rising heat and choking smoke were enough to make reason fly, but Sirena clung to hers tenaciously and dashed for the nearest stall, raising one full sleeve of her dressing gown to cover her nose and mouth.

A spark dancing lightly on the air from the blazing roof came to rest upon a bale of hay only yards away. In the blink of an eye the bale was being voraciously consumed, the sharp crackling of it lending wings to Sirena's feet.

Snatching open the door to Chispa's stall, she thought to start the little mare for the outside and turn to another, but the terrified animal stood fast, head up, eyes large and round with terror, nostrils flaring.

"Run!" Sirena called to the frightened mare. "Run!" She stepped close to give the horse a sound whack on her hind quarters, but still the horse stood firm, muscles twitching in her withers and flanks, frozen to the spot.

Sirena didn't wait any longer. Grabbing the loose halter Mike had evidently put on when he removed the tack earlier, she drew the flowing sleeve of her dressing gown over the mare's eyes and urged her forward. Chispa balked, but finally, at Sirena's insistent tugging, she began to move forward. Running along the center aisle, Sirena drew the mare toward the beckoning fresh air. To her relief, she heard other heavy hastening footsteps inside the stable, but she couldn't make out the dim figure moving through the wafting smoke toward her.

"Get the hell out of here!" Ramón snapped. He squinted against the thick smoke that surrounded them.

"The horses!" Sirena shouted, and rushed for the open door beyond, feeling Chispa's gait increase abruptly as her nostrils caught the scent of fresh air.

There was no time to put the mare anywhere. There was time only to free her and make another wild dash back into the inferno. The roar of it was now nearly deafening, the heat quickly reaching the point where it would be unbearable. They had to hurry.

Ramón pulled two resisting horses after him and bellowed, "Sirena, I told you to get out of here, and I meant stay out!"

"No!" she shrieked, to be heard above the din. Then she streaked past him, disappearing into the gray gloom of the smoke now rising on all sides of them, descending in huge puffs from the ceiling above. The entire roof was going; they had to move fast.

Sightlessly, tears streaming down her cheeks, Sirena snatched at the gate of one of the far box stalls. Flinging it open, she ducked inside, going more by feel than by sight.

A horse whinnied as she entered, the terror filling the animal a palpable thing arcing through the air between them. Sirena started toward the sound as her throat opened and closed convulsively, seeking fresh air and finding none.

From somewhere a breath of air stirred the thick-hanging smoke, and Sirena spotted the tiny new foal sprawled on the straw. At the same instant her foot came in contact with something soft but heavy and unyielding on the floor.

Coughing violently, Sirena dropped to her knees, groping before her. Her fingers struck cloth, cloth encasing a body, and her eyes cleared enough to see the dim outline of a body sprawled in the straw.

"Dear God," Sirena breathed, her voice hoarse as she half strangled on the smoke. "Mike!"

She shook him violently, but there was no response. He was unconscious, unmoving and as heavy as a sack of concrete. What had happened? Had he been caught unawares and overcome by the smoke? Had he been helping the mare foal and been kicked? Sirena could only speculate, and there was no time for that.

Overhead the fire crackled and the beams groaned with their weakening ability to support the roof. The bravado Sirena had felt only a short time earlier, snapping at Ramón's demand that

197

she leave the burning stable and not return inside, was fading as quickly as the fire was spreading. What was she going to do? She couldn't even budge Mike, and the popping of the timbers was ominous.

Like molten liquid spilled from a caldron, the fire raced overhead. Slender tendrils of flame were sliding effortlessly across the underside of the roof, blackening the rafters, eating away at the supports with alarming speed.

Frantic now, Sirena continued to shake Mike's unconscious form, trying to rouse him. She shuddered. If he didn't help himself, they were both lost, for she couldn't bear to leave him to the crackling flames. Her flesh cringed away from the searing heat that billowed over them in surging waves, and her slight frame was racked with violent coughs as her lungs continuously attempted to clear themselves of the biting gray smoke. The tiny foal, barely entered into this world, caught the scent of danger and flailed helplessly, unable to stand, its long legs still uncooperative in the effort as its mother hovered nearby, pressed against the far stall wall. Sirena felt the urge to scream, but her lungs couldn't draw enough breath to bring sound to her lips.

Somehow she got her hands under Mike's arms, levering his shoulders off the floor, attempting to draw him toward the exit. Though she strained with all her strength, she was able to move Mike only inches through the flammable straw. Tiny showers of sparks erupted from the tarred roof overhead, raining down on the stable floor. Sirena used the thick hem of her gown to slap at a small flame that leaped up near them, smothering it.

Almost gagging as a new fit of coughing ripped through her, she felt her strength waning. She simply wasn't getting enough air to renew the blood in her veins. Her chest heaved and her stomach convulsed, and she fell away from Mike for a few moments, pressing close to the floor, trying to draw a few breaths of air below the hanging clouds of smoke.

"Mike! Mike! You've got to help me!" Sirena cried out, hoping her words would touch him, stir him, where her physical prodding had not. "Mike! Wake up! I can't do it alone!" she pleaded. Through the roar of the flames, a groan issued from the suffering timbers overhead.

A heavy-booted foot slammed into the straw close beside Sirena, and a curl of smoke rose from beneath it. She turned her head enough to see the tower of well-muscled legs rising above her, topped by narrow hips and broad shoulders. Ramón's face was nearly lost in the swirling smoke, though she could make out his hand clamping a handkerchief over his nose and mouth.

In another instant Ramón was kneeling in the straw beside her. "Get up, Sirena — hurry! The whole roof is ready to go! Here, take this and tie it over the mare's eyes," he instructed hastily as he grabbed hold of Mike's arms and drew him into an awkward sitting position in the straw. "Move!" he commanded as she hesitated, mesmerized by the dancing flames.

Sirena scrambled to her feet, hampered by the voluminous folds of her frothy silly nightgown and the heavy weight of the tightly wrapped robe. Swiftly she tucked the makeshift blindfold over the mare's eyes and under the leather of the halter she wore.

"What about the foal?" she gasped as Ramón took Mike's limp weight across his shoulders and began to rise.

Ramón reached for the halter Sirena still held firmly in one hand. "We have to leave it!" he shot back. "It doesn't have a chance. Now run!" A spark ignited and flared in the far corner of the stall as if to emphasize Ramón's words, but still Sirena hesitated.

"*No!*" she yelled to be heard above the terrible din. "I'll carry him!"

"*Por Dios!*" Ramón ground the words out, but he could do nothing to stop her. He was burdened with Mike, and his other hand gripped the leather of the mare's bridle.

Sirena scooped the tiny struggling animal into her arms, pressing it tightly against her, and hastened to Ramón's side as the flames shot across the surface of the dry straw toward them. Ramón's eyes glittered with a combination of excitement, apprehension and anger, the gold of the flames reflected in their smoldering depths. They gleamed down at Sirena from the smoky swirl like the eyes of a demon.

199

"Quickly!" Ramón repeated. "The roof —"

Together they moved out of the stall as red gold flames flared up behind them to meet those dancing along the overhead beams. Ramón's strides were long and fast, his gait rolling beneath the burden of Mike's weight. Sirena matched her pace to his, her slippers skimming over the straw that crackled ominously beneath their passing feet. A snapping groaning roar rose up, and a great rush of superheated air washed over them in a rippling wave.

"Don't look back!" Ramón shouted as Sirena's head began to turn toward the source out of reflex.

Never had the simple length of the stable seemed so long. Sirena could feel the heat of the fire searing the insides of her lungs as she stumbled on, struggling for sustaining breath, knowing that if she tripped now, if she faltered, it would be the death of her. The rending crash behind them continued, splintering, shrieking and thundering into oblivion, the sound of it intertwined with the horrifying roar of the flames as they rushed to consume the dry wood. It was a dance of death . . . a flickering undulating golden lover who beckoned with sensuous movements. But to embrace him would be folly of the most permanent kind.

The double doors loomed ahead, and Sirena could sense the air lightening. The small creature in her arms felt to her as if it weighed more than the mother Ramón led so firmly beside her.

Sirena could see Ramón's head turn toward her often, but he spoke no more, and she remained silent, as well, fighting the thick smoke that threatened to choke them both. Thin cries pierced the din of the thundering flames; faintly Sirena could recognize Anita's anxious wail in the distance. They were almost there, almost clear of the clutching heat that seemed to grow more intense with each passing second.

Then suddenly the cold air of the stormy night whipped across Sirena's face in a moist slap that sent a chilled shudder throughout her tensed and sweating body. She and Ramón walked even faster, hurrying to be clear of the slowly collapsing building. Anita's glad cry of recognition reached Sirena's ears as they emerged from the veil of smoke, coughing and gasping, but all of them alive.

Ramón released his grip on the mare's halter and dropped to his knees, spilling the weight of Mike Vargo to the hard-packed earth in a gentle roll. Sirena also relieved herself of her burden, lowering the tiny new foal to the ground near its mother. Then, whirling, she grabbed the bucket Anita had dropped in her excitement. Dipping it into the trough continuously refilled by the windmill, she dashed toward the flames and tossed the bucketful of water into the inferno.

"Sirena! Get back!" Ramón was on his feet after her. "The stable is lost! You can't save any of it now!"

Dipping the bucket again, Sirena ignored his words. "We won't know that for sure unless we try!" She threw her second bucketful of water, while the stable boy scampered around doing the same, following her example.

"Get back!" Ramón ordered the stable boy. The look of black rage on his face and the ring of authority in his voice were enough to make the boy hesitate as he reached the trough again.

"We can't just let it burn!" Sirena screeched hysterically, her throat feeling as if it had been scorched. The water she flung was little more than a spit in hell, but she felt she had to try.

"The hell we can't!" Ramón ground out. Then the memory of the groans and shrieks of the perishing wood faded into nothing beside the horrible splintering moan that ripped through the old building as it settled in upon itself.

Sirena swung around to face him, her cheeks red, her blue eyes brilliant with excitement and glassy with the stinging tears brought on by the billowing acrid smoke. As the hem of her robe swung over the top of a glowering brand, sparks instantly leaped to life, racing up the length of the flowing skirt.

A startled scream tore from her lips as she whirled about, instinctively, trying to move away from the sudden heat she felt upon her slim calves. She stepped away from it, but it followed, clinging to her, moving with the sway of her body and the quick steps she took to be clear of it. An alarm clamored in her brain. She knew what she should do, but panic was rising quickly within her breast, and logic flew from her just as quickly. She knew only that she had to be free of the flames that were sliding up her clothes as fast as a droplet of water skittered across a pan of hot grease. Every primitive fear of fire, buried deep beneath the civilized exterior, bade her to run, and Sirena twirled in a flaming pirouette in an effort to do exactly that.

In an instant Ramón was beside her, strong arms locking themselves about her trim form, his weight bearing her with jarring suddenness to the dusty ground. Holding her firmly beneath him, he smothered the flames with his body.

Sirena gasped in shock, her eyes flying wide to gaze up uncertainly into Ramón's darker ones, smoldering with an internal flame of their own. She shivered with shock and the sudden cold that washed over her limbs. Not much was left of her robe and nightdress to cover her, but miraculously she wasn't burned.

Ramón's lips were set in a grim line. The planes and angles of his face were darkly shadowed in the flickering firelight as the stable continued to settle on itself, the crackling roar of the flames now the only sound to be heard. Ramón hesitated. His gaze was fixed intently on Sirena, his eyes telling her things she wasn't sure she wanted to know — or even to understand. The tense set of his shoulders as he leaned over her, the pressure of his thighs against hers, the tender touch of his fingers against her cheek, set the blood coursing wildly through her veins. And Sirena had no doubt that he knew the effect he had on her.

Without another word Ramón rolled off Sirena. Scooping her into his arms, he carried her back to where Mike was now groggily sitting up with Anita close at his side.

"Are you all right, *amigo?*" Ramón asked shortly.

Mike nodded, wincing at the pain the slight movement caused his head. "Someone hit me with something, but I'm all right."

"Good." Ramón frowned at Mike's explanation but chose not to question him further just yet. "Then I'll take Sirena back to the house," he suggested.

"I can walk," Sirena protested weakly, trying at the same time to free herself from the iron bands of Ramón's hands.

"I'll stay with Mike," Anita offered.

"No!" Sirena could feel her iron-clad resolve slipping within Ramón's embrace. "I should be the one to stay."

"Ramón, you take Sirena back to the hacienda," Anita said kindly. "Mike's all right, Sirena, and you'll catch something terrible if you stay out in the cold dressed the way you are."

Sirena blushed. She had forgotten her state of dress. Still, she didn't want to return to the hacienda alone with Ramón. It wasn't right. She knew that when Anita returned, she would take care to enter through the kitchen so as not to disturb her. Ramón, Sirena was sure, was also aware of that fact.

"I'm all right." Mike was climbing to his feet, attempting to reassure her.

Sirena sighed her resignation. She couldn't fight all of them. "All right," she relented, "but I can walk!" She pressed with all of her remaining strength against Ramón's chest, but it was like trying to topple a brick wall. "Ramón —"

"Be still," Ramón said lightly. He was already walking away from where Mike and Anita gazed at the remains of the burning stable. "If I put you down now, that gown you're wearing, or what's left of it, will leave nothing to the imagination." He cut off his words as they came up even with the stable boy, who still stood gazing at the blaze, bucket in hand.

"There's no need to strain yourself," Ramón told the lad. "Just keep an eye on it until it burns itself out."

The boy nodded in reply, grateful to set down his burden at last.

Sirena was nettled by Ramón's high-handed behavior with her, but then, that was nothing new. She gave up trying to protest his action and relaxed with the rhythm of his footsteps, curling closely against his chest, reveling in the warmth she found there and the firm thudding of his heart beneath her ear. Her arms wrapped themselves about his neck of their own volition as he held her high against his chest, his strides carrying them swiftly over the rough ground toward the beckoning lights of the hacienda.

"Where did you come from?" Sirena asked as Ramón carried her along. "I didn't see anyone near when I saw the fire."

"I was over at the foreman's house, trying to find Mike,"

Ramón answered her easily. "I was closer to the stable than you."

"It happened so fast," Sirena went on tremulously, her head resting securely on Ramón's shoulder. "The lightning —"

"The lightning didn't start that fire," Ramón informed her as they drew nearer the hacienda.

Sirena stiffened and tried to look up into his face, to read the expression there.

"Then what?" she questioned.

"I don't know." Sirena could feel his shrug beneath her arm. "But I intend to get to the bottom of it."

"But we saved the horses — no one was hurt," Sirena pointed out.

"Only because I was so near and you quickly followed." Without lowering his light burden to her feet, Ramón turned the knob and let them into the hacienda. "Think what would have happened if it hadn't worked out that way — and if you hadn't found Mike when you did. Mike said someone hit him. It would have been the same as murder if we hadn't been there."

"Couldn't the mare have kicked him when he turned around? Maybe the lightning frightened her when it started the fire."

"The mare could have kicked Mike," Ramón conceded, "but I saw the fire start, and it was burning before the lightning hit. And you," he growled, "I told you to get out of that stable twice! I know you're a stubborn and determined woman, but I didn't know you were also suicidal."

"Suicidal!" Sirena was irritated by his choice of word. "I'm no such thing." Halfheartedly she began to struggle in his grasp. "Now if you don't mind, I most certainly can walk from here."

"If you aren't suicidal, then what were you doing inside that stable after I warned you repeatedly?" Ramón questioned, ignoring her demand that he put her down. Swiftly he moved down the long hall toward her room.

"I was rescuing my horses!" Sirena retorted sharply. "What were *you* doing in there?"

Ramón chuckled softly. "I had the same thing in mind, until it began to look as if I'd be rescuing you instead! Did you think that roof would stay up just for you? My God, Sirena . . . were you burned?" He gazed down at her bare legs partially covered with the tattered scorched remains of her nightgown and robe.

Sirena shook her head, reading with accuracy the softening of his eyes. She smiled wanly. "There's no real damage," she assured him with a lightness she didn't feel. She'd been terrified back there. The flames had been roaring like demons unleashed from the bowels of hell, and the heat of the fire had tingled across her flesh in a searing example of what could happen to her.

Still, Rancho Reese was her home. Sirena knew that no matter how afraid she was, she could never just stand by and see it destroyed. The fear and trembling would come later. She felt it now, penetrating the very core of her being with a strange chill that came not from without but from within.

Ramón used his foot to nudge open the door to Sirena's bedroom and carry her inside. She was sure he couldn't help but be aware of the trembling that beset her limbs as he held her close against his broad chest.

Never in her life had Sirena been forced to face what she had this night. And now, as the reaction set in, she wished she were anywhere but in Ramón's arms. She didn't want him to see her weakness. She didn't want him to see that she felt like laughing and crying all at the same time, to know there was a weight in the center of her chest that made it suddenly difficult for her to breathe. She felt chilled to the very marrow of her bones, so cold that it seemed impossible she would ever feel warm again. Sirena clenched her teeth against their chattering as Ramón gently placed her upon her bed, unwinding her arms from around his neck.

The gentle strength of Ramón's hands soothed her, and Sirena stared up into the swirling golden depths of his eyes. Did she dare believe what she saw there? His eyes were warm and beckoning, filled with a special tenderness for her, and the usual mocking smile that curved the corners of his lips was absent. He towered above her, standing close to the bed and yet not moving closer. Sirena could scarcely believe the scene at the waterfall was merely a few hours behind them. This was

205

not the same Ramón who had stomped off angrily in response to only a few of his brother's insinuations. This was not the same man who had rejected her after rousing the pain of desire with demanding lips and searching hands. Ramón's eyes were now filled with an emotion Sirena had never believed she would see there. Longing, and perhaps. . . . She cringed from the unbidden thought, from the hope that surged within her despite her best efforts to stem it.

The sole way she could possibly be free of this feeling, free of Ramón, would be to return to New York and put Rancho Reese in the past. But even then, a small inner voice reminded her, distance would not ease the hurt. Deep in her soul Sirena knew she could put as many miles as she wanted between herself and Ramón and it would make no difference in how she felt. It would not end this terrible pain and longing.

Dark brows drawn together in a frown, Ramón gazed down at her, his proud head inclined at an angle that brought the sharp planes of his face into focus, seeming to float before her in the unlighted room. Sirena had lost the battle. Her teeth began to chatter uncontrollably; then, feeling the warmth of Ramón's eyes passing over her, she looked up at him.

"You're cold." He breathed the words so quietly Sirena wasn't even sure she'd heard them.

Carefully Ramón drew the covers from beneath where she lay, then pulled off his boots. Fully clothed, he stretched out beside her, piling the heavy covers over both of them.

"Remember," Ramón's roughened voice reached out to her in the room's dimness, "I told you once before body heat was the best thing for a chill."

Sirena felt herself being drawn up close against the length of his body, and she remained rigidly motionless, hardly knowing what to do, what to think. Her head swam with aroused sensations as his body pressed tightly against her own, so scantily clad in the remnants of her once prized nightgown and robe.

"Ramón," she began uncertainly, "I don't think. . . . I mean, today at the waterfall . . . Rualto. . . ."

"Shhh. Don't think, *querida*. And I don't want to hear about my brother," he added bitingly, before his voice once again softened for her. "*Por Dios!* Sirena, *mi adorada*, don't you know what you do to me every day, so close, so desirable? And what you did to me tonight when I didn't see you come out of that stable with the flames licking at the rafters?"

"Ramón, I. . . ." Sirena tried to protest again as the chattering of her teeth subsided with the comfort of his warm body pressed against hers.

Gently he touched his fingers to her lips to silence her. "No," he said soothingly, "you've said enough." He rubbed a silken strand of her auburn hair between his fingers thoughtfully. "I've been a fool, Sirena . . . a fool to doubt your love for Rancho Reese and your determination to continue what Austin Reese began here." He lightly rested his chin against the top of her head, drinking in the soft scent of her hair. "Austin, I think, was a wiser person than either of us."

Later, as he became aware of the quieting of her quaking limbs against his, the stilling of the shudders that had passed over her in waves, Ramón inquired, "Better?"

Sirena gazed up into his eyes. Desire flared within their depths, and she could feel the raging of his passions against her bare leg as he held her close, but he was concerned only with her needs. Motionless at her side, he wrapped his arms about her in comfort, his presence a rock against the sudden fears that had arisen within her after her harrowing experience inside the flaming stable.

Tentatively, Sirena nodded her head in answer to his question.

"The past doesn't matter, Sirena. Only the present matters. I was an even bigger fool to act as I did by the waterfall, and whatever you feel about me, I want you to know I'm sorry." He gave a wicked chuckle. "Maybe I tried to drive you away because I wanted you so much," he murmured seductively. "I love you, Sirena."

He spoke almost in a whisper, and this time there was no doubt as to his meaning. Sirena heard his declaration clearly, and her heart did a little flip-flop within her. His words sounded like beautiful chimes to her ears while her heart sang with joy.

Breathing evenly, curled against Ramón's side for warmth,

Sirena felt him drop a soft kiss on her forehead. "I'll leave you now," he said, his body tensing, sliding away from hers. "You need to rest. Dawn isn't very far off."

Instantly Sirena felt bereft at his sudden absence from her side. This was the first time she'd seen Ramón as he truly was, the first time she'd seen him without his armor of sarcasm and arrogance, the first time she'd hadn't had to bear that sneering superior smile that had haunted her in her dreams. Pain for past misunderstandings was in his eyes, and she reached out to him.

"No," she murmured almost inaudibly. "Don't go . . . don't leave me."

Ramón smiled faintly, and pain of another sort touched his face as he gritted his teeth at her gentle touch. "Sirena," he almost groaned, "Sirena, I can't just lie here with you, desiring you as I do. I'm not made of stone. If I stay —"

"I know," Sirena cut him off. "I know," she whispered softly, "and I want you to stay." She rested her head on one elbow, her hand lingering on the warmth of his arm, her eloquent eyes reflecting the love she had so feared revealing.

Ramón's hand rose to touch her cheek in a gentle caress, his eyes filled with a tenderness she had never seen reflected there. "You're sure, *mi amada?*" he breathed. "Do you know how much I've wanted this, how much I've wanted you since the beginning? I think I loved you even then."

Mutely Sirena nodded. Her throat was suddenly parched, her lips thirsting for the taste of Ramón's upon them. He drew her against the broad expanse of his chest in an embrace that was almost fierce in its possessiveness. He stroked her hair, marveling at its heavy silky mass, and Sirena drank in the heady masculine scent of him. Her arms came up to encircle his waist, to draw herself even closer to him.

"Why, my love? Why have we waited so long?" Ramón asked the question of the fates, his words hanging in the quiet of the large room.

A bit nervously Sirena laughed, then nestled against the comfort of his chest, feeling the reassurance of his arms around her while the burned smoke-scented remains of her green silk nightgown and robe hung in loose shreds about her, offering the barest minimum of coverage. Her long legs lay exposed in the dimness of the room as she half stretched across the bed, holding herself erect against him only by her grip on his waist and his arms wrapped about her.

"You thought I was a fortune hunter, remember?" Sirena teased lightly. "A shark from the city, poised and ready to rend the soft underbelly of this beautiful land before leaving with what plunder I could carry away."

Then Ramón's hand was beneath her chin, raising her lips to meet his own as they descended upon hers, capturing them in a kiss that warmed the blood as it coursed through her veins. Gently at first, his lips played upon hers, teasing, drawing her on. Excitement rose within her like a hot flame licking at her limbs and tingling across the surface of her flesh where his hand stroked her. One creamy thigh extended from the blackened edge of the silk nightgown, and Ramón's hand, strong and work roughened, found it in a fleeting caress that pushed the filmy fabric higher as his kiss deepened. It was a moment suspended in time. Sirena shuddered in his embrace, a soft whimper of surrender rising in her throat, and she drank in the sweet essence of their first joining as his tongue plundered her mouth.

One strong arm supported Sirena against Ramón's chest, and she felt she would surely collapse on the bed were it not for that arm, because the other — the free hand — kept wandering, exploring, igniting fires of desire wherever it touched as his lips traced the angle of her jaw and descended to the hollow of her throat. Instinctively Sirena arched her body against Ramón's, seeking a closeness, a balm for the erotic shivers that rippled through her body as her hands slid in delicious abandon beneath his shirt, opening it, freeing it from his broad shoulders to drop it in an untidy heap on the floor.

"Oh, God, Sirena," Ramón groaned, his deep voice thickened with his need for her.

Taking off the faded jeans, Ramón pressed forward, bearing Sirena backward upon the bed until she lay half beneath him. His lips found her mouth again before moving lower to where the remnants of the green silk nightgown still covered her breasts. His mouth captured a soft nipple where it thrust eagerly against the imprisoning silk, describing a moist circle around it as Sirena moaned softly and twined her fingers through his tousled hair. The length of his body pressed boldly against hers, growing in passion and power, wanting her, needing her. The touch of him awakened flickering passions deep within the unexplored regions of her body, and Sirena could feel the answering flames within him as he felt her response.

Impatient now with the restricting fabric of the ruined robe, Ramón untied the sash and freed Sirena from its cumbersome weight so that she lay melting against him on top of the soft velour. With one quick tug he finished the work the fire had begun on the fragile silk of the gown, tearing it away from her slender body.

"Beautiful," he murmured into her hair. "So beautiful!" His hand trailed across the soft curve of her breast, downward to the flat of her belly and beyond, sending a fresh wave of quivers through her flesh as she surged against him, seeking, straining to fulfill the needs he brought forth within her.

"Ramón . . ." Sirena gasped. Her eyes widened at the depth of the piercing desire that raced with startling demand throughout her body as his hands continued to wander, to tease, to stroke, to draw from her some inner essence she'd been unaware of all her life. "I love you," she murmured, the words forming almost of their own volition on her tongue.

"And I love you, *mi amada, mi adorada*," Ramón breathed into her hair as he slid his body upward on hers. His face floated inches above hers before his lips descended to claim her sweetness once again.

Eagerly Sirena opened her mouth to receive his tongue, hard and thrusting, reveling in the joy that seared through her, a twin to the flames that had earlier consumed the stable. Her hands slid urgently across the hard rippling plateau of his back as he lowered his body upon hers, and she clutched at the bronze-tanned shoulders that loomed above her in the darkness. A wild heat rose and flashed through her limbs, turning her blood to a molten stream that nourished her body as they joined, becoming one.

A pain all-consuming in its piercing intensity sent a shock wave rolling through Sirena, forcing a muffled cry from her lips and a single tear to her eye. Ramón hesitated, his kiss becoming softer, more deliberate, deepening to help her through the moment of exquisite pain that convulsed her. Ever so slightly he drew back, but Sirena's arms were there, wrapped around his body, holding him as if she were never going to let him go.

Then the tender flame burst forth anew, blazing to new heights as Sirena accepted Ramón fully, and they moved together in a rhythm as powerful and old as time. Sirena arched her body to get closer to him, floating free, soaring to the outermost distances of the universe. The stars were spinning wildly above her as Ramón surged forward, moaning the greatness of his pleasure in her ear, and she reached the pinnacle of her own.

As the consummation of their passion flickered and descended to an ember's glow, Sirena felt Ramón move off her. Drawing her into the curve of his arm, he brushed his lips across her forehead. She could feel his heart pounding in her ear as her head lay against his chest. Nuzzling the soft fragrant mass of her shining auburn hair, his lips planting little kisses across her smooth forehead, Ramón held her close to him, his hand stroking the smooth warm flesh of her hip.

"You haven't been with anyone," he mused, staring up at the bedroom ceiling. "You were a virgin."

Sirena laughed softly, a bit uncertainly, not looking up into his face. "New York's only twenty-six-year-old virgin," she joked quaveringly. "Was I so clumsy?"

Ramón gazed down at her with tenderness. "No," he soothed her, one hand stroking and smoothing her wild tangle of soft curls. "You were beautiful, wonderful. But the city — I thought. . . ."

"Shhh." Sirena put her fingers across his lips. "It doesn't matter anymore. Now you know."

Ramón gave a delighted laugh and drew her even closer to him, pulling her across his body to lie on top of him while he looked up adoringly into her eyes. Sirena smiled down into the golden swirling depths of his incredible eyes, longing to lose herself there forever.

"Ah," he said quietly, "Sirena, *mía,* what fools we've been. How I love you, *mi adorada.* How much I want you to be my wife. Will you marry me, Sirena?"

For an answer she leaned down to press her lips to his, reveling in the warmth of his caress and the low bubbling laughter that filled his chest as he rolled her onto the mattress again, his weight pressing her down into its softness.

CHAPTER ELEVEN

Walking briskly down the hall, Sirena could hear badly muffled sobs and soft hiccuping cries, the sounds reaching her ears before she neared the kitchen, their obvious source. Then came the abrupt slamming of the front door. Frowning deeply, she walked a bit faster.

Only a short time earlier Ramón had whispered to her in bed that he was going to go down to check on the stable; to see by daylight, before breakfast, what it would take to restore them. Upon his leaving, Sirena had stretched like a contented cat and remained where she was a few moments longer, reveling in the wonderful warmth of the bed and what the night had held.

There was no mistaking the source of the painful wails when Sirena opened the kitchen door. There, perched up on one of the stools, Anita was crying so hard her entire body was shaking.

Instantly Sirena was by her side, wrapping an arm about her slim shoulders, steadying the younger woman against her. "What is it, Anita? What's wrong?" Sirena tried to probe tactfully, but the young housekeeper's sorrow was so deep, so all-consuming, there seemed to be no tactful approach.

"Oh, *señorita*, what am I going to do?" A fresh burst of tears sprang from Anita's bright green eyes to trickle down her round cheeks. "I told him about the child. He was happy at first," she wailed. "His smile was like the sunrise. Then he thought of Carlotta. He said he wished to marry me, but Carlotta would never allow it. He said he needed time, that he would have to think about what we would do!"

Anita cried as if her heart were broken into a million pieces and there would be no mending it. Her small frame shook convulsively with the pain piercing her. "Oh, what am I going to do?" she half moaned, her words thick with the tears she had already shed.

Anita half turned, and Sirena took her into her arms, rocking her gently against herself.

"It'll be all right," Sirena murmured soothingly. "I know it will. Rualto is a good man. In time I'm sure he'll stand up to Carlotta. He loves you, Anita."

Anita sniffed, stifling her cries enough to gaze up at Sirena, uncertainty in her eyes. "Do you really think so?"

"Of course!" Sirena wished she were half as sure of Rualto's strength where Carlotta was concerned as she urged Anita to believe. "He was just here?" she questioned, surprised that Rualto had been at the ranch so early in the morning.

Anita bobbed her head and sniffed once again. "He only just left before you arrived."

Sirena cast a glance over her shoulder. She could still catch him. She wasn't sure what she could accomplish or what she would say, but she needed to talk to him.

"Are you all right?" Sirena loosened her grip on Anita. "We'll talk later. Don't worry, Anita; everything will be all right . . . you'll see."

Anita managed a weak smile as Sirena turned and left the kitchen in a rush, heading for the front door.

What kind of hell was Carlotta creating here? Sirena's brain reeled back over the past weeks since her arrival on Rancho Reese, and in a heartstopping moment she knew the answer to her question. Carlotta had made no bones about the fact that she wanted Sirena off Rancho Reese, that she intended her sons to have possession of the great sprawling ranch no matter what it took. The answer was so simple Sirena hadn't even wanted to explore the possibility. It was so painful her mind hadn't delved into that side of her ownership of Rancho Reese.

Rualto, under pressure from his devious mother, had courted her initially though he loved Anita! But Carlotta had had an alternate plan the whole time — a contingency plan, just in case Sirena wouldn't give up and return to the city. Rualto had been her last line of defense. Rualto, if he had managed to marry her, would have become *patrón* of the ranch. That was why

Carlotta would never have approved a marriage between Rualto and Anita. He would have controlled Rancho Reese through Sirena.

But then, what of Ramón? What of *his* declaration of love? An icicle of fear stabbed at Sirena's heart, but she stubbornly refused to explore the possible reasons for it. She would think about that later.

"Rualto!" she called as she spotted him lingering near his Jeep. He was gazing off in the direction of the blackened remains of the stable.

With a wan smile he turned toward her as she approached, not slackening her speed. "You've had much trouble, Sirena," he said sadly, his face molded into deep lines of concern. "I wish I'd been here to help when you needed me."

"I don't care about that now." Sirena swiftly brushed aside his expression of concern. "How could you?" she demanded, her face hard in her fury, blue eyes flashing with an anger she hardly knew how to control. "How could you treat Anita so? How could you leave her in tears when you love her? How could you even mention Carlotta at a time like that?" Sirena's surprised questioning gaze slid past Rualto to where Carlotta sat in the passenger seat of the Jeep. There was a decidedly uncomfortable set to Rualto's face, a pleading within the depths of his eyes.

"Sirena, please," he began, almost stammering. "This isn't the best time —"

But Sirena's anger at Anita's plight and Rualto's hesitancy drove away any sympathy she might have felt for him. Loving Anita was more important than trying to placate Carlotta.

"How could you?" she demanded again, ignoring the older woman's icy glare, oblivious to her move to get out of the Jeep to join them. Neither did she hear the footfalls of Ramón's approach.

"Yes —" Ramón's voice was deep, accusatory "— the same question is upon my lips." He spit the words out in staccato as his free hand dug roughly into his pocket and came out with a gold medallion hanging at the end of a gold serpentine chain. "Do you recognize this, Rualto?"

Ramón's words were somehow mocking, and then he jerked the front of his shirt open, revealing a matching medallion that winked in the brilliant sunlight of the new day. It gleamed against the dense forest of black hair curling around it.

Sirena gasped as recognition dawned. That was where she'd seen the medallion before — on Ramón last night, when she'd been wrapped so safely in his arms. He and Rualto had been wearing matching medallions; the one in his hand could belong only to Rualto. But why did Ramón have it now? Where had he found it? Sirena stared at Ramón in shock, her eyes fastened on the gold that glinted in his work-roughened palm, seeing but not understanding what she saw.

Carlotta was out of the Jeep, standing a little apart from them, her chin elevated in defiance of Ramón. Her coolness tinged the air between them, and her eyes were brilliant with a fanatic's anger.

"You accuse your brother of something? Of what, Ramón — of what do you accuse Rualto?" Carlotta held her frame stiffly erect against Ramón's accusatory tone.

"I don't have to accuse *either* of you!" Ramón snapped. "The situation speaks for itself. Your presence here, now, speaks for itself." His hand tightened around the chain and medallion until Sirena almost expected to see blood run from between white knuckles.

"Do you know where I found this, mother?" Ramón was merciless, the shock and anger at what he had discovered boiling up inside him. "There was a fire last night at the stable, but then I'm sure you know that. But did you know, too, that Mike Vargo was hit from behind and left inside that stable when the fire was set? That if Sirena hadn't gone in there and found him, he would have been dead this morning?

"Was Rualto home last night?" Ramón persisted before Carlotta could reply. "He wasn't, was he, mother, and you know where he was. You know because you were right there with him." Ramón's tone was relentless. "You were here all night, weren't you, mother? You and Rualto — you set the fire. Did you want Sirena dead, mother, or did you just want to frighten her?"

"We came here," Carlotta said with a superior air, as if instructing a backward child, "because Rualto was out in the barn taking care of a sick mare, and he saw the glow of the fire beyond the hills. On a dark night a fire isn't difficult to see, even over great distances. You know that very well." Carlotta glanced at Rualto, who stood silent and ashen beside her. "Rualto called me. We tried the radio," she continued reasonably, "and there was no answer. Out of concern we came to see if we could be of help."

Ramón spoke rapidly in Spanish — a heated reply Sirena didn't understand. Carlotta's features seemed to turn to stone before his onslaught. Then her aristocratic gaze shifted to Sirena, her lips curling upward in distaste, her icy glare holding Sirena in its grip. "She doesn't belong here," Carlotta said spitefully, her face pinched and white. Then she confronted Ramón unflinchingly.

"None of it would have happened if *she* hadn't come here. She tricked Austin," Carlotta accused. "She used that pretty face of hers and that sweet-as-honey manner, and she tricked him into leaving her the *rancho*. She doesn't belong here! We shall yet correct the mistake Austin made," she intoned, her words echoing as though issued from a tomb.

"Oh, I belong here all right, Carlotta," Sirena shot back before Ramón could say anything more. "I love this ranch. I love this land. And I loved Austin Reese. It's you who don't belong here, Carlotta. Your bile and bitterness would poison this beautiful land even before you lived your life out on it."

"A pretty speech," Carlotta said acidly, "but words change nothing!" Her eyes glowed with an insane light that caused Sirena to blanch before its intensity. "Rancho Reese has been plagued by ill fortune since your arrival, and it will remain so until you're gone." She invoked superstition as coldly as a witch bestowing a curse for eternity.

Rualto shifted uncomfortably on his feet during the ensuing silence, and Ramón seethed, his eyes shooting golden sparks that threatened to pierce his mother.

"I didn't know," Rualto breathed, contrite and conscience-stricken, his words a faint whisper beside Carlotta's echoing denunciation of Sirena. "I didn't know Mike was in there." He appeared stunned, no longer following the exchange between Sirena and his mother. "Mother, what did you do?"

"Be still," Carlotta snapped. "What do I care for a ranch foreman? He's of no consequence." She drifted forward on the flagstones that fanned out from the veranda, moving toward the waiting Jeep once again, carrying herself like a queen, the proud tilt of her head showing only disdain.

Rualto fell silent, brooding, his words only a feather on the wind of the emotional storm that enveloped them all.

Ignoring Sirena and Rualto, Carlotta shifted her gaze back to Ramón with deliberateness, waiting, expecting.

The stubbornness on Ramón's face softened somewhat as he regarded his mother, a look of sadness washing over his censuring features. He sighed deeply, his hand loosening its grip on the damning medallion.

"I'm afraid, mother," Ramón said softly, "that the only jinx on Rancho Reese is you. The seeds of bitterness and hatred are planted within you too deeply and have rooted too well. But no matter what you have done to drive Sirena away," he went on, "I tell you this." The hint of pity in his voice had changed to a command. "It's over. It will not happen again. I love Sirena. I've asked her to marry me, though I don't know if she'll have me. And this —" he held the glimmering medallion aloft as both a symbol and a shield "— will not happen again!"

Sirena could feel the terrible pain that raged within Ramón as if it were a palpable thing hanging in the air between them. She longed to reach out, to comfort him, to speak of her love for him, but this wasn't the time.

Carlotta's chin lifted, and she gazed directly into Ramón's dark eyes. "You've bedded her," she accused, "and for that you'll give up everything! I've lost a son this day. I no longer claim you as mine."

"If that's the way you want it, mother." Ramón's blunt response sent a piercing arrow of pain through Sirena's heart, as she empathized with Ramón.

"You're not welcome on my *rancho*, Ramón," Carlotta said frostily. "I doubt that you'll be welcome there ever again. And she —" Carlotta's eyes burned into Sirena "— she will never remain on Rancho Reese — this I vow." Carlotta's last words were filled with a chilling leaden certainty. "Rualto," she finished, turning from both Ramón and Sirena as if they no longer existed, "you will take me from this house of strangers."

Nodding without speaking, Rualto dutifully helped his mother back into the Jeep. In stone-faced silence she sat there, not moving, waiting.

"I'm sorry," Rualto said softly, turning back to his brother and Sirena. "I didn't realize what. . . ." He pulled himself up short, nearly choking on his words, and gave Ramón a twisted smile. "There can be no excuse," he admitted uneasily, meeting his twin's unyielding gaze. "I cannot leave her now." He inclined his head toward Carlotta.

Ramón's face reflected his understanding. His eyes were dark and filled with a bitterness Sirena had only glimpsed previously. Without another word he placed the medallion in Rualto's hand and turned on his heel, striding off in the direction of the stable.

"I'm truly sorry, Sirena," Rualto murmured. "Ramón is right: it will not happen again. I didn't realize how far it would go. . . ."

"It's all right, Rualto." Sirena's voice caught in her throat. "Things will get better. They have to," she promised, echoing the fervent wish in her heart.

Rualto smiled wanly as he climbed into the Jeep beside Carlotta, brought the engine to life and guided it around the curve of the drive in a cloud of rising dust. As Sirena stood in the curving drive staring after him, a shiver of fear inexplicably ran up her back. She felt bereft at Ramón's absence — and threatened. Carlotta was a force to be reckoned with. Sirena knew the older woman wouldn't stop her evil machinations just because of Ramón's orders.

Turning, Sirena went back inside the hacienda. Her mind was a confused blur of thoughts, and her emotions were in a turmoil. She felt she had cause to revel in Ramón's declaration of love for her the previous night; yet Carlotta had cast a shadow of doubt over the beauty of what she'd experienced in his arms. It seemed that Ramón's mother was bent on bringing misery to everyone she came in contact with.

A strange unsettled feeling swept over Sirena as she contemplated Ramón's darker side. Too often she'd seen grimness reflected within the depth of his eyes. What demons were buried deep inside? What seeds had Carlotta planted during his youth? For an instant Sirena knew the coolness of the shadow of fear. What if Ramón were declaring his love for her only to gain control of Rancho Reese? After all, he had been quick to leave her bed that morning. . . .

She brushed the unruly thought from her, striding purposefully through the front door and back toward the kitchen. She was only looking for things, dredging up apprehensions and searching for small clues that could destroy what she and Ramón had so sweetly discovered. What was Carlotta doing to them?

Fiercely Sirena shook her head. She wasn't going to let this happen. She would go see Anita first and then find Ramón. It wasn't possible to set everyone's life right with the wave of a magic wand, and Sirena needed time to think. Honesty was the medicine needed to combat the poison Carlotta spread. Alone, Sirena knew she and Ramón could talk. What had happened the previous night was no lie. It couldn't be! Ramón loved her; she was sure of that now.

By the time Sirena returned to the kitchen, Anita was in better control of herself and the wash of tears had subsided to an occasional sniffle. Delicious breakfast aromas drifted about the warm interior of the large kitchen.

Anita managed a small smile as Sirena entered the room, her boots clicking sharply on the tile floor. A large plate of scrambled eggs, buttered biscuits and crisply fried potatoes instantly appeared before her; the coffee, black and steaming, was already on the table. Anita, in her efficiency, must have placed it there when she'd heard Sirena's footsteps coming down the hall.

"There was a call for you on the radio phone while you were outside," Anita softly informed her, her words still thickly blurred by her earlier tears. "It was a man from the charter company in Tucson. The airstrip meets with approval, he said, and they will be glad to handle Rancho Reese's guests." Anita took a deep breath. "He left a number. He wants you to call. He said they can probably even give the *rancho* a special price if they can arrange a schedule that combines this stop with some others they make regularly. There's more," she finished, "but he wishes to speak with you."

"That's wonderful, Anita." Sirena couldn't help feeling a glow of excitement. It was what she had needed — a direct air link. At last her efforts were paying off! All the calls, the organizing, the letters, the dealings with Mexican bureaucracy. And Ramón's hard work, getting the airstrip carved out and in top shape, along with the hundreds of other details — finally they were meeting with success.

It was all so thrilling that Sirena wanted to dash to the radio phone to return the call that instant. But right now there was Anita and her problems to consider; the call could wait a bit.

"Sit down with me at the table," Sirena suggested warmly to Anita.

Head slightly bowed, little of her usual good humor and quick laughter evident, Anita shuffled slowly across the kitchen floor and dropped dejectedly into a chair. She stared miserably down at her hands in her lap.

"Anita, I know how difficult things must seem to you now. I know how much you must care for Rualto to have let things go so far."

Anita bowed her head, crowned with glistening thick black braids. Her green eyes glistened with more tears as yet unshed, and Sirena felt suddenly ancient beside the sorrowful young woman.

"I wish there were some magic words I could say that would make everything all right," Sirena began tentatively, "but we both know that isn't possible."

Anita forced her lips to curve into a smile, though there was no feeling in it. "Now I'm like Carlotta Savedel. I have her example to follow."

Ignoring Anita's comment for the moment, Sirena went on, "What I can do, though, is give you a few days off — with pay, of course. And some advice from my vast store of experience," she added lightly, trying to dispel some of the dour mood that permeated the sunlit kitchen. "Go visit your family for a few days, Anita. Surround yourself with the people you love and who love you. You're nothing like Carlotta. Things have changed greatly since the time of her tragedy. You have a family who loves you and friends who, I'm sure, feel the same way. I'm also your friend, Anita, and what I told you before is true: you'll have a job here as long as I'm in charge of Rancho Reese — and I intend for that to be a very long time. If you choose to stay after the baby is born, the child will have a happy place to grow up in. We won't allow the misery Carlotta perpetrated upon her sons to continue through another generation."

"Oh, *señorita!*" Anita exclaimed, some of the old joy showing through the tears that streaked her round face. "You're truly a saint!"

Sirena laughed shortly as Anita sprang to her feet and threw her arms about her neck. "No," she said lightly, "not a saint. Just a person like you, Anita, and even like Carlotta." A dark cloud of doubt passed across Anita's face at Sirena's last remark. "Now go on," Sirena coaxed. "Run along and pack a few things. My breakfast is getting cold, and it smells so wonderful I don't want it ruined."

"You're sure?" Anita hesitated. "You're sure you won't need me here?"

"I didn't say I wouldn't need you," Sirena corrected her with humor. "I said I wanted you to take a few days off, and I meant it. When you return, we'll be so busy you won't have time to think of anything but work!"

"Oh, thank you, Señorita Sirena. And who knows, maybe one day soon Rualto and I shall be married after all! Even Carlotta must melt before a grandson!"

Sirena doubted anything would melt Carlotta, but the thought sent Anita brightly off to her room, looking forward to the few unexpected days off. It gave her a bit of hope, whereas earlier everything had seemed so bleak. Maybe Rualto would find his courage; Sirena certainly hoped so.

He had helped his mother in her bizarre campaign, true. But to Sirena it was equally evident that things had progressed much further than he'd intended. It was impossible to read another's mind, but maybe Rualto had begun simply by humoring his mother, hoping she would change. He didn't seem to have realized how far things had gone until the fire and Mike Vargo's brush with death. And if Rualto finally stood up to Carlotta on one front, it was likely he would do the same on another: Anita.

Sirena sipped her coffee and stared out the brilliantly sunlit bay window into the courtyard. She had a considerable amount of her own thinking to do. It was a beautiful cloudless day, and the courtyard had a beckoning warmth. She would paint as soon as Anita departed, she decided. That would help her to think more clearly. Her thoughts returned to the painting she had done beside the waterfall, and a faint smile curved the corners of her lips as she took a forkful of eggs and followed it with a bit of buttery homemade biscuit.

By the time Sirena had finished eating and was working on her second cup of coffee, Anita appeared in the doorway leading to the servants' wing of the huge hacienda, carrying her small suitcase.

"I've spoken with Mike and told him I'll be gone for a few days," she said almost timidly. "He offered to drive me — if it's all right with you," she went on.

"Of course it's all right," Sirena responded brightly. "How else are you going to get home?"

"Thank you! Thank you again!" Anita gushed before whirling and heading for the door.

Sirena smiled and shook her head as Anita disappeared from view, heading for Mike's small house near the ruined stable. It was good to see her in better spirits. The few days off would do her a world of good.

"Where's Mike taking her?" Ramón asked as he strolled into the kitchen from the dining room, his composure returned. His boots hardly made a sound as he walked with a catlike grace across the room to where Sirena sat alone.

Sirena searched his face for some signs of the fury and agony he had suffered such a short time earlier, but she found none, save for her strange impression that the lines in his face had in some way hardened. The rest of his emotions were hidden.

"To visit her family. I gave her a few days off." Sirena refrained from adding the reasons Anita needed the days off or the part his brother played in the matter. Ramón required no further bad news concerning his family at this moment.

"I hope you haven't made any plans of your own," he said quietly, seeming suddenly distant and extremely thoughtful.

"I was going to paint. Why?"

"Mike found a couple of mares running loose near the stable this morning. That means there's a fence down somewhere and some of the mares aren't with the stud they've been assigned to. It's also damned important that we get out there right away and pick the horses for this guest-ranch project of yours. Mike and I corraled the best of the lot in a pasture out on a high mesa — best grazing on the ranch. Since we have to locate the section of fence that's down, now's a good time to head up that way and let you inspect the prospective mounts for the guests."

"Today?" Sirena asked, disappointed that her painting would again take back seat to the operation of the ranch. She realized that for a time it would have to be that way, but she was looking forward to the day when it would not be so.

"Right now, as a matter of fact." Ramón seemed different to Sirena, more tense and aloof. His eyes had a distant introverted look, and she had the bizarre impression they were repelling each other, much as identical poles of a pair of magnets. It had to be a lingering effect of the encounter with Carlotta and Rualto.

"I brought your Jeep around," Ramón added. "We can leave whenever you're ready. I threw a few things in the back so we could at least do a temporary repair when we find the section of fence that's down."

Sirena nodded. What was going on here? Why did she so suddenly feel awkward with this man she loved, a man who claimed to love her in return? It was crazy, but he seemed to be withdrawing, pulling away from her.

"I'm sorry, Ramón," Sirena ventured. "Sorry for the way everything has gone since I came here."

Ramón shrugged. Sirena could see he would rather dodge the situation than give attention to it now. "It's not your fault," he said evenly, his tones cautioning her against dragging out the matter further.

"In a way it's my fault. Just my being here has turned things upside down." Sirena played with her coffee cup, her slender fingers tracing patterns around the rim.

Ramón sighed, the lines in his darkly handsome face lending a lean, almost hawkish look to his gaze. His features were set in an implacable, almost pained expression.

"Sirena," he said with an air of infinite patience, "I warned you about Carlotta when you first arrived. My mother, unfortunately," he added with a wry twist of his lips, "has become a barracuda." It was very clear he preferred not to discuss the matter at the moment; the wound was too fresh, too raw to be exposed just yet. "She'll come around," he said firmly, though Sirena doubted his assertion was based on any fact. "It takes time. Just give it a little time."

Sirena compressed her lips into a bloodless line and stared up at him, her coffee cup clenched in her fist, her knuckles whitening with the strain. "I'll be glad to give you all the time in the world, Ramón," she told him in a tight voice that betrayed the sudden apprehensions she felt where he was concerned. "If you'll remember, I'm the one who was willing to allow that lightning started the fire in the first place and let it go at that. *You're* the one who insisted the storm had nothing to do with it, and you're the one who did the detective work. I love you," she blurted helplessly, at a loss as to how to deal with his pain and what it was doing to him, doing to *them.*

Ramón ran an impatient hand through the thickness of his hair, shot through with streaks of blue black by the light spilling in from the bay window, gleaming as richly dark as a raven's wing. "Yes," he admitted dryly, "I did the detective work." His words were weighty, carrying a much deeper meaning. "Come on." He interrupted her thoughts before she had a chance to put them together too clearly in her own mind, leaving them no more than scattered pieces of a jigsaw puzzle. "We'd better get going."

Sirena rose to follow him without comment. Sweet loving memories of the past night still floated in her memory, and she had a hard time reconciling the man she saw standing before her now with the one who had loved her during the early-morning hours. Could it have been no more than the mists of imagination? Could all that they'd shared be dissolving before her now? Sirena trembled, trying to banish the unwanted thoughts. It couldn't happen. It wouldn't! But Ramón's distant coolness chilled her to the bone. With Anita gone she almost feared being alone with him. Her hopes and dreams had blossomed forth when Ramón had held her in his arms, his heart beating fiercely beneath her ear; but now suddenly everything was different. Would things ever be right again?

In brooding silence they went to where the Jeep was parked in front of the hacienda. A dark cloud seemed to be hovering over Ramón, taking all the joy out of what had transpired between them during the night. There were none of the quiet touches or warm mutual glances or gentle morning-after kisses that Sirena had so happily envisioned.

An odd sensation of anger and shame began to build in her mind. It was not fair, her wounded woman's soul cried out in protest as they climbed into the Jeep and Ramón started the engine with a casual twist of the key. It was almost as though they were back at the beginning, as if they were taking that first Jeep ride together all over again. Last night, Sirena decided bleakly, should never have happened.

Ramón drove with his usual maniac's hand as they pulled away down the curving drive. "Shouldn't take too long," he promised tersely. "Maybe then you'll be able to get back to your painting this afternoon." His voice was throaty, and it was seemingly an effort to speak to her at all. His piercing eyes were focused straight ahead on the rough terrain as the Jeep careered along, rarely with more than three wheels on the ground at any given time.

"For God's sake!" Sirena snapped as the Jeep growled up a steep slope to a mesa, unable to bear the deep sense of shame she was nursing. She'd given herself so freely, so easily to Ramón, and it had ended this way. "Talk to me, Ramón! I understand you have many things eating at you! Don't keep it all bottled up. Tell me how I can help!"

"It's nothing I can't handle myself." Ramón glanced over at her as if seeing her for the first time that day.

"I thought you told me last night that you loved me . . . or did I misunderstand?" Sirena asked more quietly, though she still had to raise her voice to be heard above the laboring Jeep motor as the machine took the almost perpendicular climb with élan.

"I do love you," Ramón groaned, as if the words were being wrenched from him.

"Then let me help!" Sirena knew she was pleading, but she couldn't stop herself.

Ramón shook his head. "I can't. This is something I have to work out myself."

"Then what we have between us means nothing," Sirena accused, affronted by his insufferable male pride. She hesitated, then went on a bit more reasonably, "You don't think Carlotta will give up, do you? Not really. Ramón, what are you going to do?"

Ramón continued to stare bleakly straight ahead and didn't answer her right away. "I told you," he ground the words out slowly, deliberately, "it's something I have to work out for myself. Something *I* have to take care of. I don't know what I'm going to do. You'll have to trust me, Sirena."

Sirena groaned and buried her face in her hands. "Trust you? You won't talk to me and you expect me to trust you?"

"Believe me, Sirena, I'd like nothing better than to tell you all about it." Ramón wrestled with the Jeep's steering wheel and his own emotions. "But just now there would be no point. I don't know the answers myself." His face was frozen in lines of anguish. "Sirena, please believe me, I want to marry you. If you could just be patient. . . ."

The wild countryside around them rose into jagged upheavals and precipitous drop-offs. The Jeep had completed its steady climb, and now the motor was quieter as they crested the hill and Ramón steered the vehicle toward the descent on the opposite side.

"Dear God!" Sirena cried in anguish, twisting around in her seat to stare at Ramón's aristocratic profile, almost mesmerized.

227

"In one breath you tell me you have a few secrets you're damn well going to keep to yourself, a few problems you don't have the answers to, which just happen to involve me and Rancho Reese. Then in the next you ask me to marry you! What is all of this?" she demanded, losing control of the anger that had been seething within her ever since her encounter with Carlotta and Rualto early that morning. "Is it all a play staged for my benefit? Did you and Rualto work it out between the two of you? Is that it? Sort of a family agreement and enterprise?

"It didn't really matter which brother won me in the end, did it?" Sirena accused, unable to stop herself, regretting the words even as she spoke them. "Just as long as *one* of you got me *and* control of Rancho Reese! I don't know anything about Mexican law concerning marriage and property, but then maybe you thought you'd fill me in *after* the wedding! Is Carlotta a part of this little charade, too? She seems to have her hand in everything else! Oh, damn you! Damn you all!" Sirena's breath was wrenched from her throat in a sob of anguish and raw fury.

Tears threatened to come. In a small knot of horror, she sat pressed tightly against the Jeep's door, beseeching Ramón with her eyes to deny the terrible accusations that had spilled from her lips, to reaffirm his love. She wanted only for him to stop the Jeep and enfold her within the warm circle of his arms, to kiss away her darkest fears.

Ramón's lips had whitened at the mention of what had transpired that morning, and now his shoulders seemed to slump beneath the weight of Sirena's outraged words. But he didn't stop the Jeep as her heart cried out for him to do. His hands gripped the steering wheel with an iron determination while his feet played the pedals, braking, shifting, giving the machine gas to carry it over the hillock or up another short steep grade.

"I'm sorry you think that, Sirena," he said at last, the expression on his face clearly that of a man mystified. But he didn't attempt to deny the accusations Sirena had thrown in his face; his pride wouldn't allow it. "It would seem, then," he added, his words pinched and halting as he lined them up one by one like a row of children's building blocks, "that there's little hope for us now."

Sirena's heart plummeted into her shoes, and she saw the beauty they had shared the night past disappearing like a puff of smoke on the wind. As the Jeep began the long descent on the far side of the mesa, she sat mute, feeling the fluttering of her heart within her breast. Dear God, what had she done? She realized intuitively that the declarations of everlasting love she'd wanted to hear from him would only have confirmed her fears and suspicions. The Ramón she knew would never plead with her to marry him; had he done so, she could have been sure he wanted her only for the ranch. It was untrue, all of it. She knew it was, but in the face of his reticence she had struck out at him. His very silence screamed out his innocence of the charges she had so wildly hurled at him.

"Sirena, I —" Ramón began, then stopped in mid-sentence. *"Perdición!"* His eyes widened as the Jeep suddenly began to pick up speed.

"Ramón — what . . . ?" Sirena braced herself in her seat, all at once alarmed at the speed the Jeep was taking over the ruts and rocks on the narrow trail descending the mesa.

"The brakes are gone!"

Ramón's voice had roughened with the urgency of the sudden change in their situation. His hands seemed permanently affixed to the steering wheel, and his eyes didn't leave the rough trail ahead as the Jeep raced on, gathering speed with each passing second. The gears ground in angry protest as Ramón forced the vehicle into a lower gear, but that only served to slow them momentarily. A wildly spinning wheel struck a rock and sent the Jeep careening crazily close to the edge of oblivion.

Sirena cringed in her seat. Instinctively she leaned away from the side that threatened to snatch them into eternity, and sheer terror choked off the cry that formed in her throat.

"I can't hold it on the trail much longer!" Ramón's voice, rough and powerful, struck Sirena with the force of a physical blow. "We have to jump, or it'll take us with it!"

CHAPTER TWELVE

"Jump!" The word rang in Sirena's ears like a bell.

But jump where? One side of the rough trail had become a sheer wall rising up beside the Jeep; and the other was an abyss. Then the cool light of reason penetrated her momentary panic. Over the back; it was the only way. The Jeep was a small vehicle. She had to do it.

"Now! Sirena, jump!" Ramón barked the orders as if the tones in his voice would somehow propel her over the back of the speeding Jeep.

As the vehicle swayed and bumped in a series of terrifying lurches, Sirena twisted around on her seat and crawled onto the back of the Jeep, straddling the equipment Radon had thrown in earlier. Her knees banged against the roll of wire and the hammer bounced against her calf, but she didn't even pause to draw a deep breath. She knew that if she did, she would lose her courage and freeze where she crouched.

Closing her eyes, Sirena just let herself tumble off the back of the Jeep. During that suspended moment in time she remembered reading somewhere that if a person relaxed during a fall, there was less likelihood of severe injury. But for Sirena, knowing she was about to make abrupt contact with the hard rocky earth, relaxing was impossible. It seemed that every muscle in her body contracted with the knowledge, and she hit the ground in a whirling pinwheel of arms and legs, falling awkwardly with no control over her flailing limbs. Out of the corner of her eye she thought she caught a flash of motion from the Jeep that was Ramón, following her, and then the vehicle flew off the trail.

For the briefest instant there was nearly no sound. The heavy Jeep hung suspended in space, wheels spinning. Then came a crash so loud it was deafening, followed immediately by an explosion.

All of it registered in Sirena's brain like a photo negative that would one day be developed into a picture, but she didn't have time to think about it now. The pain of her impact on the hard rocky ground had dazed her momentarily. Through confused thoughts and fuzzy vision she realized she was still moving, her body rolling along as if she were a child's toy cast aside, following the natural slope of the ground toward the yawning abyss that hugged the side of the narrow trail.

A small animal cry formed in her throat, and she struck out wildly, trying to stop her unchecked descent as she helplessly tumbled toward the edge. Her hands curved into claws, Sirena snatched at every passing rock, wildly seeking purchase as her fingernails split and broke beneath her efforts to dig into the hard surface of the dirt trail.

A small corner of her mind was aware of the sound of boots crunching rapidly across rocks, but she couldn't focus on it. Her entire world had compressed into a reality of passing moments of terror. Everything seemed to be happening in slow motion; strangely, though, Sirena felt able to analyze each second, to identify every small rock that rolled beneath her, propelling her ever closer to the edge. Her own body felt alien to her, as if parts of it were working independently from the rest, thwarting her efforts to stop the unthinkable from happening. Desperately she grabbed, clutched and clawed at the hard-packed earth, causing little clouds of dust to rise up all around her. But she was inexorably slipping over the edge. She wasn't going to be able to stop her slide.

Legs dangling in open space, Sirena swung one arm wildly in an arc, her hand making contact with a small stout shrub with bruising force. For an instant her descent was arrested, though the shrub bowed alarmingly beneath the full burden of her weight.

And then, suddenly, Ramón was there.

"Sirena!" She heard him call her name, the alarm in his voice a palpable thing.

With a desperate lunge Ramón threw himself prone on the lip of the trail, thrusting a hand over the edge. His steellike grip locked around Sirena's slender wrist as her grasp on the slender trunk of the sturdy shrub began to give way.

Grunting, straining, Ramón took her full weight on his one arm. He couldn't help sliding on the flat rocky trail as he reached down with his other hand for a better grip, the toes of his boots digging into the hard surface of the earth. For a few breathtaking seconds the weight of Sirena's body, dangling free, pulled Ramón down after her, drawing his body easily along the rocky surface of the hard-packed Jeep trail.

"Don't move, Sirena," Ramón breathed through clenched teeth when she began to struggle as he started to slip. "Don't move! Let me do all the work. If you keep swinging, you'll pull us both over!"

"Ramón! Ramón, help me!" Sirena wailed, her lips suddenly dry, her mouth feeling as if it were packed with cotton.

"I will. I will, my love. Just hang on and don't move." The cords stood out starkly along his neck; speaking now was an effort.

At his command Sirena went instantly still, dangling from his grip, her feet suspended hundreds of feet above the ground below.

Oh, God, her mind cried out silently. *Oh, God . . . oh, God!*

Ramón shifted his grip on her so that he held one of her hands in each of his, and Sirena forced herself to open her eyes to the terror. Staring up into Ramón's cool and determined gaze, she saw that his arms and shoulders were already over the edge in his efforts to hold her. A steady stream of loose dirt and small pebbles was raining down on her from beneath his slipping torso.

Sirena was sure Ramón was holding on to her by no more than sheer force of will. Beneath the straining fabric of his shirt, she could see his muscles corded into knots, bracing against her weight dragging them both down.

"Hang on and don't move," Ramón cautioned again, and a small whimper issued from Sirena's lips. The muscles in her arms screamed out in protest, and pain like liquid fire streaked up to her shoulders as the grip of his hands on her wrists cut into her flesh like iron bands.

Sweat appeared in fat beads across Ramón's forehead, running down the sides of his contorted face as he gathered himself and began to pull. With incredible effort he inched his body backward up the incline, drawing Sirena along with him. Inch by painful inch he slowly drew back, then pulled her after. Dirt and rocks showered her, forcing her to close her eyes against the gritty dust.

Then Ramón had his elbows braced on solid ground. Still he pulled steadily . . . pulled, then paused, inching his body back, using the weight of it for added leverage. Sirena felt herself slowly being drawn upward. A sob of relief tried to force itself upon her, but she held it back. She wasn't up yet. Carefully she kept her body completely still, obeying Ramón's commands. The nearby ledge jutting outward toward her tantalized her with the desire to reach out to it with her feet and lever herself upward, but she didn't dare try. One slip now, one unexpected jar, and she was sure Ramón would not be able to hold her. Even worse — the realization hit her like a slap — he would not let go. He would try to hold her until the last second — and beyond. If she fell now, she would drag Ramón to his death along with her. . . .

Shifting his grip, Ramón released one wrist for an instant, quickly grabbing on to her upper arm to draw her higher, pulling her arms up over the ledge, rolling his own body back farther until only her legs still dangled over the open space. With one final effort Ramón hauled her up and rolled her into his embrace, whispering words of consolation. Sirena began to cry quietly, clinging to him as if she never intended to let him go.

"It's all right, *mi amada*. It's all right," Ramón crooned in her ear. Working himself into a sitting position, he drew her close to him and gently rocked her back and forth as though he were holding a frightened child. One hand softly stroked the glistening tangle of her hair while the other held her tightly against him. Sirena could hear the calming beat of his heart beneath her ear and his whispered words over and over again, "Thank God you're all right . . . I couldn't have borne losing you."

They seemed to stay that way a very long time. Then at last

Ramón felt her begin to relax against him. The shivers of terror that had racked her body as she met the warmth of his embrace were beginning to subside.

"Are you all right now?" Ramón's words, still husky with suppressed emotion, were spoken quietly, softly matching the beat of his heart where he held her close.

Mutely Sirena shook her head. She felt as if she'd been beaten within an inch of her life. Every muscle and joint in her body ached, and great ribbons of her skin had been torn and bloodied, but she was sure nothing had been broken. Her breath left her in a tremulous sigh.

After the trauma of what had nearly happened began to pass, bits and pieces of her sanity started to return. She felt completely encircled with warmth and love. It seemed to her that — miraculously — she'd been allowed to withdraw, even if only for a short while, into a cocoon of unreality, a soft insulated world of safety. And Ramón had created it. Sirena's heart sang. He did love her! He did! All was not forfeit between them.

"Can you stand? Walk?" Ramón's words were pricking at her consciousness, drawing her out of that safe warm cocoon and back into the world of reality and necessity. The air of cool efficiency was creeping back into his manner.

"Yes," Sirena sighed, sad that they would finally be forced to break this embrace and face what was to be done next.

Ramón dropped a light reassuring kiss on her forehead and began to shift and climb to his feet. "We'd better get going, then," he said, drawing her to her feet along with him, his arm still around her to steady her. "At least we're both dressed for it," he added with an attempt at levity, his amused glance taking in their disheveled appearances. "It's only a short climb," he added, noting Sirena's apprehensive eyes fixed on the trail they'd just come down. "After that, it's downhill all the way back to the hacienda."

Ramón slanted her a look that Sirena found unreadable. His eyes were the color of the mountain mists in the early mornings; gold was there, too, glimmering in their depths, winking at her from what seemed an incredible distance. Rapidly those few minutes of closeness were fading into hardly more than memories. Once Ramón had ascertained she was all right, except for the assortment of cuts and bruises she had collected in her fall, he had immediately begun to withdraw. Sirena could feel it in the air between them. She sensed his thoughts were once again of the blackest variety, and whatever it was he was thinking, it was more than clear he was not prepared to share it with her. The chill rising between them was almost palpable, but Sirena was too exhausted by the past string of events to attempt even a mild protest. Ramón was right in one thing: they had to get back to the hacienda before they could even begin to work things out. And she didn't want to risk saying anything that might make him withdraw even further on the long exhausting walk that loomed ahead. Should Ramón pull back from her completely now, she wouldn't be able to bear it.

"Come on, Sirena," Ramón reminded her, urging her to move. "We have to start back." But he was clearly lost in brooding; the expression on his face spoke of decisions to be made.

The Jeep could have killed them both. After the fire and the encounter with Carlotta that morning, Ramón knew better than to believe the brake failure could have been an accident; Sirena could tell by the anguish in his eyes, the set of his face. It wasn't hard to bleed brake fluid. That left unanswered only the question of who had done it.

They turned their backs on the twisted remains of the Jeep settled at the bottom of the abyss and started the walk back to the ranch.

Sirena resolved not to think about it right now. One foot in front of the other — that was the only way she was going to make it, the only way she'd be able to keep going when she felt that her beaten body was already beyond the edge of exhaustion.

Ramón's arm still around her, his strength seeming somehow to wash over onto her, Sirena started the climb with shaky steps. When she slipped or stumbled, Ramón was there to keep her from falling. His strong arm steadied her as they walked, and her legs grew stronger beneath her. The shock of what had happened was wearing off, and she was imbued with a driving desire to be home, to be sheltered within the great walls of Rancho Reese.

The one steep climb up the broken trail was the only one they had to face. From there it was almost entirely downhill. In spite of the various bruises and aches they shared between them, they set a brisk pace. Ramón strode purposefully over the rough ground, with Sirena at times trailing behind, nursing her wounds, thinking some dark thoughts of her own, until Ramón would hesitate, realizing she was falling behind, and turn back to rejoin her.

It was those few moments along the way that Sirena cherished. It was then that Ramón, contrite about neglecting her, would call a halt, a short rest, and in the middle of a sparse but rolling pasture or on adjoining rocks they would sit down together. A look of compassion and concern for her would return to his face, and more important, love again glowed in the golden depths of his eyes. The same love she'd seen reflected there the previous night, when she'd been in his arms. What had changed between then and now? Was it Carlotta? Was she reaching out to destroy them even after Ramón's rejection of her bitterness and greed? The thought nagged continually at Sirena, but she could find no answer.

The hours dragged past, and the sun was moving rapidly toward the west. Still they trudged on. Sirena's body had long ago gone numb from the continuing ache, but her stomach was a different matter. They hadn't planned on being out all day, and even what food and water they had brought along had gone over the edge with the Jeep. They'd had nothing to eat since breakfast, and now it was quickly nearing dinnertime. Sirena felt that her stomach was contracting into a discontented knot within her. Irritably she chided herself for dwelling on the discomfort: she should be grateful she was alive to feel hunger and not be annoyed by it.

But she was hungry, and she ached all over. She wanted only to get fed, cleaned up and then seek the comfort of her bed. The entire process, since she'd given Anita time away from the ranch to work out her own problems, would probably take hours. In a dispirited moment Sirena wondered if Rancho Reese was really more than she could handle. It had been one thing after another from the beginning, and there were no signs of letup. If anything, with the Jeep crash things seemed considerably worse.

"Home is just over the next hill." Ramón nudged Sirena gently when he saw that she'd withdrawn as he had into a world of private thoughts. "You didn't get much time to paint this afternoon," he observed apologetically, putting an arm around her. Ramón's words held a bit of the wry humor Sirena had come to expect from him.

She sighed and warmed to the strong arm that encircled her, wanting to melt within his embrace, to relax against him and to revel in the feelings of the past night. But there was an intense remote quality about him that stopped her from following the impulse.

From the top of the small hillock the ranch rolled out below them like a scene from a child's storybook. The hacienda stood majestically at the end of the sheltered valley on a low swell of land, its dominance over the area unquestionable.

As they approached, they could see a Land Cruiser parked in front of the sprawling ranch. Sirena was puzzled, for the vehicle was not one she'd seen on the ranch previously and was nothing like the open-topped affair that Rualto drove. It sat much higher off the ground than the usual squatty Jeep, which could barely manage two passengers, and its sand-colored body, gleaming with obvious attention, was entirely closed in against the weather. Sirena didn't relish facing visitors in this condition, but it appeared that there would be no avoiding it.

With a dispirited sigh she wearily covered the remainder of the distance, Ramón's arm resting lightly about her shoulders. She felt a slight tensing of his muscles and realized he knew who owned the Land Cruiser. And by the way his grip tightened, Sirena didn't think the Land Cruiser belonged to anyone Ramón was any too eager to see.

CHAPTER THIRTEEN

The deepening shadows of twilight were casting long corridors of darkness over the mountains and slanting across the hacienda's veranda as Sirena and Ramón covered the last steps into the curving drive. There was no movement from the Land Cruiser, nor from the house, and Sirena was beginning to wonder where the driver had wandered off to when she spotted movement on the veranda.

She discerned a tall figure through the darkness toward the twilight that still set the yard aglow. He moved with a panther's grace, almost gliding through the evening's stillness, and suddenly Sirena recognized Rualto's distinctive tread. He blended into the shadows because, oddly, he was dressed completely in black, from his high-necked shirt down to the immaculately tailored pants and softly gleaming black-leather boots that moved silently over the flagstones. On his head was an equally black broad-brimmed hat. His face beneath the hat was as immobile as ice, his swarthy complexion a darker shadow in the evening's fading light. The black costume made him appear like a ghost drifting before them.

"Rualto." Ramón's greeting was wary.

Rualto's eyes glittered like diamond chips, reflecting back what light remained. His gaze held and appraised each of them, his face a map lined with concern at their battered disheveled appearance, then relief that they stood before him at all. Deep unfathomable pain was etched across his features.

Rualto gripped Sirena's arm. He intended to shield her from whatever had brought Rualto back to the ranch.

"The Jeep?" Rualto questioned. His face was a mask of frozen anticipation, the words forced from between lips long dry with suffering.

"The brakes failed, and the Jeep went into a canyon. We're

both very lucky to be alive." Ramón spoke in a monotone, his eyes fixed on his twin, the burning light in their depths accusatory.

Rualto's face instantly went pale, and a look of anguish such as Sirena had never seen creased itself across his angular features. He gasped audibly, falling back a step as though being dealt a blow.

"*Maldito sea!*" he murmured, burying his face in his hands. The curse was wrenched from him, little more than a papery whisper. Raising his head hesitantly from his hands, he gazed anxiously first at Sirena, then at his brother. "You're sure you're all right?"

"Yes, Rualto," Sirena answered. "A little battered, but fine."

Rualto nodded dumbly, then his face began to crumple, the set mask of expression dissolving to leave . . . what? "I could have lost all of you," he groaned, his words stiff and broken. "My God, all of you! I would have stopped her had I known. . . ."

The lines in Ramón's face went rigid, his eyebrows knit together in a frown that was somewhere between anger and puzzlement. "All of us? What are you talking about?"

Somehow Sirena knew what Rualto was talking about. Somewhere deep inside she knew, and she had no doubt that Ramón knew, as well. A chill ran through her body. She felt herself begin to shiver in Ramón's grasp; she didn't want to hear the awful truth from Rualto's lips.

"On the way home Carlotta confessed to me that she had punctured the brake lining of Sirena's Jeep, that the brakes were sure to fail. When we left, I didn't know of the horrible thing she had done, just as I hadn't known she intended to start the fire when we came here last night. Also, I didn't know she had struck Mike Vargo," he explained, unable to meet his brother's eyes.

"When she told me of the brakes, I insisted we turn around and return. We were nearly home then. I turned the wheel and our mother grabbed it, trying to pull it back. I lost control of the Jeep. It went over an embankment and into the creek at the deep point near home, rolling over. I jumped clear. *Madre* was pinned inside. I couldn't lift the Jeep from her. By the time I was able to get help from the house, mother had drowned," he finished with a controlled calm that lowered the curtain of unreality on the entire scene.

"Carlotta? Dead?" Sirena mouthed the words quietly without even realizing she had done so. The only reaction from Ramón was a tightening of his grip on her arm, enough to cause her to wince and try to draw away from him.

"She's dead?" Ramón managed to choke out, his free hand clenching and unclenching at his side. In spite of his exhaustion, the shock of what he'd just heard pulled his backbone up ramrod straight.

Sirena tried to shake off Ramón's grip, wanting only to withdraw into the comforting sheltering walls of the hacienda and let the horror of what had happened sink in. How ironic that Carlotta had died in her Jeep at almost the same time the Jeep she and Ramón had been driving had gone over the edge of the trail into a canyon. A wave of pity washed over her. Only Ramón's quick action had saved their lives. If not for that, mother and son, as well as she herself, would have died within minutes of one another. And what of when she'd been dangling over the edge? Had it been then, during those terrifying moments, that Carlotta had drawn the water deep into her lungs and. . . .

In the core of her very soul Sirena could feel the trembling beginning, transmitting itself into waves that rippled throughout her body. The past few days had been too much to bear. The fire . . . the Jeep crash . . . and now this.

A smothering silence descended over them. Ramón's face was ravaged with conflicting emotions. The mother who had disowned him was dead. Sirena sensed all that had been brewing within him — the unconfirmed certainty that Carlotta had been responsible for the nearly disastrous brake failure, the final knowledge of just how deep her bitterness and hatred had gone. He was stunned, like a man punch-drunk and swaying.

Slowly Ramón began releasing his painfully tight grip on Sirena's arm. Carlotta had rejected him because he wouldn't step into her shoes, embrace her bitterness of the world. From the outset it had been obvious that Carlotta favored Rualto over Ramón. She had been able to play on Rualto's loyalty and, yes, pity, to manipulate him. Ramón had turned from her hatred, and in so doing he had, in her mind, turned from her. And now Carlotta was dead. It was over, all of it. The pieces were broken and scattered.

What was left for Ramón and her now? What would she and Ramón be able to salvage from it all? A heavy weight bore down upon Sirena's heart. Ramón turned from her, leaving her to stare unseeingly at Rualto. Nothing about Rualto's features had changed; nothing in his expression had altered. And yet there was a crumpled look about him, a hopelessness that haunted his eyes.

Not sure what to do, Sirena stood frozen to the spot. Should she stay there with Rualto, run after Ramón or retreat into the shelter of the hacienda? Her nerves were raw, her throat constricted with a kind of agony she had never experienced previously. Then she saw the door behind Rualto open, and Anita slipped out onto the veranda.

"Excuse me — I heard voices," Anita apologized softly. Her eyes darted to Rualto, anxiety reflected in them.

"What — what are you doing here? I thought you left with Mike this morning," Sirena stammered. She noted with relief that Anita's appearance had arrested Ramón's retreating footsteps.

"I forgot something," Anita explained. "This shirt I made for my mother," she added, holding the beautifully embroidered shirt aloft for their inspection. "Mike was kind enough to drive me back for it. I'll leave first thing in the morning . . . if that's all right."

Sirena nodded numbly.

"Is something wrong?" Anita asked anxiously. Her eyes moved from Sirena to Rualto, then to Ramón's dim figure on the fringes of the darkness, where he hunched in a raw animal pain that could only be felt but not expressed.

Sirena hesitated, not sure she should be the one to deliver the news.

"Carlotta is dead," Rualto intervened before Sirena could say anything.

Anita's bright green eyes widened in horror. A tear appeared at the corner of her eye, a tear shed for Rualto's grief, and ran down her cheek.

Ramón, in his excruciating mental torture, turned and walked away into the darkness, a lonely figure, rejecting all comfort.

Until he was swallowed completely by the night's shadows, Sirena stared after him. She longed to hold him; to share the pain of all that had passed, just as Anita now filled Rualto's arms; to help him shed the tears of release. Then alone she withdrew into the safe and comforting walls of the hacienda.

Oh, how she longed to follow Ramón. Her heart constricted within her with the effort of allowing him the solitude he had chosen.

CHAPTER FOURTEEN

Sirena stared at the almost completed painting set up in front of her in the courtyard and hesitated before dipping her brush once again into the color on her palette. The painting was the one she had done at the waterfall; it seemed ages ago that she had recreated the idyllic scene on canvas. Beside it on the small table that held her palette was the jar containing Austin's letter, and the cryptic scrawl on the envelope's white surface constantly drew her curious gaze. She would open it soon, she resolved, fascinated by the strange spell it cast. It both attracted and repelled her, which was silly, really; nothing Austin would have had to say to her could be all that bad.

For two days Sirena had been alone now, blissfully alone. The dramatic events of the recent past were beginning to fade, to become a blurred dream that could never have happened, except for the fact that she knew it *had* happened. Carlotta was in a cold grave to prove it.

Sirena shuddered at the thought. As the shiver passed through her, she was grateful her paintbrush wasn't touching canvas. She would never forget the day of Carlotta's death as long as she lived.

The following morning, as planned, Anita had gone home to visit her family — only this time Rualto had taken her. And Ramón had not turned up for breakfast that morning or since. Nothing had been said, no explanation tendered; he had merely disappeared. From Mike, Sirena had learned he had ridden off into the hills alone.

With a sigh Sirena went back to contemplating the canvas before her, eyeing the tiny figure she had begun to paint. There was a heaviness about her heart that brought a tightness to her throat, but she was determined to shed no more tears. A pad of paper lay on a small table nearby; on it she was jotting occasional thoughts regarding the new guest ranch. Rancho Reese and her painting would fill her life, but, she admitted to herself, it would take a long time for the pain in her heart to subside . . . a long time to accept that Ramón was finally gone from her life. She was better off without him, Sirena tried to tell herself again and again.

Touching the fine brush to the canvas, she delineated a few details, bringing life to the small figure of a woman floating in the sparkling pool of water and a smile to the lips of the man who shared it. What fragile things memories were, even memories as recent as those born at the waterfall. Sirena wanted to get the painting just right; to preserve the memory while it was still clear in her mind; to reflect just a small portion of the love she and Ramón had so briefly, openly, shared. It was one painting she would never sell. Once it was finished, she would hang it in her study and remember only the beautiful moments, few though they were, not the bad.

Still the glass jar beckoned, and Sirena regarded it with an almost wary appraisal. Many were the times it had pricked her curiosity. While caught up in the turmoil of preparation for Rancho Reese's new future, she had all but forgotten it. Through her worst trials she had not broken the jar; there hadn't been time even to consider it. But now. . . . Laying down her brush, Sirena picked up the jar and with no more hesitation dropped it to the flagstones.

The glass shattered with a strange muted sound, the tinkling arrested by the grass that grew between the slabs of stone. Extricating the envelope, Sirena ignored the pieces of glass. She would clean them up later. Quickly she tore open the envelope and held up the letter in the sunlight to read.

My Dearest Sirena:

It is my fondest hope that you are reading this letter because you are getting married — to Ramón. That was my greatest wish for you both. If that is the case, you need read no further than my congratulations. Had you not accepted Rancho Reese, it would, as you know, have been divided evenly between Ramón and Rualto. But from that wonderful time that you stayed with me and I saw your love for this country shining through in your beautiful paintings, you have been my first choice. Ramón and Rualto will have a vast ranch in any case, which they will inherit from Carlotta.

If it is not marriage and you have read on, then it is trouble. I cannot anticipate all things, but I can warn you: beware of Carlotta. I don't know to what lengths she will go in her bitterness. Once I thought her to be a hurt and vulnerable woman, capable of love and compassion but badly damaged by life. I learned, though, that the years have hardened her beyond my ability to comprehend. There is no way to tell how she will react once she knows of your inheritance.

Understand Rualto, for he is a good man, only weak where his mother is concerned, but depend on Ramón, for he is his own man — a man so imbued with honor he would stand against the forces of hell itself in the cause of right.

It is my hope that these words have at least brought you understanding.

Austin

Sirena folded the piece of paper and slipped it into the pocket of her smock with a sigh. Why hadn't she opened it sooner? It would have revealed so much. But no, she had made a game of it, amused by Austin's melodramatics. Now all he had told her had become painfully evident.

"No, Austin," she murmured absently, mixing some new color and lifting it onto the tip of her brush, "I won't be marrying Ramón after all." Then she stepped back and gazed fixedly at the small figures in the picture, a new pain pricking her heart. She lost herself gratefully within the flowing lines and brushstrokes of the painting. Time stood still, and she was content to stand in the flow of eternity, free of her agony of loss, oblivious to a small particle of its passing.

Then, little by little, Sirena became aware of someone intruding on her reverie. A momentary confusion brought her around on her heel, paintbrush poised in the air, searching for she did not know what.

Sirena didn't have to look far. Ramón stood just outside the kitchen door in the courtyard, regarding her with eyes as limpid and inviting as the blue waters of the painting she'd been working on.

"If you aren't careful," he said in a dangerously familiar, softly mocking tone, "you'll fall right into that painting. And I'll never be able to follow you there."

"I wasn't aware you'd want to follow me anywhere," Sirena said tightly, turning from him. She could feel all the old pain surfacing within her again at just the sight of him, the sound of his voice.

"Why?" Ramón queried softly. "Because I seemed to abandon you a couple of days ago? I'm sorry, Sirena." He moved closer to her, and she could feel the warmth of his presence. "I had to have time to think. Carlotta was my mother. I thought 1 knew what she was trying to do near the end, and by the time I was sure, I felt like murdering her myself. Then she was dead. It was almost as if I'd wished her so."

"Why didn't you tell me earlier, when you began to suspect?" Sirena chanced a careful glance in Ramón's direction, letting the golden depths of his misty gray green eyes capture her own for a moment. Hastily she returned her fixed stare to the bright colors of the canvas before her. "Why didn't you say anything when you left?"

"I couldn't have told you anything then that you'd have wanted to hear." Ramón brought his hands up to rest lightly on Sirena's shoulders. "I didn't even know if you could still love me after all my family had put you through. Rualto told me mother admitted to him that the idea of the accidents had come to her when the Jeep had slipped into the washout at our arrival. It was almost impossible to tell which occurrence was accident and which planned . . . until the fire. Rualto had hoped to humor mother at first, to take her where she wanted to go and, he hoped, prevent any real tragedy, but he only succeeded in providing her the means to her end."

The grip of Ramón's hands, the gentle pressure of his long

aristocratic fingers, demanded a response. "Well . . . can you still love me, Sirena? After all you've been through, after all I've told you? I said once I loved you and wanted to marry you. Could you marry me now?"

Sirena dropped her paintbrush and stared up into Ramón's troubled face. She didn't know whether to laugh or cry. He was all she'd ever wanted, and she was so filled with love for him that she felt ready to burst from the sheer joy that filled her breast.

"You were afraid I couldn't care for you because of Carlotta? Oh, why? Why would you ever believe that? I thought you'd left me — that you couldn't bear to be near me after what my coming to Rancho Reese had cost. If it weren't for my coming here. . . ." Sirena hesitated. "But you are my love! It always has been you, and it always will be you. My love couldn't change. Of course I will marry you . . . if you want me."

"*Por Dios!* How I love you," Ramón whispered into the softness of Sirena's hair, gathering her closely to him, feeling her melt against the length of his body as he held her. "We'll be married very soon," he said eagerly, "and we'll make this the finest *rancho* in all of Mexico!"

Sirena laughed exultantly, but she found the strength to enforce a bit of practicality. "It'll take time," she breathed, "but we'll do it together."

"We'll do it together, and it'll take no time at all," Ramón countered.

"But, Ramón . . ." Sirena protested, and he silenced her with his lips gentle upon hers.

"No buts, *querida*. I have enough money for a lifetime, for two lifetimes — money I made from investments at Austin's advice when I was younger. I never knew what I was going to do with it all until now."

Gently Ramón drew Sirena down into the sweet-smelling grasses that carpeted the courtyard. His lips found the silky hollow of her throat as his hands slid over the smooth contours of her back, drawing her even closer to him.

"Don't you think we should go upstairs?" Sirena teased as she found herself pinned lightly to the earth beneath Ramón's

247

weight, Austin's letter crinkling between them. Breathless between kisses, she whispered, "It would be much more comfortable there."

"Later," Ramón promised, his warm breath caressing the delicate curve of her ear. Then his lips descended upon hers with a gentle persuasion that brought a song to her heart, matching the lilting tune of the small yellow bird that drank from the bubbling waters of the nearby stream.